TEDDY BEAR STORIES FOR GROWN UPS

TEDDY BEAR STORIES FOR GROWN UPS

compiled by Catherine Taylor

PAN BOOKS
IN ASSOCIATION WITH MICHAEL O'MARA

To Edward Bear with Love

First published 1993 by Michael O'Mara Books Limited

This edition published 1994 by Pan Books
an imprint of Macmillan General Books
Cavaye Place London SW10 9PG
and Basingstoke
in association with Michael O'Mara Books Limited

Associated companies throughout the world

ISBN 0 330 32937 5

1 3 5 7 9 8 6 4 2

A CIP catalogue record for this book is available from
the British Library

Printed and bound in Great Britain by
Cox & Wyman Ltd, Reading, Berkshire

Contents

INTRODUCTION   vii

THE BEAR IN THE WINDOW   1
Anne Forsyth

SHOOTING TEDDY BEARS IS NO PICNIC   15
Abigail Harman

HAROLD'S BEAR   27
Pauline Macaulay

A FRIEND IN NEED   41
Anne Goring

TITANIC BEAR   47
Pat Rush

THE BATTLE OF JERICHO   51
Peter Clover

CONFESSIONS OF A BAD BEAR   57
Allan Frewin Jones

LOOK ME IN THE EYES   71
Jill Drower

FIT FOR A PRINCESS   87
Pat Rush

ONE BEAR'S WAR   89
Elisabeth Beresford

CONFESSIONS OF AN ADULT BEAR COLLECTOR   101
David Elias

THE TEDDY BEARS' PICNIC   107
William Trevor

HIGH-SPEED TED   125
Pat Rush

TEDPERFECT   129
Alan Hackney

THE SERVANT PROBLEM   145
David Roberts

SALUTE TO A MILITARY BEAR   155
Mary Ross

WORTH A BASH   165
Rebecca Fraser

CUDDLES   169
Marie Macneill

OF MONKS AND TEDDY BEARS   173
Gillian Elias

THE BARD   181
Jane Beeson

A SYMBOL OF UNLONELINESS   195
Pat Rush

TED AND ANGELINE   199
Dinah Lampitt

STUFF AND SAWDUST   205
Valerie Thame

ACKNOWLEDGMENTS   213

Introduction

As countless grown ups know, teddy bears are not just for the children. They may have arrived originally as a present for a child, but one of the distinguishing features of a teddy bear is how its owner's attachment to it almost invariably lasts long into adulthood. Often, even when the teddy itself has disintegrated into a shapeless, eyeless, earless lump, the affection it inspired still remains.

When I first began, tentatively, to put this book together I was amazed at the response from the people I contacted (all of whom were grown ups!) So many seemed to find teddy bears an inspiring theme for a story and, what is more, were willing to put pen to paper and prove it. An advertisement in a newspaper also drew some fascinating responses (though sadly, nowhere near as many as Peter Bull attracted when he advertised in the *Times* twenty-five years ago). From the stories and letters which came in, it became obvious that teddy bears lead lives as individual as their owners.

Some teddy bears have led extremely exciting, even dangerous, lives. I was told of one teddy bear who lived an idyllic life on the French Riviera until the Second World War forced his young owner and her family to flee their homes, sadly leaving Teddy behind. However, Teddy survived the frontline, and was later rescued by his twelve-year-old mistress on a daring midnight expedition to retrieve the family possessions. Another wartime bear was rescued by the owner's elder brother during an air-raid, much to the consternation of their mother. Yet another bear, poor Bolop, spent his early years being cut open and stitched up again while his owner practised his surgical skills. It was worth it in the end though – Bolop's owner grew up to be a consultant surgeon.

Binky and Breakfast's owner kindly sent me their photograph – they date from 1925 so they are now well-worn but they are obviously still great characters. Their owner tells me: 'Binky... early acquired a reputation for naughtiness. There was nothing he would not do – "he even said a rude word about Heaven," I told my mother in shocked tones.' Breakfast was a very different character: 'For all the years I played with him, he was trying to pass the entrance exam to Cambridge, with a signal lack of success. When he was supposed to be working, he was occupying the lavatory, reading the newspaper.' Despite trying to get into Cambridge University, Breakfast also stroked the Oxford boat to victory in the annual rerun of the University Boat Race which took place on the nursery floor.

Today there is a great resurgence of interest in teddy bears – both new and old – not just as objects of affection but also as collector's items. Teddy bear shops have sprung up all over the place and there is even a teddy hospital at The House of Bruin in Loughborough, Leicestershire, where sick teddies can receive expert medical attention. David Elias in his 'Confessions of an Adult Bear Collector' shows just how easy it is to fall prey to this delightful hobby. But you do not need to be a collector to love teddy bears.

The wonderful range of stories that teddy bears have inspired has surprised and delighted me – as I'm sure it will you. There are mystery stories, funny stories, romantic stories, true stories and even some darker tales. But whatever their theme, all the stories acknowledge the very special relationship that exists between a bear and its owner. As Abigail Harman puts it in 'Shooting Teddy Bears is No Picnic': teddy bears are 'warm and cuddly, always there to be loved and always ready to listen to your moans and woes. With a teddy bear there's always a furry shoulder to cry on. They never interrupt; never tell you to snap out of it . . . they are sympathetic and silent.'

My own teddy was my constant companion in my childhood, and established himself as such a character that I think it's fair to say that he truly became part of the family. Never a very handsome bear (at the age of one, I firmly rejected a fully jointed bear in favour of this bright yellow cuddly teddy that can't even sit up unaided), he is now almost furless and very, very patched from numerous much-needed operations carried out by my mother. But I know he would be delighted that at last there is a book which confirms what he has always thought: teddy bears are worth writing proper grown-up stories about.

Catherine Taylor

The Bear in the Window

ANNE FORSYTH

'I HOPE I'M doing the right thing. I hope I am.' The beads of sweat dappled Mr Twentyman's forehead. He ran his finger under his collar and, for the umpteenth time, checked his waistcoat pocket to make sure he still had his ticket.

'Of course you are. Don't worry, Mr Twentyman.' Alice stopped flicking her feather duster over the dolls' tea sets and smiled reassuringly at him. Inside, she quailed slightly. It was a big responsibility to be left in charge.

'I don't like leaving the shop,' he said. 'I'm not easy in my mind about it.'

He gazed round the ranks of toy soldiers as if they would rise and mutiny as soon as his back was turned.

'And leaving you on your own,' he added. With her fair hair and blue eyes, Alice looked rather like one of the china dolls that sat on the counter. But she was a capable saleswoman and appearances were misleading.

Beneath the pink-and-white prettiness, Alice was something of a rebel, with a lively mind. More than anyone in the world, she admired Sylvia Pankhurst. 'If only I could go out and do something like her!' she said to herself. 'I would chain myself to railings, march for the cause – anything! But I'm stuck here.' She picked up the duster again and whisked it over the clockwork toys. She knew she was lucky to have a job. Times were hard and there were young brothers and sisters at home.

'You know you'd only worry if you didn't go,' she urged her employer. Mr Twentyman's sister was in hospital, and he had decided he must visit her – leaving the shop in Alice's charge for a week.

'You, Ray, be sure you help all you can,' Mr Twentyman turned to the message boy.

'You can count on me,' said Ray, a cheerful lad with a shock of red hair.

'And don't break anything,' added Mr Twentyman gloomily. He glanced round the shop as if taking leave of it. Alice followed his gaze. They sold hoops and tops and skipping ropes. And there were shelves of model soldiers, and cowboys and Indians, and pink-cheeked wax dolls with pintucked dresses, and wooden-jointed dolls, their cheeks painted a hectic red. But for something really special, like a splendid train set, or a grand dolls' house, people had to travel to the city, to one of the big stores. J. Twentyman's toy shop, tucked away in a side street, would never make a fortune.

Sometimes Alice marvelled that Mr Twentyman ran a toyshop. The owners of toyshops should be round and jolly and exude goodwill. Mr Twentyman was nothing like that, but then the toyshop had come to him through his late wife's family. He looked on it as a respectable source of income, rather than as a fount of joy.

'There,' said Alice kindly. 'Don't forget your umbrella.'

'Ah, well,' he said gloomily. 'What's to be must be.'

She watched him as he anxiously checked his pockets again, then she waved him goodbye.

Alice continued to watch the stooped figure as he turned the corner, his stick tap-tapping rhythmically against the kerb stones. She felt rather sorry for him. If only she could do something in his absence to boost sales. What a pleasant surprise for him when he returned!

At least, she thought, I can do something about the window. First, clean it out, then arrange a more attractive display – the dusty printing sets and magic tricks had occupied the main part of the window for as long as she could remember.

She opened the catch and, armed with dustpan and brush, climbed over the sill. If only she could think of a real attraction

2

that would make the customers stop and look and buy.

'Out you go!' she commanded, sweeping up an army of toy soldiers. 'And you, too!' she ordered a solemn baby doll. She crawled about the window, removing the plates of plaster food, now covered with a film of dust, the painted tops and rag books whose colours had faded in the sun.

Ray watched admiringly. 'Cor, you've got a nerve,' he said.

'That's quite enough from you,' said Alice with some asperity. After all, she was in charge.

'What's she up to?' An old woman watched from across the road as she whitened her doorstep. 'Look at her, crawling about, showing her ankles.'

'He'll not be pleased,' said her neighbour. They sighed in unison.

Across the way, Alice was too busy to be aware of their disapproval. Already, she was wondering what sort of window display would really attract customers. How pleased Mr Twentyman would be! There must be something among the stock – she had never fully explored the top shelves for Mr Twentyman seldom did a stock-taking.

'Ray, would you help me?' she called. 'If you'd bring the ladder.'

She climbed up, and had begun searching among the dusty cardboard boxes when the doorbell jangled and she nearly lost her footing.

'A customer! And so early in the day!' she thought. 'A very good sign.'

'Oh!' she sneezed and, recovering herself, looked down on the young man with the dark crinkly hair.

'Excuse me.' He offered a hand. 'Can I help you down?'

'No thank you, I can manage. You startled me, that's all.'

'I do apologize.' He gazed admiringly at the pink flushed cheeks and the tendrils of fair hair on her forehead.

'I'm the traveller from Hopkins and Handley,' he said, as she hopped nimbly off the ladder.

'Oh,' said Alice, a little disappointed. 'I thought you were my first sale of the day. Where's old Mr Jenks?'

'He's retired.' The young man began to open his case.

'Mr Twentyman's not here today. He does the ordering,' said

Alice. 'But as you're here,' she went on, mustering up her dignity and trying to look as if being in charge was no novelty at all, 'I could order, I suppose, to save you coming back, that is . . .'

Mr Twentyman had not expressly forbidden her to order more stock, but that was only because it had not occurred to him.

'Anything new?' she said, as if she dealt with travellers every day of the week.

'Why not?' she told herself. After all, she was in charge.

The young man delved into his case. 'The very latest,' he said. 'Now I think you'll agree this is something really exciting.'

'What is it?' Alice stared.

'It's a toy bear,' said the traveller.

'It's – well – different.' She looked at the long-limbed creature, the plush body, the large head, the boot-button eyes, and the soft felt pads on the paws.

'Very new, just arrived.' The young man made the bear's arms move backwards and forwards. 'Came from Germany to begin with,' he said. 'Firm of Steiff. They're making them in America too – the Ideal Toy Corporation, they're very go-ahead. They'll soon be making them here, I shouldn't wonder – the plush for the body comes from Yorkshire anyway.

'Quite easy to manufacture,' he went on. 'A large sack for the body. Four thin sacks for each limb. They were the hit of the Leipzig Toy Fair.'

'A child would like it,' said Alice. 'Something to hug.'

'The thing is,' said the salesman, 'it's a toy a boy can play with too.'

Alice nodded. 'What do you call them?'

'Teddy's bears,' said the salesman. 'After Theodore Roosevelt. Seems he was on a bear hunt, found this small brown bear, refused to shoot it. There were pictures in all the papers.'

'Teddy's bears.' Alice smiled. She made up her mind. 'All right. I'll take one.'

'You won't regret it,' said the salesman. 'They're going to sweep the country. The newest craze.'

'Well, we'll see.' Alice might be young, but she was shrewd, and she knew an over-enthusiastic salesman when she met one. Time would turn him into a Mr Jenks who had sold tin soldiers with a weary air, as if youth had long since departed.

4

'My card,' said the young man. 'Mr Edward Porter. If you require any more stock just let me know. I'll be along in two shakes.'

He shook her hand, holding it a moment longer than was really necessary. Alice didn't notice. She was thinking about the window display. Of course! The bear could be the centre of the display – a real novelty to bring in the customers.

Flags! She knew they had some, somewhere in the back shop. There were certainly Union Jacks, left over from King Edward's coronation.

'Yes, yes, of course.' She smiled at Mr Porter, and he thought he had never seen eyes of such deep blue – cornflower blue, in fact. He had a feeling for things poetic, had Mr Porter.

As soon as the door had closed behind him, Alice collected the sailor dolls, the guardsmen dolls and one or two china dolls and set them on either side of the window. She sent Ray to search for the Union Jacks and, by great good fortune, he found the Stars and Stripes as well.

She put the bear in the centre of the display, the American flag wedged between body and forepaw.

'New from the United States of America,' she wrote on a large placard and propped it in front of the bear. Then she went outside to admire the effect.

Several urchins were playing kick-the-can down the street. They crowded round to admire the display.

'What's that, miss?' One of them pointed to the bear. 'What's that funny-looking animal?'

'It's a bear, the very latest,' Alice said. She looked at them for a moment. An old tin can wasn't much of a toy. Yet some children had toy trains and real sailing boats and footballs.

With a sigh, she went indoors again. 'Now for the customers,' she told herself. 'But not many of those around,' she thought sadly.

How the day dragged! She sent Ray out on an errand, and finished tidying the shop. By early afternoon there had been only three customers – a child buying pencils, two small girls ooh-ing and aah-ing over highly coloured scraps. They all stood wide-eyed before the window display.

Alice began to have misgivings. 'It's early days yet,' she

braced herself. 'But I do hope he sells before Mr Twentyman comes back.'

The bear looked steadily ahead from the boot-button eyes. Surely any child would love him, thought Alice. He was just asking to be picked up and hugged.

Yet again, she flicked a feather duster over the tiny rooms of the dolls' house, over the plates of plaster food and the miniature tea set. She paused by the toy theatres. These were her favourites – especially *The Sleeping Beauty* and *Jack the Giant Killer*. She sighed. Being in charge wasn't as exciting as she had expected. It was turning out to be a very long day.

But then the door opened, and two small children, a boy about six and a girl about four years old, came into the shop, shepherded by their governess. 'Oh . . .' the little girl's eyes widened.

'Come in,' Alice smiled encouragingly. 'What can I do for you?'

'We've got some money from Uncle to buy a present,' said the boy.

'Then you've come to the right place,' said Alice. 'I'm sure we can find something you'll like.'

'Nothing dirty or dangerous,' said the governess hastily.

Alice ignored her.

'Look at this!' The boy hung over the model station with its brick tunnel and station buildings complete with clock tower.

'And here's a toy farm – maybe you'd like that?' Alice pointed out the placid black-and-white cows standing in a green plaster meadow.

'Or a Noah's Ark, maybe?' suggested the governess. 'That's a nice Bible toy. You could play with it on Sundays.'

'Or a boat. This one really sails.' Alice picked it up. 'Or, I wonder, have you seen the bear in the window with the flag in his paw?'

The small girl had been silently sucking the strings of her bonnet. 'I saw him,' she volunteered. 'Can I touch him?'

Alice reached into the window and brought out the bear. 'He's a new kind of bear. He came all the way from America.'

'America?' said the boy. 'Really and truly?'

Alice smiled at him. 'Yes, he did. He came all the way by ship with some other bears. There are lots of bears like him in New

York. But he is one of the very first to arrive in England. His brothers and sisters all stood on the quayside, waving their pocket handkerchiefs, as the boat set sail for Southampton.'

'What did he eat?' asked the boy. 'He must have been very hungry coming all that way.'

'Ship's biscuits, of course,' said Alice. 'And rum to drink.'

The governess sniffed her disapproval.

'I mean lemonade,' Alice amended hastily.

'I can smell the salt on his fur,' said the boy, gazing in admiration.

'Now that's enough,' said the governess briskly. 'You must choose a toy. If there is nothing here, we can always go to town.'

'He is a very brave bear,' said the boy, paying no attention, 'to come all this way on his own.'

'He *is* a very brave bear,' said Alice, 'and very adventurous. Once he got lost in a forest. Another time he rode down Fifth Avenue, in New York, in a carriage. And he came on a train all the way from the West.'

'What about his brothers and sisters?' asked the boy.

'Oh, yes,' said Alice, 'he has lots of brothers and sisters. All the other bears begged to be allowed to come to Europe. So they are arriving next week. We will have a special party for them in the window. You must tell all your friends to come and see it.'

'Let's buy him,' said the boy, 'before anyone else does.'

'Not a Noah's Ark?' said the governess. 'Or a nice sailor doll, or a farmyard?'

'The bear,' said the boy, who knew his own mind.

'A very good idea,' said Alice, wrapping the bear in brown paper.

As soon as they'd gone, she danced round the shop, humming to herself. She knew she could sell more of these bears. So she sat down immediately and wrote out an order, 'Six bears – urgent delivery,' and sent Ray to the post before she had second and more prudent thoughts.

The next afternoon the doorbell jangled and Mr Porter's cheerful grin announced his arrival. 'Right on schedule, as our American friends say. Six Teddy's bears, as ordered, and you won't be disappointed, Miss, I can tell you . . .'

'Oh!' Alice smiled at him. 'That's very speedy service.'

'Prompt to please, that's my motto,' he said.

'You haven't been in the job long,' she guessed.

'Not very long,' he said. 'But it's a good job with fine prospects as long as you work hard.'

He looked up as he unpacked the case – yes, cornflower blue was not too strong a description, and he fancied the eyes were looking at him admiringly.

'I'm sure,' she said gently, 'you are a very good salesman and they are lucky to have you.'

Mr Porter's ears reddened as he lifted the bears out of the case. 'Now that'll be . . .' he did a quick mental sum.

'If you would just invoice us as usual,' said Alice with dignity.

'Of course.'

She stifled any doubts. 'I'm certain they'll sell. And if we should want to re-order?'

It would be pleasant to see the young man again – but all in the way of business, of course.

Mr Porter found himself writing out the order form with a trembling hand. He almost increased the discount there and then, but he was a salesman when all was said and done, and he resisted the temptation.

'I think a picnic scene,' said Alice dreamily.

'What's that?' He went on, 'Of course they're imported just now, but no reason why they shouldn't be made in this country as soon as the trade catches on. They're planning to make them with growlers soon – we've had news from our agents.'

'Growlers?'

'You know – ' he imitated a bear growling. 'To make them more lifelike.'

'What will they think of next?'

Reluctantly, he closed his case. 'I'd best be off then. I wonder if I might call again, to see you.' There was a slight emphasis on the 'you'.

'Please do,' said Alice.

Mr Porter strode down the street, whistling. It had been a very good day.

Back at the shop, Alice rearranged the window. This time she created a picnic scene. She placed the bears in the centre of the window, and around them spades and pails and shells. In no time a small group of children had gathered. From then on, there was a crowd in front of the window, their noses pressed to the glass.

Next morning the first customer arrived early. He was a middle-aged man with a prosperous air about him.

'Someone told me you sell these new-fangled bears,' he said. 'Just the thing for my godson.' He pulled out a wallet.

'Straight from the States,' said Alice. 'Mr Twentyman is very much in the forefront when it comes to new ideas. There isn't a toyshop between here and Birmingham where you'll find more up-to-date toys than we have here.' She began to get carried away. 'We are, I'm fairly certain, the only shop in the area to stock these bears.'

'Oh, you fibber,' said a still, small voice.

'Is that so? Enterprising man, Mr Twentyman. Congratulate him for me,' said the customer.

'Have you no shame?' said the still, small voice. 'Just think what Mr Twentyman would say.'

To be honest, Alice had given very little thought to her employer, she had been so happily occupied during the past few days.

But next morning there was a postcard. Mr Twentyman's sister was rallying. He would be back on Friday and, in the meantime, he hoped all was well in the shop.

Alice felt slightly guilty, but he was sure to be pleased with the way she had handled things in his absence. By the beginning of the week she had sold four more bears and customers had bought other toys too. She had done a brisk trade in boats and hoops and clockwork toys, and Snap and Happy Families. The news of the bears' arrival spread throughout the neighbourhood, and small children begged to be taken past the window.

Alice liked having the bears in the shop, and she'd found out more about them. How the first bears had come from the Steiff factory in the Black Forest. How Herr Steiff's son had gone to the zoo at Stuttgart, specially to study the bears there.

But, in the midst of the excitement, came another postcard: 'Returning 4.30 train tomorrow. J.T.'

Alice did hope he would be pleased but, for the first time, she began to have serious misgivings. And when, the following afternoon, the familiar black-garbed figure loomed on the threshold Alice knew by his face that there was trouble ahead.

'Welcome back!' she said. 'And how was your sister? Better, I hope?'

'I met that old gossip across the way.'

'Oh,' said Alice, after a pause.

'"Won't recognize your shop," she said. "that girl, she's been up to all sorts of things behind your back . . ." Just what,' he demanded, 'has been going on?'

'Going on?' Alice tried to sound puzzled, in the hope of delaying the explanation.

'You know quite well what I mean. She said something about bears.'

Alice pointed to the remaining bear in the window. She had sold all the rest. 'Selling like hot cakes,' she said, trying to keep the tremor out of her voice.

'You ordered – you ordered stock without consulting me!'

'Well, yes,' she stammered, 'but such a success . . .'

'How dare you!' His face darkened. 'I go away for just a short time, and this is what happens!'

'But,' said Alice, 'they've sold very well . . .'

'That's neither here nor there,' he said grimly. 'We'll see about this. I can't trust you, Miss . . .'

Half a century later, Alice might have said,' You can keep your job,' and walked out in high dudgeon. But jobs were hard to get. What would they say at home if she were dismissed, and probably without a reference? So she swallowed hard and said meekly, 'I'm sorry.'

'Sorry, indeed, sorry's not enough.' He stormed upstairs. Young Ray's eyes widened. 'I heard that. What a row! What's going to happen?'

'I don't know. I don't indeed.' Alice was very near to tears. She picked up the remaining bear from the window display. 'Oh, you have caused a lot of trouble.' She hugged the bear. She could well understand how a child, perhaps sick or lonely, might find the bear friendly and comforting.

But, just then, the door opened, and a slim woman, elegant in black and white, came into the shop. 'Is this where I buy the bears? I've heard all about them and I want one for my nephew.'

'Of course,' said Alice. 'This is the very last one.' She tried to keep her voice level – she was aware that Mr Twentyman had come downstairs again.

'Isn't he a darling!' said the woman. 'Such a good idea – a lovely toy for a child. And you have such a charming, old-fashioned shop.'

Behind her, Alice could hear her employer sniff.

After the customer had gone, he said, 'Maybe I was a bit hasty. You'd better tell me what's been going on.'

Mr Twentyman always did his accounts at the end of the month and, when he had totted up the final column of figures, he sat back, frowning thoughtfully. Then he called Alice into the office.

'Sales are up,' he said brusquely. 'Can't say fairer than that. What you did was wrong. But, in the circumstances, we'll say no more about it.'

'Thank you,' said Alice and, although she seethed inside, she didn't dare say anything in her defence.

There was a large gap in the window now. Alice really missed the bears. They had such a comical appearance and their long, rather solemn faces had such character.

Of course they'd catch on, anyone with any imagination must know that. Just what a child would like – not so prim as the pink-cheeked dolls, easier to hug than a stiff wooden doll. 'If it was my shop,' she thought, 'I'd have it filled with bears – black bears, brown bears, bears with growlers. What fun it could be!'

Next time Mr Porter called at the shop, Mr Twentyman was firmly back in command. There was no sign of the girl with blue eyes.

'It was you sold my assistant them bears,' said Mr Twentyman.

'Well, er, yes.' Mr Twentyman could look rather formidable and the young man quaked a little.

'Doing well, are they?' he enquired.

'I grant you that,' said Mr Twentyman. 'Yes, I can honestly say they sold well.'

'Then,' said the young man eagerly, 'I suppose you wouldn't care to re-order?'

'You suppose right,' said Mr Twentyman. 'You can't be too careful in this business. It's all too easy to be left with stock you can't sell.'

'But . . .' said the young man.

Mr Twentyman shook his head. 'They're a novelty. It's best to stick to the lines that sell well all the time. Good-day to you, young man.'

Mr Porter closed his case. He knew when he was wasting his time.

The following Sunday evening, Mr Porter walked his young lady home from chapel. Even then, his thoughts were not far from work.

'I've had a very good month of sales,' he said. 'I sold another half-dozen of those Teddy's bears. To an old-fashioned sort of shop – the owner's a bit of a stick-in-the-mud, but the assistant, well, she was prepared to take a chance. They sold like hot cakes.'

'Oh?' said his young lady. She tried to take a polite interest in his work.

'Really go-ahead, that young lady in the shop,' he went on. 'A good-looking girl, too,' he added.

'Oh?' She withdrew her hand from his arm and stared straight ahead. 'Well, if some girls like to put themselves forward, I'm sure that's all very well.'

'No need to be jealous,' he said cheerfully. Time might teach him tact, but he had a long way to go.

He took the young lady's hand in his. 'I've had a very good run at the firm. Mr Handley's giving me a rise. He says he's very pleased with the way I'm getting on with the customers. What I'm trying to say . . .' he broke off.

'What?' enquired the young lady softly, 'What are you trying to say?'

'What I meant was . . .' he started again, and suddenly he couldn't continue.

She tried to prompt him. 'You were saying you're doing well in the firm. Making a real success of the job . . .'

'Well, yes.' There was a pause for a moment, and then he said the first thing that came into his head. 'These bears – I know they've sold well, and they'll be all the fashion for a bit, and then I wouldn't be surprised if the craze is over. They're just another American idea. You'll see.'

'I'm sure you're right, Edward,' she said, gazing at him adoringly. 'You always are.'

He thought, after he left her at her door, that he had been a fool. She would have made any man a good wife. And he had excellent prospects, a lot to offer. What on earth had made him draw back?

A few days later, he selected the largest and best of the bears from his stock. 'I must be mad,' he said to himself, as he squared his shoulders and set off for Mr Twentyman's toyshop.

* * *

'Not bad, not bad at all.' The young woman stepped back to admire the display. 'People have been wonderful, the way they've agreed to lend things – really valuable things, too. It's going to be a good exhibition.'

'Thanks to you,' said the reporter who'd come along to cover the exhibition. The girl blushed. 'A Century of Toys' had been her idea.

He went on, 'It's odd really. You'd think the toys would be battered but they're not. Look at these farm animals – the paint's scarcely worn. And these boats – you could still sail them.' He picked up a toy engine. 'Now, this is a real collector's piece.'

'They were much cherished,' said the girl. 'But it is marvellous that so many are still working. I like these mechanical toys.' She pointed to an earnest-looking monkey, holding a pair of cymbals between its paws. 'But the bears are my favourite. These ones' – she pointed to three bears in a glass case – 'are very old and very valuable. See how different they are from today's teddy bears – the longish head, the floppy limbs. They must have looked very fine when they were new, but they've been hugged a lot over the years, I expect.' She grinned. 'This one,' she said, lifting the bear in front, 'is my favourite of all. He's special. I brought him in. He belonged to my great-grandmother and he was one of the very first bears imported into Britain.'

'Really?' said the man. The bear was badly faded but he wore a jaunty bow tie which gave him a dashing appearance.

'I wish I'd known her,' said the girl thoughtfully. 'Gran used to talk about her. Apparently, when Great-Grandma was a girl, she worked in a toyshop and she bought a whole lot of teddy bears when the owner was away. She nearly got the sack. The bears were a novelty then, of course, and girls in those days weren't supposed to show initiative.'

She went on thoughtfully, 'I think Great-Grandma had a mind of her own. She joined the Suffragettes later on.'

'But she must have been sentimental, too,' said the man. 'If she kept the bear, I mean. There must have been a soft spot somewhere.'

'Oh yes,' said the girl. 'There must have been, because she kept the bear on her dressing-table for the rest of her life, even when she was a very old lady. So Gran told me. Only Great-Grandma didn't buy the bear herself. A young salesman gave it to her – the one who persuaded her to buy the bears in the first place.'

'A piece of family history,' said the man. 'And a nice little story there.'

'You could say so,' the girl agreed. 'That young salesman became her husband and, of course, my great-grandfather.'

The reporter smiled as he put his notebook away. 'Quite a romance. Listen,' he said suddenly, 'I don't suppose you'd be free for a bit of lunch?'

'Why not?' The girl smiled at him and he noticed for the first time how her blue eyes sparkled.

'I'll just tell my colleague,' she said. 'Someone has to be here all the time, the toys are so valuable.'

As he held the door open for her, he said, 'By the way, I don't know your first name.'

'It's Alice,' said the girl. 'Same as my great-grandmother.'

The bears sat immobile in the display cabinet. Some had tattered ears or an eye missing. The brown fur had faded and the felt on their paws was worn.

But anyone with a trace of imagination could have supposed he heard a murmur of approval. And Alice's bear most certainly nodded his head and winked. After all, he had seen it happen before.

Shooting Teddy Bears
is No Picnic

ABIGAIL HARMAN

T HEODORE FELL over. Again.

I sighed, moved out from behind the tripod and helped him up. After dusting him down and getting him to stand in exactly the same position as before, I hurried back to the Nikon to take the shot. Then, just as I had him perfectly focused he slipped again, sliding slowly and majestically forwards onto his face. I shouted at him irritably but he paid no attention and, by the time I had got him back to his feet once more, the sun had gone behind a cloud and the light had changed completely.

I had been especially keen to take some pictures of Theodore and Lucy together in the garden; in natural light against a background of plants and bushes. Now, I had to decide between going all the way back to the house, dragging out the Bowens lights, the reflectors and the rest of the equipment and rearranging the entire set-up, or waiting impatiently for the sun to reappear. I opted to wait; at least the sun, if it came out, wouldn't need to be hauled almost a hundred metres like my 15 kilos of lighting.

I glowered at Theodore but, being a lady, refrained from cursing the inconsiderate b— under my breath. He stared back at me with a haughty, nonchalant look whilst Lucy, as always, smiled vacantly in my general direction. I ignored her and shook my head to vent my frustration. It's maddening when photographic models act up and show the kind of total disregard for the photographer's problems that these two were showing.

I waited a while and then, just as I was about to trudge back to the house, the sun slipped out from behind a cloud. I could see it wasn't going to be out for long so I quickly bent to the viewfinder, rapidly adjusted the aperture, checked the focus once more and – watched Theodore slip drunkenly sideways and topple on top of Lucy. The two of them rolled on the grass in an abandoned, blue-movie embrace and ended up under the variegated laurel.

That was it. This time I did swear. I packed up the camera, collapsed the tripod and, with Theodore and Lucy under each arm, marched back to the house.

No, Theodore isn't some drunken, pint-sized photographic model and Lucy his no-better-than-she-ought-to-be girlfriend. Nor are they professional, pain-in-the-posterior child models. Theodore and Lucy are teddy bears and if you think photographing teddy bears is an easy way to earn a living then you'd better think again.

Shooting teddy bears is no picnic.

I have been earning a living as a professional photographer for about twelve years and, like all professionals, can recount countless stories about the people I've had to photograph. Most photographers have a love-hate relationship with their subjects and, in a funny kind of way, it isn't so different with teddy bears.

I love teddy bears and always have, ever since I was a little girl. They're warm and cuddly, always there to be loved and always ready to listen to your moans and woes. With a teddy bear there's always a furry shoulder to cry on. They never interrupt; never tell you to snap out of it; never come up with some ditzy, smart-alec solution to all your problems. They are sympathetic and silent and never, never disappear for the day to play golf. But there's no doubt that, when it comes to being photographed, they can be irritating, awkward, uncooperative, and often just plain cussed. Exactly like people.

I started my career photographing people. Or, more accurately, bits of people.

My first professional job was as a medical photographer in a large teaching hospital where the surgeons seemed to have this bizarre passion for cutting out vital organs and then asking someone like me to take pictures of them. Scores of pictures, all in full-colour and from every angle imaginable. Goodness knows why. You'd think they'd have seen enough of people's innards without compiling family albums. Usually the organ was pinned to a screen or placed on a table so it could be shot with a rostrum camera; but I'm convinced that, if they could have got away with it, the doctors would have had me snap them proudly displaying the organs and grinning at the camera like shark fishermen on the Great Barrier Reef. In the end I decided that the only reason they had all the pictures taken was so that they could disappear behind the bike sheds and swop them: 'Two kodachromes of my spleen for one slide of your old alcoholic's liver.'

Sometimes in the hospital I had to take pictures of complete people; people with all their parts still intact. That was one of the easiest jobs I ever had. They were all so wonderfully cooperative, they didn't move or twitch or blink their eyes or anything. Maybe it was because they were dead.

Later, I was a fine art photographer in a museum where my job was to photograph priceless works of art. In that job it wasn't the subject that twitched and blinked; it was the photographer. Every time I had to pick up a Ming vase, the value of which was a row of numbers longer than a roll of film, my palms turned sweaty and I shook like a leaf. Heaven knows how I never broke anything. How I longed for the calm of the hospital morgue where, compared to shooting works of art, snapping cadavers was dead easy.

With a photographic background like mine it was odds-on that I would end up doing something out of the ordinary; though given the nature of my previous work you might have expected me to turn up in the British Museum, taking pictures of mummies. As it is, I eventually finished up with my own studio taking pictures of teddies.

It all came about when I started my own business, making greetings cards from original prints of my photographs. First I started with local black-and-white scenes of Cambridge and the surrounding villages, and then later I shot rustic scenes of lambs and horses and old agricultural implements. The cards were popular. One day I noticed a friend's teddy bear snuggling into a corner of the sofa in her lounge. He was a lovely-looking little fellow and reminded me of Georgie.

Georgie was the teddy bear I'd had and loved to pieces when I was young. He was a delicious Geoffrey bear, about 14" high and fully jointed, with quite long arms which bent in towards his tummy and a really cute, slightly bashed-in face. His fur, which was sandy coloured and rough to the touch was, in places, almost bald from too much love. He wasn't the best-looking bear in the world but he did have character. And he was mine.

Tragically, Georgie disappeared, never to be seen again, on the day my husband and I moved to our present house. Somewhere between our old house and the new one, Georgie went out of my life forever. It's not an uncommon story but a sad one all the same. Even after all these years I miss him and sometimes wonder if there isn't somewhere an enormous house removers' warehouse filled with teddy bears. If there is, I hope they're all happy and having a good time.

Looking at my friend's bear reminded me of the time when, as light relief from photographing kidney stones and lengths of large intestine, I would take black-and-white shots of Georgie. I remembered how, depending on the quality of the light and the position of the camera, I was able to get him to look quite different in almost every picture and how, with his expressive, lived-in face, it was possible to get Georgie to convey distinctive moods; to make him 'say' different things.

I asked my friend if I might photograph her bear and perhaps use the picture on one of my greetings cards.

Afterwards I noticed two things. Firstly, that the picture of the teddy became one of the most popular of my cards. People, it seemed, liked photos of teddy bears. Secondly, when I looked at the picture and compared it to the 'live' model, I could see how much of the teddy's 'character' had come through to the celluloid.

I had shot the picture in black and white. Almost all my work is in monochrome. I rarely work with colour film; usually, colour works best when it's used for events or scenes, that's why holiday snaps are always so much better in colour. Black and white, on the other hand, records impressions, feelings, sensations; it emphasizes tones and shades of light and dark. The quality of the light, whether it's natural or in the studio, is so much more important in black and white; it casts rich, subtle shadows and creates strange vibrant shapes which form an intrinsic part of the picture. Black-and-white photography is really like painting with light; its unique properties are especially good at depicting character and capturing mood.

Teddy bears are characters. And creatures of mood. Our moods. Repeatedly they're the recipients of our feelings; cheerfully dancing around the room in our arms when we're happy, serenely absorbing our tears in their fur when we're sad, silently watching over us when we sleep. They take on our moods and turn into characters and when I took that picture I discovered, or perhaps rediscovered from the time I had photographed Georgie, that black-and-white photography was the ideal medium with which to capture the distinctive character of teddy bears.

Of course it helps having my own darkroom. Being able to do my own processing meant that I was better able to produce the image I had seen when I shot my friend's bear; to reproduce the mood I had tried to capture in the picture. Using black-and-white film allows me control in printing: I can use different papers, alter the contrast or add printing screens to give a special soft or grainy effect. Often I sepia-tone the prints which gives the picture a warm, old-fashioned feel or sometimes I hand-tint the teddy's bow; one splash of colour in a picture of grey tones and subtle shadows.

Having discovered that people liked photos of bears, I 'borrowed' a ragged, disreputable teddy that has belonged to my husband since he was a child and which he calls Doodum. (No, don't ask). Although my husband maintains that he has neither interest nor affection for this poor, crumpled creature, I notice that Doodum sits in pride of place on a shelf above the word processor in his study. Unfortunately, I forgot to tell my husband I was borrowing Doodum; when he discovered the bear was missing, I had to struggle to stop him telephoning the police, Interpol, MI5 and the Joint Defence Chiefs of Staff. Any poor policeman or government official, confronted by my panic-stricken, middle-aged husband screaming, 'Someone's teddy-napped my Doodum,' would have immediately had him carted off to a nice padded room for a long, long time. I was only able to settle him after a few large brandies and a touching reconciliation with Doodum who, in the end, he let me photograph. I suppose the incident should have told me something about people's attitudes towards having their teddies taken away to be photographed.

Doodum's picture was not only popular as a greetings card but, again, I noticed that the photograph had really brought out his disreputable, debauched but highly attractive character.

After that I borrowed a number of teddies from my family to set up a series of 'bear shoots'. It was then I discovered that, like people, not all bears are photogenic. Some, though handsome in the flesh – or should that be, 'in the fur'? – could not transmit their physical appeal to celluloid. Usually they were the newer bears. Today's teddies, many of them sold in specialist teddy bear shops, are attractive enough but somehow, when photographed, they appear flat and characterless. The most interesting and photogenic bears are almost always the older ones; those with a history.

I think older bears have a special appeal. Maybe it's because they've been loved so much by so many for so long? Many teddies have remained in the same family since they were new, passing down through the generations, moving *safely* from home to home, travelling with their owners to the far-flung parts of the globe, all the while garnering masses of affection along with their rubbed-ball fur, their badly stitched-back-on arms and their wobbly stuffing. Others, like those that go missing in a house move, change from one family to another where, I like to think, they are just as much loved and cuddled. In either case teddy bears accumulate an enormous reservoir of love as they suffer the scars of life, mutely observing our joys and sorrows passing in quotidian procession before their boot-button eyes. Those older teddies have brought decades of solace and delight. They have witnessed history – and it shows. It shows in their faces: some are cheerful, some doleful, some sad, some quizzical; almost all human emotion can be detected on some teddy bear's face somewhere and, with the right light and set-up, it can be brought out in a photograph.

Gradually, and after much trial and error, I became quite good at knowing in advance which bears would make suitable models. I found that the really photogenic ones are in a minority and, because they're older, usually the most prized and precious. Usually, but not always. Some of my best bears have been rescued from years of solitary confinement in dusty lofts by people who had forgotten that they existed. It's nice to think that, if nothing else, my work has brought a few teddy bears back into the light. However, the shortage of good bears meant that I had soon exhausted the supply from my family. I began asking close friends and neighbours if I might borrow their bears.

Everyone was pleased to be of help although, of course, they all knew that I hoped to produce pictures of their teddies which would sell as greetings cards. In fact they were flattered that I thought their bears were good enough to be photographed though, as word got around, the job did call for some tact. A few neighbours and even some complete strangers turned up at the house with their bears, asking if they might be photographed. Some of the bears were excellent but others – well, what can I say? No one wants to be told that their teddy is too monstrous, too battered, too dopey-looking to make a good picture. It's like telling a mother that her child is ugly. Usually I chickened out and took a couple of quick shots of the bear and gave them to the owner as a gift. It's an expensive solution, but the price of diplomacy has always come high.

Recently I have been commissioned by Athena International, the card people, to produce a series of teddy bear photographs under the title, 'Abigail's Bears'. The owners of the bears I've featured in the series have all been delighted that their teddies can be seen on cards in places as far apart as Paris, Tokyo and New York. However, as a sign of my appreciation, I always give the owner of any bear that appears on one of my cards a large eight by six print of their teddy.

Usually photographers, when taking pictures which include people and which they intend to sell, either pay a modelling fee or request people who appear incidentally in the picture to sign a 'model release form'. This gives the photographer permission to use the person's image in a picture which might be sold. Up to now I haven't had to produce a 'bear release form'. Most people are very relaxed when it comes to lending their bears for a 'shoot' but there are a few who have been as anxious as first-time mums with their babies.

Following the affair with Doodum the next hint I got of this phenomenon was when a neighbour, from whom I had borrowed a lovely little Horst bear, called early in the evening to ask for her bear back. I explained that I hadn't yet photographed him, whereupon she said that her bear 'couldn't possibly stay out all night'. As she was being kind enough to lend him to me I took him home and dutifully collected him the next morning. His owner came with me and watched nervously as I set her bear up against a terracotta pot in the conservatory for some low-angle shots.

She wasn't the only owner to watch me anxiously as I carefully set up the shot, positioned the bear and clicked away feverishly. One was particularly anxious that, as I wanted to keep her bear until the light was just right for the shot I had in mind, I wouldn't allow him to mix with any of the other bears in my keeping 'in case he caught something'.

The worst and most embarrassing incident, and one which caused a minor scandal in our village, happened when I borrowed a beautiful little Bruin bear. As nearly all the bears I come across are decidedly 'male' I was pleased to find that this one was 'female'. I enhanced her feminity by fixing a bow to the fur close to her ear and putting a small veil over her head before taking some 'happy wedding day' shots which featured her together with a rather handsome Steiff bear. They made a perfect couple and, after the wedding shots, it occurred to me to take a picture of them in bed together. Nothing salacious or *risqué*, just a few shots of innocent affection. I waited until the early morning sun was streaking across the counterpane, balanced this with some back-fill light and took some marvellous pictures. The handsome, furry couple were side by side, half propped up on the pillows and with their arms around each other. It was all wonderfully warm, cuddly and innocent.

The first mistake I made was to show the pictures to the little bear's owner. She was horrified. She would not, she said huffily, have let her bear out 'if I'd known she was going to be naughty'. I was distraught; it was the first time that someone had been upset by one of my pictures. I was in danger of losing a friend and close neighbour. The next mistake I made was to tell my husband.

My husband is a writer and, like me, works from home. It's a good arrangement; the house is big enough so we don't fall over each other and we can go for hours without meeting. He's a lovely man really and I like having him around; it's just that, much of the time, he drives me nuts. Like most writers he has a great feeling for words and absolutely no feeling for the social niceties. He thought the whole incident of the bears in the bed was hilarious. He started calling me 'Goldilocks' and told me that I was the only person in the world who could turn teddy bears into pandas.

I had no idea what he meant. He explained that I was definitely guilty of 'pandering' which means to act as a go-between in some illicit sexual intrigue. It used to be a serious crime and still is in parts of America. (See what I mean? In the middle of a desperately serious social crisis my husband is the kind of fruitcake who starts quoting useless rubbish like that.) To make matters worse he told all his drinking cronies that I was running a bordello for bare teddies. I started getting some very peculiar looks from the neighbours.

The matter was finally resolved when the bear's owner learned that the handsome Steiff bear with whom her teddy had been photographed in bed belonged to Lady—, a member of the local gentry. The knowledge that her bear might have been *in flagrante delicto* with a bear belonging to the minor aristocracy went some way to mollify her, though it was some time before relations returned to normal and she forgave me for pandering to her bear's baser instincts. Even now, months after the incident, my husband gleefully recounts the story of the 'bare teddies' to our dinner-party guests whilst I still can't bring myself to produce a card featuring the picture, even though I think it's charming, evocative and not the least bit in bad taste.

Location, even when it's a bed, is very important in teddy bear photography, and I try to shoot my bears in as many different locations, both interior and exterior, as possible. This is especially true now that so much of my work is commissioned by Athena and I am producing so many 'occasions cards', such as – 'congratulations on passing your exams', 'happy eighteenth birthday' – and so on.

In the early days, when I was shooting for my own cards, I found the bear and then created the picture. Now that I am commissioned I am given the subject and have to find the right bear to fit the part, like a producer looking for the right actor for a film. Bears featuring in the 'good luck' cards must have an intense, yet relaxed, look, as if they are working hard but are confident of achieving their results. Quizzical-looking bears often suit this kind of role. Happy bears suit the 'well done' cards, whilst the doleful bears are perfect for the 'miss you' or 'get well' cards.

It's only when I've chosen the bear best suited for the role that I can decide on the right location. I have shot teddy bears at the seaside, waving farewell to the ferry at Harwich, as well as at the end of the runway at Stansted Airport, waving goodbye to a Jumbo jet. Some of my teddy bear pictures have been taken in Cambridge colleges or in the Botanical Gardens; others in stately homes or outside East Anglian churches. Many pictures were shot around my own home: in my photographic studio, in the garden and in the conservatory.

Beyond a bow tied around the neck or in the fur, I never dress the bears for a shoot. A full suit of clothes may work well for Messrs Rupert and Paddington Bear but, in the main, I don't think dressing a bear up works too well in photographs. Generally speaking, clothes hide the bear and conceal his character; the very element I am trying to capture. Props on the other hand are vital. A pair of spectacles or sun glasses; a little hat, a small bunch of flowers, a few inches of lace for a wedding veil, all add to the atmosphere of the picture and the character of the bear.

One of the more complicated pictures I was commissioned to produce was for a 'congratulations on passing your driving test' card. It took my commissioning designer and me ages to find a large enough child's car in which a couple of teddy bears could sit. At last we found one. It had been hand-built by a local crafts-man for his children and, instead of being pedal-powered, was driven by batteries. It was marvellous; it even had a 'dicky' seat in the back which could take a third teddy. It looked like one of those old-fashioned Bentleys.

Apart from the car I also needed some helium-filled balloons, 'L' plates, flowers, an old-fashioned driving cap and a couple of pairs of driving goggles. When I had got all the props together and selected the three teddies to feature in the pictures, I decided to shoot the scene outside some old-fashioned wrought-iron gates near the house. As I could get a supply of electricity from nearby I used my portable lights to enhance the natural light.

Foolishly I asked my husband for some help in humping the lights and props to the location. The thing about writers is that, when a friend calls for a drink, they'll drop everything but, if a wife asks for some help – then they're always at a critical point in the novel or script. In the end I persuaded him to give me a hand. Idly he watched me setting up the lights and arranging the teddies. Then I think he must have had a sudden rush of blood to the head. Suddenly, he began imagining that he was Martin Scorsese or Cecil B. De Mille. 'Shoot it this way,' he ordered, 'with the sun over there, the lights here and the shadows falling there.' After I had humoured him, he insisted on shooting it from another angle. This went on for about an hour until, finally, he got bored with playing at film directors and ambled off, leaving me to rearrange the car and teddies into the set-up I had originally thought out. Doodum would make a better photographer than my husband.

I was there for another seven hours, arranging and rearrang-ing the teddies in various poses in the car. I took about forty shots. One was commissioned.

Arranging the teddy bears into the poses I want can present problems and, as they are borrowed, I have to be very careful not to do anything to damage them. It can take hours and much patience to get teddy bears to sit or stand in the position I want; to hold their heads at exactly the right angle, to have their arms in precisely the right position; to have their bows tied just so. To achieve the best effects I must admit to the occasional judicious use of fine thread to fix their heads or arms in the posture needed for the picture. Sellotape is also a useful and non-damaging fixative, and so is blu-tack which is great for helping to keep the teddies still and secure.

That's what I ultimately used on Theodore. When, finally, I shot him and Lucy in the garden I stuck two wads of blu-tack to the bottom of his pads to help him keep his feet. It worked wonders but, to make sure he didn't revert to his old trick of toppling over at the critical moment, I also wedged a thin stick into the ground behind him and jammed it up against his bottom. It worked wonders. Theodore, with the demure Lucy sitting prettily by his side, stood tall and erect for the entire shoot.

Though I could swear it was the stick in his bottom that wiped the arrogant, supercilious smirk right off his face.

Harold's Bear

PAULINE MACAULAY

HAROLD HAD been lying dead in his Pimlico flat for several days before his body, on the lounge floor, had been spotted by a window-cleaner. This is what I was told when they finally tracked me down to the conference I was attending in Manchester. A police constable came with the sad news under the mistaken impression that I was Harold's cousin. In fact, Harold had no living relatives but, as I was one of the few privileged visitors to the Pimlico flat, his landlady had presumed we were related. Not so. I was, however, his oldest friend.

Yes, we went back a long way, Harold and I. From primary school to Cambridge and ever after. We met on a regular basis, usually attending a concert together or the opera . . . and then going back, either to his flat or mine, to eat take-away Chinese.

'But what happened?' I asked. 'How did Harold die?'

'There were no suspicious circumstances,' the policeman informed me. 'It was an accident. Cause of death was brain haemorrhage, caused by the gentleman falling and hitting his head on the metal radiator.'

'Falling?' Harold was not given to falling. He was only forty . . . hardly a geriatric and I said as much. How had he fallen?

'We surmise that he tripped. There was a bear on the floor, Sir.'

'A what?'

27

'A bear . . . one of those toy teddies.'

'Yes, but surely . . . Harold didn't blunder about. He was the kind of person who looked where he was going.'

'He was unsteady on his feet, Sir.'

'Are you suggesting he was inebriated?'

'Definitely, Sir. No doubt about it.'

'But Harold didn't drink.' I practically shouted it.

There was a silence. The policeman looked at me pityingly, the way he might if I were suffering from a mental disability.

There had been a time, years ago at Cambridge, when Harold had had a severe drinking problem . . . culminating in his losing the only girl he'd ever wanted to marry. After that he'd embraced the AA movement and given alcohol up completely.

The phrase 'Once an alcoholic always an alcoholic,' echoed in my brain. It was undoubtedly what the policeman was thinking. He didn't say that, of course. He said, 'I'm very sorry, Sir.' And after I'd assured him that I would take care of all necessary arrangements, he made his departure.

So . . . a dear person had left me and, with him, the best friendship I'd ever had.

I arranged the funeral, of course. There was no one else to do it. Hardly anyone came. His landlady, a mousy-looking girl from his office, his solicitor and myself. Not much of a send-off really, but then Harold would have preferred a quiet affair.

A short while after that, the solicitor informed me that Harold had left a will and that I was the only beneficiary. Not that his estate amounted to very much. Very little, in fact. A modest High Interest Savings account, a few bonds and the contents of his rented flat. But I was very, very touched. Eventually, and with the solicitor's permission, I steeled myself to go over to Harold's flat.

There was something unutterably sad about being once again in a place where I had spent so many convivial evenings . . . and had so many quiet chats about the arts, music in particular, which we both loved. There was an air of desolation about the flat now, though to anyone else it would have appeared charming. A bijou apartment, consisting of lounge, balcony, kitchenette and bathroom. The pleasant living-room was furnished with a knee-hole desk, a couple of easy chairs, a campaign chest and a divan which converted into a bed. There was a splendid music centre, with very up-to-date equipment, which had been Harold's pride and joy. I decided to put on Mozart's Requiem as a tribute to my dear departed friend.

Sitting on Harold's bed I lit a cigarette, a vice we had both shared although we tried to control it, and listened to the music. I wondered where to start. Sorting out a dead friend's things is a painful business. As my eyes ranged the room, my glance took in the bear, lying on the floor as the policeman had described it, in the vicinity of that wretched radiator. Harold's bear. I knew he'd got one, of course. I remembered it from when I used to go to Harold's house for tea as a child. Bruin, as he called it, always had a place at the table. In fact, it was around for most of our activities . . . as a mere onlooker, of course. Now it lay on its back like a wounded soldier. I say that because it had a bandage round its head. The ludicrous thought struck me that the bear had fallen first and hit its head on the radiator and Harold had bandaged it up. Well, he wouldn't have then put it back on the floor surely.

The more I thought about Harold's accident the more it didn't make sense. But that was because I just couldn't accept that Harold had been drunk. Harold didn't drink! As I walked around the flat, however, I saw with my own eyes the evidence to the contrary. On the kitchen table stood an empty whisky bottle . . . another one with only the bare dregs remaining was on the floor next to the lavatory, while a dirty whisky glass lay upturned on the carpet. Well, there you go. After years of abstinence, Harold had suddenly lost control. In some fit of depression? The odd thing was that, when he did drink, it had never been whisky. In Cambridge days it had always been Bacardi rum. He'd had this absolute penchant for Bacardi rum. Some old Navy salt had got him on to it, he'd told me, on a sailing holiday he'd had off the Cornish coast.

Well, people's tastes change. I cleaned the place up a bit and then thought I'd better make a start on the desk, although I really disliked the idea of going through Harold's papers. Nevertheless, it had to be done and, as soon as I pulled open the first drawer, I knew it wasn't going to be too bad. Everything was so ordered, neat and tidy, the way Harold always was. Bills clearly paid on time and receipts kept. Paper-clips, drawing-pins, elastic bands, etc., all in suitable containers. No rubbish.

It was when I opened the drawer containing Harold's personalized stationery that I found this letter to myself. For some quite unexplainable reason I had lifted up the cover of the writing-pad. And there it was . . . not so much a letter . . . just a few terse lines. 'Dear Alan, Please phone me just as soon as you get back. I need help. I'm desperate. Harold.' Help with what? I pondered without success. Desperate? Because he'd started drinking again? But Harold was a very staunch member of AA and had attended their meetings for years. It would have been them, not me, that he'd have turned to if his desperation was over that. And why hadn't he posted the letter? There were envelopes and stamps. And if he'd changed his mind about sending it, it would have been in the waste-paper basket. Perhaps he never got any further because he was interrupted. He'd had a visitor before he'd got as far as the envelope. There'd been a knock at the door perhaps . . . and he'd done what we all do with something personal like that. We close the cover and shut the drawer on it.

'Well, we'll never know now, will we Bruin?' I said to the bear who was the only other person in the room. He looked at me with his shiny brown eyes and said nothing. It occurred to me that he probably knew more about it than anybody.

A few days later, I had a visitor at my home . . . a Miss Spencer. She had telephoned, asking if she could come and see me. Something to do with Mr Riley she had said, Mr Riley being Harold. It turned out she was the mousey girl who'd attended the funeral and my second impression was even mousier than the first.

We had a cup of tea and Battenburg cake, which had been a favourite of Harold's so it seemed appropriate. Miss Jennifer Spencer, or Miss Mouse, was twenty-two or three, I hazarded a guess. She was small and neat in a beige suit with a cream-coloured blouse, beige stockings and brown court shoes. Her light brown hair was cut in a bob and she wore roundish spectacles. Obviously shy and a bit ill at ease, I could see it would

take her a while to come out with whatever was troubling her.
I hoped it wasn't a tale of unrequited love. It wasn't. After
rambling on about the office, she cleared her throat and said,

'I think Mr Riley was afraid of something.'

'Something or somebody?' I enquired rather sceptically.

'Somebody. He thought somebody was after him.'

'After Harold? Whatever for?'

Miss Mouse sipped her tea and there was a long pause while
she picked a few crumbs of Battenburg off her skirt.

'I'd better tell you what happened, Mr Hooper.'

'Please.' I refilled her tea cup and passed her the sugar.

'You know that our firm has a branch office at East Croydon?'

I didn't. I knew that Harold worked for a shipping firm in the
city, just as Harold had known I was a lecturer on medieval
history, but we seldom discussed our jobs. To save time I
nodded.

'Well,' Miss Mouse continued, 'Mr Riley had to visit our office
there from time to time and, as his typist, I usually went with
him. We travelled together, there and back, from Victoria.'

'Yes?'

'The last visit we made was a few weeks ago. We'd just got off
the train on our return from East Croydon. Mr Riley stopped to
get something out of his briefcase and suddenly he said, 'Oh
Christ, what have I done now, Jennifer?'

'And what had he done?' I prompted.

'He'd picked up the wrong briefcase.'

'The train was packed,' Miss Mouse went on, 'it always is, you
know, with commuters. Like sardines really . . . Obviously Mr
Riley didn't realize . . . Anyway, he said he'd just have to find
out who it belonged to and see if whoever it was had got his. I
said, "Would you like me to do that for you, Mr Riley?" but he
told me to get off home, he would deal with it himself. It was
after that, that things started to go wrong.'

'Wrong in what way?'

'Mr Riley got his own briefcase back, all right. It arrived by
taxi at the office but, when I asked him if he'd traced the owner
of the one he'd taken by mistake, he said, "Yes . . . and I wish to
God I hadn't." There was a long pause from Miss Mouse while
she cut another slice of cake into very small pieces.

'Did he elaborate?' I asked her.

'No, he didn't. He gave the impression he didn't want to talk about it any further. He was quite snappy, actually.'

'And then?'

'Well, the first thing I noticed was that he stopped going out to lunch. Mr Riley always used to go to a little place a few streets away called Bruno's. Italian . . . a lot of people from the office used it. I thought . . . well, maybe Mr Riley's going on a diet or something, although he was quite slim, wasn't he? But then he started acting a bit oddly and asked me if I'd go to the window and see if anyone was watching the office. "But why should anyone do that, Mr Riley?" I asked him. And he replied that he'd already spotted someone doing it. So I did what he asked of course, several times a day. I mean I was working for him, wasn't I?'

'And did you ever see anyone?'

'Well, I think I did, yes. One late afternoon, just before packing up time. I did think I saw somebody.'

'Looking up at the office?'

'Well, lurking outside the building. When I told him, Mr Riley had a quick look himself, then he said, "That's him, the same bloke who's been following me home. And I'll tell you something, Jennifer, it's on account of that damned briefcase!" Then before he could say anything further, Mr Hanson, that's Mr Riley's immediate superior, came into the office and asked Mr Riley to come into his office and have a drink and a chat right away, before they both went home.'

And that was all Miss Mouse knew about this mysterious affair because she never saw Harold again and there had been no sign of anyone lurking about when she'd left the building. The next day she was told that Mr Riley was taking a few days off because he hadn't been feeling too well. He had requested a meeting with Mr Hanson for that very reason.

'And do you think he told Mr Hanson what he had told you?'

'If he had, I'm quite sure that Mr Hanson's secretary would have told me.'

'And when you finally heard about Mr Riley's unfortunate death, did *you* say anything?'

'No.'

'Why not?'

A look of obstinacy settled across the mouse face. 'Because I thought that, if Mr Riley had wanted them to know about it, he'd have told them himself.'

Touché! Bravo, Miss Mouse. I looked at her with renewed respect. 'That was very loyal of you, Miss Spencer.'

Obviously I had been singled out for these confidences because I was *not* the office, who might not have taken it seriously. I thanked her for telling me and tried to reassure her. 'It's possible that someone was trying to intimidate Mr Riley,' I said. 'People behave like that sometimes. I'm sure there was no connection between that and his tragic accident.' This was not what I thought at all, but the relief on her face was well worth the lie. 'By the way,' I said, as I showed her to the door. 'Did you notice Mr Riley drinking? I mean, did he keep a bottle of spirits in his desk or anything?'

'Oh no,' said Miss Mouse. 'The only thing I ever saw Mr Riley drink was coffee.'

'So what do you think, Bruin?' I asked the bear the next time I was in Harold's flat. 'Should we go to the police?' The bear looked at me with the same expression he always had – rather fierce. He made no comment but then he never commented on anything I said to him. He'd probably had more of a rapport with Harold, all the years they'd lived together.

As I stacked Harold's books and music into a couple of packing cases, I thought to myself that the police probably wouldn't be very interested in the story of the loiterer. There were loiterers all over London. Besides, in their eyes Harold had been a drinker and therefore subject to seeing pink mice, elephants or, for that matter, mystery individuals hanging about on pavements. The fact that Harold's typist had also seen a man probably wouldn't carry any weight either. 'Probably a flasher, Sir,' they'd say, 'waiting for young girls to come out of the office.' And the story of the briefcase? A pretty common occurrence on crowded commuter trains. So the other party got annoyed about it? Who can blame them? But what about that letter to me? 'I'm desperate.' 'Desperate to stop drinking,' would certainly be the police explanation. I had to have more to go on than that. I carried on with the clearing up, keeping a lookout for any clue that Harold might have left behind . . . but so far there was nothing.

Most of the furniture would have to go to auction, I decided, but I would keep the music centre and the collection of compact discs because Harold would have wished it. Also, his rather fine camera.

It was quite late when I decided to pack it in for the evening. I'd had a hard day lecturing at college and was ready for something to eat before I went to bed. I said goodnight to Bruin and then, on impulse, decided to take him with me. After all, he was mine now and he must feel lonely without Harold.

I plonked him rather unceremoniously into a plastic bag, turned off the lights, locked the door and left. My home was only a few streets away but, to save cooking, I decided to pick up a meal from the little Chinese take-away that Harold and I had always patronized. It was a pretty chilly old night and there were few people about, but I suddenly became aware that there was someone walking behind me. I stopped suddenly, pretending to be engrossed in the lighted windows of a men's outfitters. The footsteps behind me stopped, too, and then I knew . . . I was being followed. I increased my pace and the footsteps behind me increased also. I didn't look round but made it to the take-away like a bat out of hell.

I gave my order and asked Mr Wang, with whom I was on good terms, if he could possibly order me a taxi. He did so. I waited inside until it arrived and then, clutching my dim-sum . . . plus the bear, I left the café. There was no sign of anyone in the immediate vicinity when I stepped into the taxi and, as it made the short journey to my home, wondered if this business of Harold was affecting *my* imagination. I missed him dreadfully. Once inside my own front door I felt better . . . and better still when I'd eaten my supper. I thought I'd let the food settle before I went to bed. I made a cup of cocoa, sat down and lit a cigarette.

I should have been concentrating on the lecture I was going to give the following morning . . . instead, I found myself once more going over in my mind the events that had led up to the death of my friend. I was absolutely convinced it had not been an accident. The remark Harold had made to Miss Mouse, when she'd asked him if he'd traced the owner of the briefcase, kept repeating itself in my brain. 'Yes . . . and I wish to God I hadn't.' In that reply, it seemed to me, lay the clue to the whole mysterious business.

From then on, Harold had been nervous and fidgety at work, had stopped going out to lunch and was convinced that someone was following him. Of course, if he had taken up the booze again, this could have been put down to paranoia, but there had been no signs of drinking in the office and, what is more, Miss Mouse had herself seen someone who appeared to be 'lurking about'. There could be only one explanation for all this, in my opinion. There had been something incriminating in that briefcase. In his attempts to trace the owner, Harold had found it . . . and, in so doing, he had signed his own death warrant!

So why hadn't he gone to the police? Because he was himself guilty of taking something that didn't belong to him and seeing something he wasn't supposed to see – and Harold was no 'telltale tit'? I remembered way back at school when he and I had caught a boy cribbing. I was all for hoisting him up in front of the Head, but Harold had said, 'No. He knows we know, that's punishment enough'. He believed in letting sleeping dogs lie and giving the other chap a sporting chance. Harold was a gentleman.

Whatever he had found in that briefcase, short of it being a matter of national security, would have been safe with him. He would have told no one. He would not even have told me, I was certain of that. The owner of the briefcase, however, and perhaps other interested parties, would not have been certain at all. So steps would have been taken . . . A phone call to Harold first of all. A suave, anonymous voice on the end of the line. 'Mr Riley, what would you say to a nice new numbered account in a Swiss bank?' To which, Harold would have replied quite firmly, 'No, thank you.' Under no circumstances would he have accepted a bribe from anyone. 'You have my word as a gentleman,' Harold would have said, 'that will have to be good enough for you.'

But for the party or parties concerned, the word of a gentleman would not have been good enough. It would have meant nothing, since they were probably villains, or the dirty tricks brigade, or both. So orders were given. Harold was followed and, when it seemed opportune, the orders were carried out . . . possibly the same evening that Harold had written that letter to me.

'Did the doorbell ring?' I asked the bear. 'Or did it open silently, catching Harold unawares? . . . Was it one man, or two?' It must have been two, I concluded (since Bruin didn't enlighten me) and they brought the whisky with them.

'Let's all have a drink, Mr Riley. Sit down now and have a nightcap before you go to bed.'

And if the invitation was declined?

'I'm afraid we insist.'

So Harold had a drink whether he wanted it or not . . . and another one and another one and another one after that. It was all the drinks he hadn't taken in all those years of abstinence. But it wasn't Bacardi rum . . . it was whisky they poured down his throat and, if it spilled around a bit . . .? 'Never mind about that, we've got another bottle.

'Had enough now, have we? Let's get up from the chair then, it's party-over time. Stand over there, will you Mr Riley, in front of the radiator, if you please? We'll show you where . . . just a few steps to the left. That's better. Only for a minute, Mr Riley, and then you can lie down. We will assist you to lie down . . . All be over soon.' And it was. Each let go of an arm and each grasped an ankle. In one quick, simultaneous movement, Harold was assisted off his feet, his head hitting the radiator hard as he fell.

They hung around for a bit . . . in case he got up. When they were quite sure he would never get up again, one of them chucked the bear at his feet and they left. Risk eliminated!

'Is that how it was, Bruin?' There was no reply to my question. The bear lay supine and silent on the bed, an arm and a paw behind his head, saying nothing. He must have heard all Harold's confidences over the years . . . all his worries and wishes. An attentive listener who never nodded off, who never voiced opinions of his own, never argued and never answered back. To Harold, he must have been the perfect silent friend. Now he was my friend. Looking at him I wondered how old he was. Perhaps he was a Steiff bear and worth a lot of money. Well, I'd never part with him if he was, but it would be interesting to know. The only way to tell was to examine his ears and see if there was that little identifying tag.

'And to find that out,' I said to him, 'we'll have to take that bandage off your head.' Carefully I unwound the slightly grubby piece of crêpe. I saw at once why it had been put on. The bear's head was like a boxer's . . . distinctly battered . . . and straw and sawdust fell from both his ears. Once upon a time, Bruin had had a fight . . . with another bear perhaps, at a children's tea-party in Harold's youth.

'I hope this won't cause you any pain,' I said to him, 'but if we want to find out your pedigree I'll have to explore further.' I poked my finger cautiously into his left ear as far as it would go . . . more straw and sawdust . . . nothing else. But in the right one I felt resistance . . . and exploring further I felt what seemed like a small cylinder. Carefully, I extracted it. It was nothing to do with Steiff, I saw at once. It was a spool of film. So, Harold may have been a gentleman, but he had been a cautious one. He had photographed what he had found in the briefcase, never, I was absolutely certain, with any intention of using it . . . but as a form of insurance if things were to take a wrong turn as, indeed, they had.

I reflected that, in the first instance, the other party concerned would have expected Harold to have photographed what he had found in the briefcase and to have followed this up with a demand for a cut of the profits. That would have been behaviour they understood. But when Harold actually turned down their offer of 'hush money' on the pretext of being a gentleman, they would have been genuinely puzzled and distinctly uneasy. Was this fellow playing for higher stakes by playing their own game for them? Well, they weren't going to risk that.

I sighed. Whatever the scenario, for Harold it was too late now. It was not too late for me, however. The film would be developed first thing in the morning. We would see what we would see. Industrial secrets? I pondered. Indecent exposures of some well-known VIP seemed more likely. It would explain Harold's reluctance to tell. For a gentleman like Harold to have stooped to initiating a revelation of that sort would have been tantamount to kicking a cripple in the crutch. Well, I hadn't seen the originals and I didn't have the same scruples in any case.

'You keep this for tonight, Bruin,' I said, placing the spool carefully back in the bear's ear and winding the bandage once again around his head. Tomorrow we shall go to the police and the process of avenging Harold will begin.'

It wasn't until I looked at the clock that I realized how late it was, or how tired I had become. It was definitely time for bed. I undressed, brushed my teeth and turned down the bed, placing the bear next to my pillow. Drawing the curtains back I switched off the light and looked down at the street. Quiet as a graveyard . . . not a soul anywhere . . . no loiterer lurking about. Vaguely relieved I climbed into bed. The soft glow of the street lamp was sufficient for me to see the bear's brown eyes as he lay beside me. 'Good night, Bruin,' I said and almost immediately I fell asleep.

Was it two or three in the morning that they came . . . my uninvited guests? No noise . . . no broken glass . . . no splintering of wood, super efficient . . . just a faint click as they switched on the bedside lamp and there they were, two men in raincoats and leather gloves, one on each side of the bed.

'Sorry to disturb you, Mr Hooper,' a voice said.

I sat up and saw that one of them had a revolver.

'You're the men who murdered Harold Riley!'

'Lie down, we're not here to get acquainted.' They shoved me back on the pillow. I pulled up the blanket, perhaps I should play possum.

'Put your left arm out of the covers.'

'What for?'

They did it for me.

'Going to give me the whisky treatment are you? Well, I could do with a drink.'

They smiled simultaneously. 'We never repeat ourselves,' the one with the revolver said. The other one took a syringe and a phial from his raincoat pocket.

So that was what they had in mind for me. I was to be an overdose case, depressed at the death of a dear friend. 'I don't know anything,' I said to them, 'even if I was Harold Riley's best friend.'

'That may be, Mr Hooper,' the man with the syringe had filled it and was pushing up the sleeve of my pyjama, 'but you're what we term a loose connection. Better be safe than sorry.'

I attempted to struggle, but the other man pinned me to the pillow.

'I can't get a vein up,' the man with the syringe said, smacking my forearm, 'I'll have to make a tourniquet with something.' His eyes fell on the bear. He picked it up and unpinned the bandage, causing a trickle of sawdust to fall on the pillow. 'This'll do.' He wound the crêpe tightly around my arm as I tried once more in vain to struggle.

The man with the syringe smiled like a sympathetic dentist. 'You won't feel a thing,' he said, plunging the syringe into a vein, 'no pain at all, I can promise you that.' He withdrew the syringe, pressed my fingers around it and let it drop to the floor.

He was right about the pain, there wasn't any . . . just a numbness and a feeling of floating. The men in raincoats never said goodbye, but they weren't there anymore and they must have switched off the bedside lamp before they left because the room seemed to have grown darker. My eyes found it difficult to focus, but I could still see Bruin lying comfortingly close. It seemed to me that his expression was less fierce than usual. There was a look of compassion on his face and the hint of a tear in the clear brown eyes. I wanted to speak to him, but no words came out. I felt incredibly tired and knew I was fast going to sleep. I was quite contented. My final thought, before I closed my eyes for the last time, was that the Bear knew. He had the secret and one day he would avenge both of us.

A Friend in Need

ANNE GORING

LAST YEAR it was Singapore, this year it's one of the most luxurious hotels in the Florida Keys.

'If you want privacy and good service, you stay at the best places,' Lucy always says. Firmly. These days she's very firm. Decisive. Bright. It's one of the reasons she's got on. You don't get your own thriving PR agency by sitting around dreaming about being successful. You set goals and go for them. Lucy's words, not mine. I've a more relaxed view of life.

Our goal today is just to get on the plane to Miami. There's a flight delay and we're sitting with Tom, who has kindly offered to run us to Heathrow, having a coffee before we go through to the no-man's-land the other side of Customs. We're flying Business Class, of course. The days of cramped charter flights backpacking round Greece and cheap packages to the Med are long since gone. Don't get me wrong, though. We had some great times. Fun times. When you're young and carefree, that's the way it should be. When you get older, the punches life throws at you take the edge off pleasure. You become cynical, worried that happiness somehow has to be paid for by grief. That, sadly, is what Lucy believes, though she didn't once. Not before Paul.

I'll never forgive Paul for what he did to Lucy. Overnight she changed. The laughter went from her eyes, the joy from her life. He broke her heart, I know. She cried bitter tears on my shoulder

41

more than once. And even if I felt helpless to do more than let her cry, she was grateful. 'I don't know what I'd do without you, Jo. You're such a comfort to be with.'

It's nice to be needed, though if Paul had had his way, Lucy would have discarded all her friends. Paul was jealous and possessive, and I knew from the moment I clapped eyes on him that he was a louse. He did his best to belittle me and ridicule me. I suppose it was because he saw me as some sort of hangover from Lucy's past. The part he could never share.

Lucy told me the whole of it afterwards, though I guessed as much at the time. It's to her everlasting credit that, despite Paul's jealousy, she stubbornly went on nurturing her friendships.

Me? I'm Lucy's oldest friend. The quiet one. They say pretty girls always go for a dull, plain companion, but it's not that. We just like each other's company. Always have. In any case, when we were both young, I was the bright, good-looking one and she was the girl the boys teased because she was gangly and shy and wore braces on her teeth.

But time and growing confidence, not to mention success, have worked magic on Lucy. Those idiot boys are probably balding and overweight by now. I've got a bit of a world-weary look too – but Lucy! Wow! Like me, she won't see thirty again, but she's stunning. I'm proud to be with her. She's tall, graceful, fine-boned, with an aura of cool, smiling self-confidence that men seem to find both irresistible and provocative.

Ultimately, of course, when they discover that the air of reserve is actually an invisible, armour-plated shield, they give up on her. Which is why these days she has this undeserved reputation for being hard-boiled and stony-hearted.

No one since Paul has ever discovered the warm, vulnerable, tender person who still lives behind those impenetrable defences. Though I get the feeling Tom's come pretty close recently.

Lucy's tired, you see. She really needs this holiday. This year has been especially hectic with the agency expansion, her secretary on maternity leave, new accounts . . .

I reckon it was sheer weariness that made her give in to Tom's dogged persistence. He's taken her out to dinner once or twice, even whisked her off to the coast one Sunday, with Lucy protesting crossly all the way that she'd absolutely no time for gallivanting . . . But I saw the wistful look in her eyes when she told me, briskly, what a waste of time it had been dawdling over a picnic on the Downs when she could have been bringing her filing up to date. I saw, too, how carefully she looked after the flowers he'd bought her at a roadside stall, and how reluctantly she threw them out when they'd wilted.

It's very noisy at the moment. I don't like crowds. I like peaceful, bookish corners. I want our flight to be called, so that we can be on our way. All the same, I'm fascinated by the conversation going on between Tom and Lucy.

It's not so much what they say. That's a bit stilted, in fact; the sort of desperately banal stuff people talk about when they're on the point of parting and neither wants to be the first to make a move. No, it's the little tense silences, the movements of hands and bodies as they sip their drinks, as though there's a dialogue going on at a different level. But I'm the only one to hear it because I'm a listener and a watcher rather than a talker.

Tom's a vet. She met him at a cousin's wedding back in the spring. I've only seen him once before today – not actually met him, mind – just a glimpse from the window a couple of weeks back when he dropped Lucy off.

Tom's red-haired and stocky and his clothes are more off-the-peg than Savile Row. Very different from Paul, who was devastatingly handsome in a dark, broody, Byronic way and who prided himself on being a sharp dresser.

Tom looks as though he means it when he smiles. And he has caring hands.

I notice hands a lot. When he carried the cases from his car just now, I saw how square and clean and strong they were. I would believe Tom if he told Lucy he cared for her.

Paul's hands were too greedy and grasping. I never believed him when he told Lucy she was the love of his life, though *she* did, of course. It took her two years to find out that the only person Paul ever truly loved was himself. Until he found someone else – younger, livelier, *newer*. He walked out on Lucy without even having the guts to tell her to her face. Just left a measly note when she'd gone out. I hate even to recall her distress after she'd read his slimy excuses.

Lucy looks terrific today. She's done it on purpose. Disguise, you see. She's wearing a new outfit. For eight hours in a Jumbo, I ask you! Who dresses up formally for long-haul travel these days?

She doesn't fool me. She's using this elegant façade like a shield, protecting herself. The real Lucy's hiding away from Tom behind it. She's felt, recently, that she may be a bit vulnerable where he's concerned and she has no intention of being overcome by silly emotional ideas in the fraught atmosphere of an airport.

It's terribly sad. I can feel the sadness – his, hers. Mine. It seems such a waste of two nice people who obviously enjoy each other's company and who might, just might, become more than mere friends, given a little encouragement.

But what can I do? They're grown up, intelligent, capable. Yet I feel that unless I do something, Lucy will go away and not look back. She'll have two weeks being pampered, recovering her strength and her resolution, rebuilding her armour plating. She'll think rationally – oh, so rationally – about Tom while she's lying by the pool, walking by the ocean, watching fiery sunsets over the Gulf of Mexico. She'll come to the sensible conclusion that she doesn't want to risk being hurt again.

Poor Tom. I realize now that he's a bit shy. He's not smiling. He looks quite solemn and his kind eyes are troubled. He'd be kind to Lucy. And protective and gentle, like I guess he is with all the frightened animals he deals with. He's no practised charmer with women, though. That's half the trouble; he can't find the right words. And if he doesn't hurry, it'll be too late.

Oh, no! They're announcing our flight.

Lucy almost jumps to her feet, grabs her flight bag. 'Well, this is it!' she says brightly, with a false-sounding laugh. She holds out her hand. 'Thanks for the lift, Tom.'

'My pleasure,' he says, equally brightly. 'But I'll see you as far as I can go.'

He reaches for the bag. She makes to snatch it away. They both end up with a handle each and that's when I seize my chance.

I've been watching them through the gap where the zip hasn't been quite pulled over. Now, with Lucy and Tom tussling over the handles, the zip bursts right open and out I pop with the pressure of everything Lucy has crammed into the bag.

For a moment I hang suspended. Me, Joe Soap or, as Lucy when she was five wrote on a label when we first went travelling together, Jo Sope, Lusie's tedy. She wouldn't ever go anywhere without me. Not then. Not now. Especially flying, which she privately feels nervous about.

I fall ignominiously to the floor.

A big, strong hand gently picks me up. I feel a bit embarrassed and a little nervous. I mean, I'm not exactly a pretty sight. Paul thought it was stupid and childish that Lucy still kept a battered, bald, one-eyed teddy bear. They once had a row and he chucked me in the bin with the rubbish. Lucy rescued me after he'd gone and cried because my arm was all bent and it never did recover. She hid me away in a drawer after that whenever he was around.

I relax after a minute. Tom's smiling, but it's a surprised and happy sort of grin. He looks from me to Lucy. Colour has swept up her face. Posh new suit or not, she looks about fifteen.

His grin fades, his eyes are tender. He's seeing Lucy as he's never seen her before. The real Lucy. My Lucy.

He says nothing at all, but it's hard to believe I ever thought him shy as he takes her in a big, hugging embrace and kisses her. And she lets him. Whoopee, she lets him!

From my rather inelegant position dangling by one paw over Lucy's left shoulder, I feel her relax. I relax myself and unashamedly eavesdrop. I've been doing it all my life, so I don't see any reason to stop at this interesting juncture.

I won't go into details. It isn't seemly. All I will say is that there's a lot of reorganizing of plans going on. For a moment it's touch and go whether we will take the flight, but Tom has quite a masterful way with him once he gets cracking. He says he needs a break as much as she does, he's always wanted to see the Florida Keys and he'll fly out for the last week of her holiday. Most satisfactory.

I resign myself to being re-stowed in the flight bag, but surprise, surprise, Lucy tucks me under her arm for all the world to see. I get a good view of all the gooey farewell bit before we go through the formalities.

In the departure lounge, Lucy whispers, 'Well, Jo Sope, what do you think of that, eh? And it's all your fault, you wily old thing.'

I look as modest as I know how.

'I hope I'm doing the right thing,' she says with a sigh. Then she brightens. 'But you heard him, old friend. He still keeps the blue plush rabbit his granny gave him when he was three. A man like that can't be all bad.'

My sentiments entirely. A blue rabbit? Mm, well, I guess I can stand the competition.

Titanic Bear

PAT RUSH

No one can remember whether this little bear ever had a name. Certainly he was rarely played with. But few bears can have had a more exciting life. For, on a night when over 1500 people drowned in the icy waters of the North Atlantic, this teddy somehow managed to survive the sinking of the *Titanic*.

His exact origins are not known for certain, but it is believed that the gold mohair bear – which had a metal frame under its fur – was made in Germany by Gebruder Bing. The company originally produced household tinware. But later it began to manufacture enamelled toys, and it was also one of the first to turn its attention to teddy bears. Since this little bear was made just three or four years after the creation of the very first teddy, he is clearly a very early example.

Eventually, however, he made his way to Paris and it was there, in 1907, that a seafaring uncle of little Vittorio Gatti bought the bear as a present for his nephew.

Vittorio was never permitted to play with his gift. Rather, it was treated as an ornament – something to be looked at and admired. But there is little doubt that he loved the bear dearly. When, five years later, his father Gaspare accepted a job as catering manager on the White Star Line's brand-new liner, the *Titanic*, Vittorio chose the little bear as his parting gift to his father. It was to be a good-luck mascot for the voyage ahead.

Italian-born Gaspare Gatti had worked in some of the most prestigious restaurants in London – among them the famous Café Royal. But the White Star Line's offer was too good to refuse. The new luxury vessel was, after all, the star of their fleet – one of the largest vessels afloat, and also proudly proclaimed to be absolutely unsinkable, thanks to the provision of sixteen watertight compartments.

Gaspare's wife Edith, however, appears to have remained unconvinced about the liner's safety provisions. In the week before it set sail, she dreamt more than once of the disaster that was to come. Nevertheless, on 10 April 1912, her husband left from Southampton as planned. Tucked inside his tobacco pouch, which he kept in his coat-tails, was his son's little teddy.

The story of the subsequent voyage is, of course, well documented. Speeding towards New York at some 22 knots – trying to win the Blue Riband for the fastest Atlantic crossing – the vessel struck an iceberg at 11.40pm on the night of 14 April. A 300-foot gash below the waterline allowed water to pour into several of the forward compartments, and in less than three hours the *Titanic* had disappeared.

Gaspare Gatti was last seen standing on the deck, wearing his top hat and with a travelling blanket over his arm. In his hand was a small case. Clearly he was still hoping to be rescued. But there were lifeboats for fewer than half the passengers and crew, and matters were made even worse by the fact that many boats were not filled to capacity. As both a crew member and a man, Gatti stood no chance of finding a place.

His body was the 313th to be recovered and he was buried in Halifax, Nova Scotia, alongside other victims of the disaster. Eventually, his effects were returned to his widow Edith who had, on the night of the disaster, again been woken by her terrible dream.

Still safe inside the tobacco pouch, however, she found her son's tiny teddy – remarkably unscathed by his terrible ordeal. Edith was to keep him with her for the rest of her life – a poignant reminder of the man she had lost.

By the outbreak of the Second World War Edith Gatti was

living in London, and it was there that the little bear underwent his second great ordeal – the destruction of the Gatti home by one of the Luftwaffe's bombs.

Once again, however, he managed to survive, and he stayed with Edith through several less traumatic moves of house before eventually finding tranquillity when she retired to the Yorkshire Dales.

Edith died in 1962, and it was then that the little bear was returned to his original owner, her son Vittorio. When Vittorio died in 1974 the bear passed to his widow, Marjory, and became a source of constant delight to her five grandchildren and an ever-growing number of great-grandchildren who all wanted to hear his fascinating story.

Then one day Marjory happened to see a television programme about teddy bears, and she began to wonder about the background of her own little teddy. Was he, perhaps, of an interesting make? Would anyone be able to tell her more about him? She decided to contact Ankie Wild at the Museum of Childhood in Ribchester, Lancashire, to see if she could help.

She told Ankie nothing about the bear's adventurous life but, even so, Ankie knew as soon as she saw him that he would make an interesting addition to the museum's collection. She immediately asked if the teddy was for sale.

Until then, however, Marjory had not thought of parting with the little bear, and at first she was not at all sure that she would want to let him go. Then, during a family visit, a quarrel broke out about who would become his next custodian. Marjory realized that she would face an impossible choice. She also wanted to make sure that *all* the family would be able to see the bear whenever they wanted. What better solution, therefore, than to accept Ankie's offer?

So it was that, on 14 April 1990 – seventy-eight years to the day after the *Titanic* went down – the little teddy arrived at another new home. He soon became one of the stars of the museum.

Articles have been written about him in magazines from as far afield as Australia and Japan. Teddy-lovers and collectors of *Titanic* memorabilia have flocked to see him. And to mark the

eightieth anniversary of the *Titanic* disaster, soft-toy manufacturers Merrythought produced 5000 replicas which have been
sold all over the world.

Slightly larger than the original, and without the metal frame,
each of the bears is housed in a special handmade presentation
box which tells the story of the original bear and of that fateful
night in April 1912.

It is a remarkable tribute to a truly remarkable little bear.

The Battle of Jericho

PETER CLOVER

JERICHO WAS a tatty, soft brown bear. One of his ears stuck straight up in the air and the other flopped right over. His fur was quite worn in places and he was very, very old. He belonged to Violet.

Violet was already a grandmother herself and Jericho had belonged to Violet's mother before her, so he was almost prehistoric. Violet was very fond of Jericho and took him almost everywhere. Sometimes he went for rides in the shopping trolley. Sometimes he drove the car, and sometimes he went to the hairdresser in a carrier bag. But most of the time he simply lazed among the cushions on Violet's big, brass bed.

When she was a little girl, Violet had ten teddies which she took to bed with her every night; she had to sleep right up against the wall to stop herself from falling out. But now she only had Jericho and that was enough.

One afternoon, Violet's best friend Florrie came around to help clear out the cupboards. Violet still had all of Alf's old suits hanging in the wardrobe and there were heaps and heaps of clutter to be got rid of. The Church Jumble was glad of the offer and was coming around later to collect the boxes for the garden fête.

That evening when Violet settled down with her Horlicks she made a terrible discovery. Jericho was gone! She looked for him everywhere, under the bed, in the wardrobe, in all the cupboards and drawers. She even searched through the cupboard under the stairs but Jericho was quite lost.

Violet was very sad when she finally went to bed. She kept waking up throughout the night, thinking of him and missing him dreadfully.

On Saturday morning, Violet and Florrie went along to the garden fête. It was a big affair in the playing-field behind the village hall with lots of stalls and curious side shows offering various prizes to be won. Florrie hoopla'd a 2lb jar of strawberry jam, then won a packet of gypsy creams by spearing the ace of hearts to a dartboard. Violet wasn't having much fun though; she was missing Jericho too much. Florrie vaguely remembered packing a soft brown teddy bear into the bottom of a cardboard box but was feeling far too guilty to say anything. Instead, she threw herself into the Bingo and within minutes had won a huge nylon teddy bear with purple fur and a beautiful lime-green bow. The bear was almost as big as Florrie. Violet didn't like that teddy bear at all; in fact, at that moment, she didn't really like Florrie very much either because she kept on winning things, and deep down Violet had a sneaking suspicion that Florrie knew something of Jericho's disappearance.

Violet went off on her own to look at the stalls away from Florrie who wandered off winning things here and there. Florrie was carrying a Dundee cake and a goldfish in a pickle jar now as she struggled past a toy stall full of knitted animals and soft rag dolls in colourful bonnets. She cast an eagle eye over the contents of the stall and there, at the very back among a collection of misshapen teddy bears, was Jericho. He had a ticket around his neck asking 50p. Florrie became so excited she almost dropped everything as she fumbled through her purse for the money. She only had 25p as she'd spent all her money winning things – the stallholder wasn't open to bartering.

Florrie looked around frantically for Violet but it was already too late. Something terrible happened! Jericho had been bought by a little girl in pigtails who was walking off with him in her arms.

Florrie hurried after her and tried to explain that Jericho really belonged to Violet and would she like to swop the tatty old bear for a big, brand-new purple one with a lime-green bow? But the girl in pigtails said 'No!' She had bought Jericho with her own money and she was going to keep him. Florrie tried to reason with the little girl and offered to swop the purple teddy and all the prizes she'd won for the tatty old bear. But the girl looked mean and still said 'No!'

Then Florrie became desperate and offered £5. The pigtails twitched and the girl suddenly looked interested.

'I'll think about it,' she said.

Florrie told the girl that she lived along Alexander Street, and said she would sit the purple bear in the front window so that she would recognize the house. Then she raced home as fast as she could.

That afternoon, 'pigtails' called round. She was prepared to sell Jericho but not for £5. She wanted £50 – in used notes. Florrie showed 'pigtails' the door, but that wasn't the end of it, not by a long chalk. The next day 'piggy' pushed a note through Florrie's letterbox. The note had one of Jericho's ears pinned to it and read . . .

> If your friend ever wants to see the bear
> again, Grandma, cough up the fifty quid
> or it's curtains!

There was a roughly drawn map of the park showing Florrie exactly where the money should be left, and the note was signed ominously,

> The Terminator.

Poor Florrie was horrified. She felt awful about Jericho and really wanted to get him back for Violet, but £50 was a lot of money.

The next day a bag full of woolly stuffing was shoved through the letterbox along with a further note which read . . .

> O.K. Grandma? You had your chance.
> It's sixty quid now and the bear's
> getting thinner and thinner. Will call
> at 3 o'clock to collect. Be there
> with the dosh!
> The Terminator.

Florrie suddenly felt very faint. Violet was coming round just after three, and the 'Terminator' would be there with an emaciated Jericho as hostage. Oh, it was all such a muddle. Florrie's legs went all wobbly and she had to sit down. Then, with her head in her hands she started to cry. The tears just came and Florrie realized that she had never been so worried about anything in her life as she was right now.

There was £40 in the Christmas Club and, if she borrowed £10 from the week's housekeeping, she could get Jericho back and Violet would be none the wiser. She didn't care about the money any more, she just wanted to put an end to this terrible mess.

On the dot of 3 o'clock precisely, the doorbell rang and Florrie came face to face with the Terminator. The stupid girl had put on a balaclava so she wouldn't be recognized, and held Jericho tightly with one hand while a fat magic marker in the other threatened to ruin what was left of his remaining fur.

'You'd better come in,' said Florrie.

The girl took a quick look around the room.

'Are we alone?'

'Of course we're alone,' said Florrie. 'Here, take the money and give me the bear.'

'There's only fifty here,' said the girl. 'Where's the other ten?'

'But I thought . . .'

The Terminator threw the money on the carpet and, as Florrie knelt to pick up the notes, the front door opened and in walked Violet.

'What's going on?'

The girl tried to dash through the open door but Violet was too quick. She slammed the door shut and leaned her full weight against it. Florrie was on her knees sobbing and the girl was brandishing the magic marker like a dagger.

'What's going on?' asked Violet. Then she saw Jericho and her heart leapt. Her eyes darted from Florrie to Jericho to the dwarf in the balaclava to Florrie then back to her beloved bear.

'Will someone please tell me what's going on.'

Florrie blurted everything out in one long, sobbing sentence and begged Violet forgiveness. The Terminator was hopping nervously from one leg to another.

'I'll settle for the fifty then,' she croaked.

'Settle for fifty!' said Violet, pulling herself up to a full, rounded 5 feet. You should be ashamed of yourself. I have known that bear all my life. He has lived through two world wars and a lot worse besides. He's been a comfort to me, my children and my children's children and shared more secrets and dreams than you could possibly imagine; and if you think for one minute that you can extort money from myself or my dear friend then you are very much mistaken. If, after all these years together, Jericho and I must part company this way, then so be it. Do as you wish, but you won't get a penny for your trouble.'

'How about twenty quid then?'

'Goodbye, Jericho,' whispered Violet as she showed the girl to the door.

'I'll rip off his arms and legs!'

'Not a penny, you little monster,' said Violet, then she snatched Jericho and gave the girl such a shove that she flew out into the street without her feet touching the floor.

The door slammed shut and Violet hugged Jericho in her arms. Florrie couldn't believe her eyes and just looked vacant. Then the flap on the letterbox sprung open.

'Just you two wait 'til I tell my mum!'

'Oh sod off,' said Violet, grabbing a handful of balaclava and pulling it right through the letterbox, ripping it clean off the Terminator's head.

'Owwww! My ears,' screamed the girl. Violet and Florrie fell about laughing. Twenty minutes later there was an ominous ring on the doorbell. It was the Terminator and her mother, 'the Incredible Hulk'. The woman was enormous, built like a galleon at almost 6'. She wore a hand-knitted mohair jumper in vivid purple, big enough to accommodate an entire family. Her skintight ski-pants were lime green and her stilettos were brilliant white. Her hair was mauve, almost luminous.

'I understand you've stolen my Natalie's bear,' she boomed.

Natalie had a grin on her face which stretched from ear to ear. Violet went cold and held Jericho so tightly that her knuckles turned white.

'She tells me she bought that bear with her own money. You

can't just go around taking other people's property just because you fancy it, you know!' She saw the purple bear with the big lime-green bow sitting up in the armchair. 'Come on, hand him over or I'll get the police.'

Sadly, Violet offered up Jericho in her outstretched arms, struggling to hold back the tears.

'Oh very funny, very droll,' said the mother, then marched across the room and hoicked the purple bear from the armchair. Natalie's grin suddenly vanished.

'Mum,' she began to protest, but it was no good. The Incredible Hulk was already dragging her through the front door and off home.

'I can see why you were so upset, darling, he's luverly,' said Mum, giving the bear a big hug and a kiss. 'I think I'll call him Elvis.'

The battle of Jericho was over.

Confessions of a Bad Bear

ALLAN FREWIN
JONES

S O. HERE we are then. And a pretty sorry state I'm in, too, if all that stuffing scattered about is anything to go by. And if I'm not much mistaken that's a very familiar paw sticking out from under the bed. Very familiar. One might almost say I know it like the back of my hand. I should do. It *is* the back of my hand. With arm attached. Still, nothing a bit of nifty needlework can't put right. The eye will be a problem. They turn over the stock so quickly these days that it's going to be a *bugger* to get an eye to match, and God knows where my one is now. Down a mousehole, I wouldn't be surprised. Carried off by cockroaches. Yes – they've got cockroaches. They don't know it, but they do. Up and down the walls like Regency stripe once the lights are out.

And an ear half-hanging off. Christ! It's a bad bear's life, alright.

Still – you can't complain, in a way – they do *warn* you about the possibilities. Sitting there – ranks and ranks of us in the factory. Hope for the best, they said, but be prepared for the worst. Well – that's my life stitched up good and proper. Done up a treat.

There I was, at Hamleys (note that: Hamleys – not your average street-corner toyshop rubbing tentacles with the Monster from Outer Space and getting covered in chewing-gum) up on the shelf beaming away. And was I cuddly? Do kids wee in swimming pools? Does pigeon shit stick to an Arran sweater? I'll say I was cuddly. And handsome? You could see the kids drooling from twenty yards away. 'Mummy, Mummy, *that* one! *That* one *there*!' Or more likely, 'Daddy, Daddy,' or 'Granny, Granny.' They've got no prejudices, kids. Money's money no matter whose pocket it comes out of – and a teddy bear's a teddy bear.

And I was a very toothsome teddy bear indeed, dearly beloved. Sorry, a bit of Kipling slipped in there. Well – the *Just So* stories were their favourites. No, I tell a lie. *Their* favourites were the porn mags they found in their Daddy's shed. The *Just So* stories were their father's favourite – which is why he read to them about How the Elephant Got His Trunk and How the Leopard Got His Spots. And they'd pretend to go to sleep so he'd sod off and leave them to fumble through 'Wobblers' and 'Hugeness in Rubber' and 'Blimey, Look at the Jugs on Her.' Amazing how fascinating they found all that at the age of six. A long time ago now (he said, with a crocodile tear plipping out of his one remaining eye).

But here I am, wittering on about *them*, and you don't even know who *them* are, do you? James and Jemima. No, don't laugh. It wasn't their fault. I mean, people don't get to choose their names, do they? Perhaps they should. Would that be a good idea? Give them numbers until they're about ten or eleven, then everyone get round a table and decide on suitable names? I can give you a suitable name for James – no problem. A name like Mad Bastard, for instance. Now Jemima I liked. Fair dos. She was a cutie right from the start. Looked the part, too – long golden hair and a face you could suck like a lollipop. Sweet as . . . oh, sugar and spice – you know how it goes. Sugar and spice and everything nice.

We had our ups and downs like everyone does. It'll be a long while before I forget the bleach incident, for instance. But, come on, she wanted to know what I'd look like blond. You can't really blame her for that. Curiosity, that's all it was. Childish innocence. And the same when she decided I needed a haircut. The less said about that the better. I'm quite sensitive about my bald patch – although that's a piece of cake compared to what I look like now. Stomach split open. Guts hanging out. One arm gone west. One eye gone east and my ear hanging by a thread.

Still – I *got* him for it. In the end.

I'm a bad bear, I am.

What was that I said earlier about a swift spot of needlework putting it all to rights? I should be so lucky. If they knew what I'd been up to they'd be using me as oil-rags before the day was out. And a couple of handfuls of teddy bear stuffing up Gerald the Giraffe's backside. That'd wake him up. That'd put a stop to him doing the splits on the windowsill. Makes your eyes water. Oh yes, I've got a cruel tongue on me when I'm in the mood. But it's not my fault. It was *him*. It was that little fiend, James.

Look at him now, though. Poor old James. Where's your nasty cackle now, Jimbo? Eh? You've gone very quiet, my lad. Don't you fancy sticking a scalpel in me, Jimmy? Plucking my eye out by the string, perchance? Come on, Jim – get up and rip my other arm off at the shoulder. What? Can't be bothered? Sulking, that's what it is. He always was a sulky blighter. Sulky and spiteful and sorely in need of something sharp and hard right between the eyes. Wallop. Hold that. And me caught red-pawed. Except for one problem – one *tiny* problem. Teddy bears can't hold things. They don't give us fingers. Just that useless halfmoon of felt at the ends of our arms. Try beating someone to death with *that* in your spare time. Thank you and goodnight. If you're going to *do* anything, it can't be anything that involves holding things. We lack the wherewithall. Good job too, I can hear some of you thinking – those of you with cuddly little kiddies tucked up in their beds and Mr Edward Bear sitting at their pillow glowing with homicidal intent like Strontium 90.

But you've got it all *wrong*, I tell you. We're not like that. It's *me*. I'm a bad bear. Something nasty got packed into me along with the kapok. Lovely word that: kapok. I quote: a silky fibre obtained from the hairs covering the seeds of the tropical bombacaceous tree. That's what kapok is. It makes you think, doesn't it? Can you imagine all these English explorers with their handlebar moustaches and pith helmets, traipsing about in the tropics last century. And one of them says: stone me,

Cuthbert – this bombacaceous tree has hairs on its seeds that would go down a treat back home for stuffing teddy bears with. I know – let's call it *kapok*.

I digress. Well – wouldn't you, with half your bombacaceous tree seed-hair hanging out of your stomach?

Where was I? Oh yes – James and Jemima. I remember everything, you know. Right from the moment Daddykins lifted me down from the shelf. No time to say goodbye. I hardly knew the others, anyway. We're not encouraged to fraternize. It's a very competitive business in a place like Hamleys. You use up all your energy just sending out waves of 'Buy me, buy *me*' without having the time to chin-wag with the Brenda Bears and Boris Bears and Bruno the Big Brown Bears of this world.

The twins were only about four years old – but already James was flying his awkward-bugger colours. Hopping from sandal to sandal and going, 'I want *that* one,' he was pointing to an ugly bleeder twice my size with a face that would have frightened Atilla the Hun. It was just the *size* he was interested in, you see. He didn't care that it looked like a bulldog that had got its face caught in a food-mixer so long as it was bloody enormous.

That was his first tantrum. The first I saw, anyway. Right there on the floor in Hamleys. What a sight. I tell you – you see some things from a shelf, but I'd never come across anything like that. Writhing on the floor, kicking his little heels, screaming and hollering so you'd think someone was torturing him to death. I wish someone had been. And Jemima was hanging on to me, and being quiet and lovely and smelling of wonderful things. And I was thinking – I've got the salubrious end of *this* stick, and that's for sure.

I loved her straight away. That's the thing with us teddy bears. Love and affection. You can't beat it. And I loved that kid right from the word go. She was beautiful – bright as a button. She'd come out of the bath smelling like a little piece of heaven and all warm and glowy and I'd be tucked in next to her and she'd fall asleep cuddling me. Sorry. Look – I'm getting a bit choked-up here. You see? I'm not such a bad sort, am I? That's the thing with us bears – we don't *act* – we *re*act. We're cuddly little reflections of a loving child's affections. Crikey – that's almost poetry, that is. I ought to be in advertising. No, but *seriously*. She was adorable. I'd have done anything for that kid. And could she talk? My life, that child could chatter. I'll swear, even when she was little, she told me things she never told anyone else. That's why I didn't mind so much about the bleach. You can't help but forgive them when they're like that, can you? Go on – you know you can't. James, on the other hand. Yes, well – *James*.

Where was I with James? Oh, yes. On the floor. Screaming. He didn't get pug-ugly, though. I'll say that for Daddykins – he did occasionally know how to put his foot down with a firm hand, if you see what I mean. Actually, I think Daddykins was in need of defibrillation after he'd clapped eyes on the Hamleys-Horrors' price tag. I'll tell you – I'm not cheap – but that big ugly bugger made me look like a special offer.

James had decided he didn't want nuffin' if he couldn't have the Big One. 'I don't *want* a diff'rent one. I don't want anything *at all*. I *hate* you.' Yes, all that. And a fair dose of 'Nobody likes me, I'm gonna go down the bottom of the garden an' eat *worms*,' too. I'd have let him. In fact, I'd have insisted on it and hoped they choked him.

You think I'm being uncharitable, don't you? Yes you do. I can tell. Aww, you're saying, he was only a likkle kiddie. He'll grow out of it. Well, let me tell you – he didn't grow out of it – he most definitely grew *into* it. And I should know. Don't forget. I was there.

'Would the little girl like a bag for her teddy?'

'No.' No, the little girl wouldn't like a bag for her teddy. The little girl just wanted to carry her teddy in her arms. God – but she was so sweet, you know? This story is never going to get into some cutsie-wootsie anthology of teddy bear stories, is it? Not in a million years. The Umpteenth Pan Book of Horror Stories, maybe. With a good following wind. Which is a shame, because it's all true and now no one's going to hear my point of view.

Not that I'm worried about getting caught. I mean – come on – be realistic. Who's going to think I had anything to do with it? Get into the real world, can't you? I know what they'll say. They'll say he was on his hands and knees on the floor looking for something he'd dropped when he must have bumped against the table so hard that it jolted the typewriter right off the edge and crash, bang, wallop – right on the old craniumaroo. Right through the back of the old skullaroonie. Kersplat. Crunch. Blood everywhere.

Actually, that's not true. The blood-everywhere bit, I mean. Neither was the bit about him bashing against the table. It was all rather well thought out, actually, although I say so myself. Me sitting there half-mangled on the table but with enough go left in me to give the typewriter a quick nudge with my foot while he was getting the paper out. A swift nudge so the Tippex bottle fell on the floor. And when he bent over to pick it up – a nice, hefty kick from yours truly and a good few pounds of antique typewriter does a plummet job off the edge of the desk and it's all over.

It stopped him typing that letter, anyway. Hold on, I've just realized. No wonder you're thinking I'm some right evil sod. You still think he's a little kid, don't you? You're probably sitting there thinking he's about ten years old or something. Go on – I'm right, aren't I? That's just what you were thinking. Well, pardon me for missing it out, but a good few years, beers, cheers and tears have flowed under the bridge since Master James here kicked up that big stink in Hamleys. Fourteen years to be precise.

He always hated me, you know. It was as if, locked deep inside him, he's always felt a complete prat 'cos of the spectacle he made of himself in the toyshop – and the only way he could cope was by taking it out on me. This stomach wound of mine isn't recent, you know. Oh no – that was when he was about seven. Listen, I'll give you a quick insight into what Master James was like. Me and Jemima were playing doctors and nurses – like you do when you're seven. Well – doctors and patients, anyway. I was the patient, naturally. Up to my ears in bandages. Mummy bear. Get it? Bandages? Head to foot? Oh, never mind. I was the patient, anyway. Well, it'd have been a pretty static sort of game if I'd been the doctor, wouldn't it? Jemima lying on the floor saying: 'Doctor, I've got carbon dioxiditis and lumbago in both ears,' and me just plonked there staring into space. 'Cos that's the thing, you see – we mustn't ever let humans know we can move about on our own. What? *Whaat*?? I should cocoa. You'd be out of the TBU so quick your paws wouldn't touch the ground. That's a court-martial offence, that is.

And it's OK – we get the nights to ourselves – a couple of tots from the drinks cabinet – quick read of the paper – bit of television if you're lucky and no one's any the wiser. Mum thinks dad's drunk the whisky. Dad thinks mum's pulled the newspaper all out of order and both of them are suspicious that it's the twins who've been watching videos. No problem at all. And when the kids get a bit older and get packed off to school you get the days off as well. You end up, by the time they're about seven or eight, doing about . . . oh, say – three hours of an evening and a full day Saturday and Sunday. So, you can't complain, can you?

There I go again. Losing the thread. You shouldn't let me rabbit on. That's what they said about me in the factory, you know. Always rabbiting. And some wag reckoned my fur had come off a rabbit – which explained everything. It was funny, in the factory – they said: 'You'll come to a bad end, you will. You're just not *serious* enough – not *steady* enough. If you're not careful that impetuous streak in you will see you to no good end. You might be a toy to your owner, but to us you're a . . .' what was it? '. . . a Representative.' Sounds grand, doesn't it? A Representative. And my trainer, he says to me – I can see it, clear as daylight, he says, one night your owner will say: 'Goodnight, teddy,' and you'll go: 'Night-night, kiddo,' and all hell will break loose. Well – he was wrong about that. I kept mum and I didn't move a hair – even when that little bugger broke in on our game of hospitals and decided he'd liven it up with a scalpel he'd nicked off his dad's drawing-board.

'I think teddy needs an operation,' he said. And when Jemima tried to stop him he tied her to the end of the bed with some left-over bandages and actually cut me open in front of her. Can you beat that? She was crying her eyes out, the poor little mite, and he was hauling out great lumps of stuffing and laughing his head off. It didn't hurt me – not physically, I mean – I'm a teddy bear, aren't I? We don't have a nervous system as such. But you do get this really weird, *weak* feeling when someone's eviscerating you – weak and sort of out-of-it. Woozy. Apparently, if they take enough stuffing out you just pass out and that's your lot.

Ex-teddy bear. But Jamie didn't get the chance to do the full works on me. Jemima was kicking up such a racket by then that Mumsie came hurtling in and James was given what we call in the trade an exemplary punishment. And I was restuffed and sewn up. But I've always had a weak stomach since then.

So, that was Jamie when he was seven.

He was always getting at Jemima through me. Hanging me out of an upstairs window and threatening to drop me. Stuff like that. Fixing it up so that I was hanging by the neck from the ceiling light when she went into her bedroom. Stamping on my head. Shoving me in the microwave. Nothing that actually *hurt* me all that much – except for a few scorch marks and certain bits of my anatomy that I don't suppose will ever again be the shape that God intended. But, you know, us teddy bears get a sort of psychic link to our owners – so what I felt was the anguish of a little girl whose best friend was being tortured and abused. Yes – that's right – best friend. You knew that, didn't you? A kid's best friend is her teddy. Come on – it's *true*, I tell you. Teddies never let you down.

Teddies never let you down. Poignant, isn't it? It is when your owner goes through her sophisticated phase. It happened with Jemima between about ten and . . . oh . . . fourteen. Too grown up for a teddy bear. But then, after that, she was old enough for me again and I was winkled out of the bottom of the wardrobe and sat at the end of the bed with Gerald the Giraffe and assorted whey-faced girlie dolls. There was a difference, though, once she was in her teens. I sort of moved from being her best pal to being one of a static row of mascots. The magic had gone, I suppose. She *knew* I was just a stuffed *thing*. Well – that's what she *thought* she knew. You know different now, don't you? And I hope that after you read this you'll take your old ted down off the top of the wardrobe and give him a quick cuddle – just for old time's sake. We feed off love and affection. Don't forget that.

Every time a child tells a lie a fairy dies, so they say. I don't know if I believe that or not. It all sounds a bit whimsical to me – but if it's true then it must have been like a bad day on the Somme when James was at full throttle. And the odd thing with James was that he didn't *need* to be like that. He was a clever kid. Sailed through school with a force nine wind behind him.

Unlike poor old Jemima who had to work like a maniac to pass anything. Lovely, lovely kid, but not a great brain, if you take my meaning. Not top of the form. She had to run like mad just to be average at school, while Jimbo cut through it like a scalpel through teddy-bear hide. So why he was so jealous of her is a bit of a mystery to me. Except that people liked her and no one could stand the sight of James. 'Everybody hates me!' he'd say. And I'd be sitting there thinking: too bloody right, mate. And is it any wonder? But I didn't say a dicky-bird.

So, why is he lying here with a 1930s Exelsior typewriter down the back of his neck and his head like a Spanish omelette? And what was this letter I was so eager to stop him writing?

Like I said, Jemima had to work her socks off to get anywhere. And she wanted to be a psychiatrist . . . or a psychologist, or something. All these ologists confuse me. Anyway, she wanted to be something or other that meant she needed to get to College. And, I'll tell you, she worked like a lunatic. Nearly went barmy with the strain. Then someone told her about these pills that would keep her awake and keep her brain going. Some sort of zoom pills. Dexadrin, or something. Well, the long and the short of it is that she spent about six weeks permanently high on these little sweeties. Working 'til all hours. Burning the midnight oil and the candle at both ends and all that kind of stuff. Meanwhile, Jimmy was out gallivanting with his friends.

It's the classic tortoise-and-hare scenario. Jim was so certain he'd walk his exams that he did sod-all work. Well, you can guess the rest, can't you? He absolutely *bombed*. No kidding. Failed the lot. Couldn't believe his eyes when the long brown envelope plopped on the mat. He went *mad*. And can you imagine how he reacted when he found out that Jemima had passed everything? Jealous? Jeezus – jealous doesn't come into it. He went berserk. Accused her of everything from tattooing cribs on the insides of her eyelids to sleeping with the examiner. If his boat was sinking he was going to make damn sure Jemima went down with him.

He found the little silver box she kept the pills in. He was a nosy, prying git. No one's property was safe from him. Talk about not knowing the difference between meum and tuum –

that guy couldn't tell night from day. I hope you spotted that bit of Latin I chucked in there. I might have a touch of an accent and I might be somewhat of a scruffbag, but I'm not *thick*, pal. That's for sure. I pick these things up, know what I mean? You do that when you spend most of your time sitting and listening. You want to try it sometime. Gob shut and ears open. You'll learn a lot. That's the problem with you humans, if you don't mind me saying so – love the sound of your own voices. Hasn't it ever occurred to you that God gave you ears that are permanently open and a mouth that you can easily shut? Doesn't that *tell* you anything? Sorry – I'm getting personal. Don't worry about it.

The letter? Yes, I'm coming to that. Me and Jemima are sitting in her room and she's so happy to have passed her exams that she just *has* to give me a cuddle. See? Where does a young lady go in moments of pure bliss? Boyfriend? Do me a favour. Mumsie and Daddykins? No chance. It's ted that gets the full force of hurricane happiness when it comes sweeping across a lovely kid like Jemima. Yes, I know she's not a kid any more, but old memories die hard and I can still see her carting me along Margate Pier. Me under one arm, an ice-cream in her mush, singing something about the wheels on the bus going round and round, round and round, round and round . . . She used to drive me batty with that song. I used to make up my own verses: the brakes on the bus go fail fail fail . . . I've got what is called gallows humour, I suppose. Perhaps that bombacaceous tree was used for a lynching at some time and it rubbed off on me. Who knows.

James comes storming in, bent on revenge 'cos he's screwed up and she's on her way to College. 'I'll fix you,' he says. 'I'm going to write to the Board and tell them you were on *speed* all through your exams. You're not going *anywhere*, Jemima.' And then he grabs me and starts bashing the life out of me. You wouldn't believe this maniac was eighteen years old. Or maybe you would.

They have a fight over me. I can see the headlines: Tug of Love Ted. No, that's not right. The last thing James did was *love* me. So they're lurching about and my earhole comes off and an eye pops out and – rip – the old appendectomy scar opens up again.

Then he gives her a clout and she falls over and he's out of there with me and into his own room. And you wouldn't give credence to the things he's calling me and her. You won't find much of it in a dictionary, anyway. He gets me by the arms and gives this huge yank, laughing like a drain when my arm comes clean off. And I'm thinking – God give me teeth and claws and this kid would be mincemeat. But, like I said before, teeth and claws aren't an option.

He drops me on the desk and goes downstairs to fetch his mum's old typewriter. He figures, I guess, that a typewritten letter to the Authorities telling them about Jemima's little pills will carry more weight than a handwritten one. He may have been right. He never lived to find out.

Which is why I'm sitting here like patience on a monument waiting to see what's going to happen next. Now that's one thing us teddy bears have got in *spades* – patience. Mumsie and Daddykins should be back soon. I love it. Will Jemima be pleased or what? Big ted saves the day. And no one will ever know. Am I a big, bad, brilliant bear, or what?

It's dark. I'm still sitting here on my own, and it's dark. We live for a long time, you know. A long time. Unless we're physically dismantled we carry on living until we just rot away. That's a long time. A long time to sit and think about your mistakes. I heard about a bear once whose owner choked on his eye. Little thing, it was. The eye, I mean. He never got over it. So – how am I going to get over this?

Of course, you don't know what's been going on, do you? When was I talking to you last? It's got to be about a month ago. Hard to tell. We don't chop time up into neat little parcels like you do. Oh, look, you say, it's twelve *noon*, I must do the shopping. Or: it's half-past four, where are those children? No. None of that. But if I concentrate I reckon I can make it about four or five weeks I've been sitting here. Since they came and took Jimmy away. And my Jemima, God help me.

Never interfere. That's the cardinal rule where I come from. Never, ever interfere. Say nuffin'. Do nuffin'. That's a teddy bear's lot. Just *be* there for them when they need you. Sounds easy, doesn't it? Just *be* there. So – yes, I broke rule Numero Uno. I kicked that typewriter off the desk and squished Master Jimbob's napper flat as a welcome mat. More like a mashed melon, to be honest with you. I doubt the carpet will ever be the same.

Jemima found him. Not long after he shuffled off to Buffalo with an Exelsior 6000 on his head. Funny thing is, she came rushing in, yelling and clutching a carving knife. Strange, that. No way – trust me – no way on God's green earth could that girl ever in a million years do damage to anyone with a carving knife. Come on. I know her. I know more about her than anyone, and that's a fact. I reckon it was just to put the frighteners on him. Try and stop him writing that letter. That's all it was. She'd never have *used* it. Never. So, anyway, she comes steaming in and finds him on the floor and she just sits on his bed and howls.

A bit later Mumsie and Daddykins get home, and they pile up the stairs to see what all the racket is about and find Jemima sitting there and James lying there. And, believe me, Jemima is well out of it. It's like she's flipped, or something. You know – flipped her lid. The shock, I guess. I hadn't accounted for her doing a loopy on me.

Well, before you can say: 'Anyone for squashed melon?' the police have been called and there are flatfoots lumbering around the place and Jemima's being carted off for questioning. Some ambulance people turn up with a stretcher for Jim's body and a plastic bag and a spatula for his nut and it all goes horribly quiet.

What was that I said the other day? You know, the day that I *did* it. What did I say? A quick turn with a needle and thread and I'd be right as ninepence? Some chance. Daddykins locked the door from the outside and no one's set foot in the place since. I'm not bothered by the dark. Night or day, it doesn't make any difference to me. But we don't like silence, and that's a fact. Silence can kill you quick as hunger. And what with that and not knowing what had happened to Jemima, I was getting into a pretty rare old panic, I can tell you.

Last night it was, that I finally got the news. Sheer luck, actually. I mean, they didn't make a point of dropping in on me to *tell* me. It was only Jemima who made a point of telling me everything. But I've got a nasty feeling she's not going to be in a position to tell me about this one for a while. Mumsie and Daddykins were standing outside the door. Talking. That's how I got to know about it.

You see, the police didn't go for the bump against the table and oops, pardon, my typewriter idea at all. Apparently they reckoned it was *impossible* for that to have happened. Which meant it hadn't been an accident. Which meant it was either suicide or murder. Your average Pot Noodle wouldn't take more than ten seconds to figure out that people don't commit suicide by hitting themselves over the bonce with typewriters – so the police managed to discount that theory in a day or two, leaving – you got it – leaving murder.

Do I sound calm to you? A bit matter of fact? Don't you believe it. I am tearing myself apart over this. Have you cottoned on to what happened yet? Have you guessed the end of my bad, sad story?

They found her pills. Prosecution exhibit number one, m'lud. They found her sitting over his corpse with a carving knife in her hand. Circumstantial evidence, sure, considering the murder weapon was a typewriter, but when they asked her *why* she had a carving knife in her mit, apparently she looked at them with those pretty blue eyes of hers and said: 'I was going to kill him with it.' And when they asked her how he came to be lying face down on the carpet with a weighty item of antiquated office furniture embedded in his sconce, she said: 'I'm glad he's dead, he hurt my teddy.'

God! I could have wept blood.

They've taken her away, my beautiful, wonderful Jemima. Taken her to some distempered institution. Unfit to plead – that's what I heard Daddykins say through the door. They thought she was unfit to plead. In short, they thought she was a psycho. They thought she beat her brother's brains out with a typewriter because her mind had been scrambled by drugs.

You idiots! You stupid, rag-brained idiots! It was me. Open this door. Let me out of here! I did it! I did it.

Jemiiiiimaaaa. . . . . . . Jemiiiiiiiiimaaaaaaaaaa. . .

Medical Note: The attached piece of work was produced by Jemima Evans who is currently detained at Her Majesty's Pleasure at Bamboro Psychiatric Prison, following the murder of her twin brother James. I thought it might be of interest.

Look Me in the Eyes

JILL DROWER

I T WAS mid-afternoon and the sun was still scorching the terrace umbrellas along the Copacabana beach front. The Morrison family had slumped into moulded plastic seats on Avenida Atlantica's broad mosaic pavement, unaware that they were being studied from a short distance away.

Washington Silva was watching the Americano couple fussing over their young son. Washington Silva was eight years old and he had two ambitions. The first was to be selected to play soccer for Brazil in the World Cup. The second was to stay alive that long. Washington Silva was closely shadowed by his little sister, Cidinha. They were waiting for the right moment to approach. Gringos always stood out a mile, their sunburnt flesh, as inviting as red sirloin, alerting the senses of all the scavengers in the area. You could smell a gringo for miles.

Washington and Cidinha both knew that timing was everything. Move in too soon and they get jumpy. Move in slowly, meekly, appealingly and you're home. Leave it too long and the bigger kids beat you to it, or the head waiter chases you off.

The American family were studying the English version of the menu. Linda looked down at her son. 'Put Lazarus Bear down, Junior, he's not going to run away.' She gently took the bear from him and placed it on her lap. The name Lazarus did not hold any particular religious significance. It was just that, when asked what he wanted to call the bear, Junior had mumbled three syllables that sounded like a mixture of 'Lettuces', 'Lassoo Zeus' and 'Lassie says'. His parents helped him out with the name Lazarus because it sounded less doglike than plain old Lassie.

'Junior, what are you having? Stop messing around and decide. No, sweetheart, mango ice-cream might disagree with you.'

Junior was a strapping lad. If you'd put them back to back, Junior would have stood over a head higher than Washington. You could never have guessed that Junior was the younger child, the same age as Cidinha in fact.

'I wanna coke, Mom.'

Cidinha had moved in and was waiting near the table. Patient, dignified, sooner or later they'd notice her. Her real name was Maria D'Aparecida, and that's what she was – a little apparition that momentarily penetrated the consciousness of the affluent world and just as quickly vanished without trace. Cidinha was accomplished for a six-year-old. She had it down to a fine art. The gringos would suddenly notice her dark-brown chin perched neatly on the white of the café table. There was something about the way her face shone up at them and the way she looked straight into their eyes that made her totally irresistible. For one instant only, they would want to take her in their arms and comfort her, whisk her away to Vermont, New Jersey or Portland and bring her up as their very own child. It was a fantasy that vanished with the unfolding of a 1000-cruzeiro note.

Cidinha had caught the tourist lady's eye at last.

'Hey, Glen, take a look at those kids. How old do you think that little girl is?'

'Dunno, six going on sixty? Before you know it we'll be wading knee-deep in street kids.' Glen was right. There was something hydra-like about this high-profile poverty. For every one of the nine little faces you despatched with a dollar, another two would appear in its place.

'But, Honey, we don't have a choice. Just look at the state of them.'

'Yes.' He was trying to work out what five dollars would be in cruzeiros. 'But don't kid yourself that we're helping them this way. What they need is something drastic.'

'What are you trying to do, knock down the first domino?' his wife joked.

It was at this point that Washington noticed something was wrong. Cidinha was no longer gazing up into the faces of the gringo family. She had missed her cue for the upstretched palm. Instead she was staring down at the tourist lady's beach robe. The rim of the chair-seat pressed against the woman's red thighs so that they spread out generously. Cidinha wanted to prod them and pinch them. They must be soft. Cidinha looked at the cosy arms and bulging breasts of the lady and at her kind smile and thought that she would like to be cuddled by that tourist lady. She looked down at the teddy in the lady's lap and thought she would like to cuddle that little teddy, that *ursinho*. Washington guessed what she had in mind and was ready to beat it the moment she moved to snatch the bear. But the gringo boy caught Washington's glance and pulled Lazarus Bear off his mother's lap, clasping the toy tightly to his chest. The waiter was approaching. The two urchins darted off like minnows in the shallows.

The hotel suite overlooked the seafront. It was midnight and the American couple stood resting their arms on the sill and watching the negotiation on the street corner below. Linda was wondering what it must be like for the women to sell their bodies to feed their children. Glen was wondering what it must be like to be one of the punters, unaware that these stunning hookers were all young men with an uncanny knack of taking in the tourists. Like everything else in this carnival mask of a city, what you pay for is not necessarily what you get.

'Unzip me, would you please, Glen?'

'Sure, stand straight, honey.' She stepped out of her cocktail dress and moved towards the bathroom. Glen heard the taps go on.

He idly lifted Junior's bear off the table. There was something about the eyes. They were ludicrously out of proportion to the head size and the head, in turn, was way way too big for the length of the body. This was one of nature's tricks, borrowed by the manufacturers of soft toys. It was a way of giving the new-born a cuteness that cut across the whole world of mammals and made them so appealing that, if orphaned, they would be able to tug at the heartstrings of an adult from another species and therefore survive.

Glen thought of the lean street urchins with their vacant hungry stares and their skin sores. He thought of the little girl who'd approached their table, undernourished and covered in parasites.

'Look me in the eyes all you like, Lazarus. It's not my fault.'

'What, honey?' Linda was calling from the shower. 'Forget it,' he answered. He didn't know why he'd said it.

Lazarus Bear stared up, eyes unseeing. Glen walked into the adjoining room and placed the teddy on the pillow next to his sleeping son.

Within half an hour Glen was in bed, asleep. He was twitching and his eyelids flickered, his dreams peopled by topless mulatto women dancing the samba. They wore giant feather head-dresses of pink-and-green plumes, and they did impossibly wonderful things with their hips as they danced along. Great bands of these women floated towards him, moving slowly, wiggling their butts deliciously. Glen was worried. His pockets were bulging with dollars. He could not conceal the notes. He could see the mulatto women moving alarmingly close, arms waving in the air, dancing to the pounding rhythm, dancing devilishly towards his dollars.

His wife, Linda, was tossing and turning. She had not been sleeping well. It was not just her stinging back. The city was a disappointment. It made her feel uneasy. They had come here for a good time and to see the world. But it was the kind of good time that made her think too much, the kind of world that didn't bear close examination. Of course she would not say any of this to her husband. She wouldn't want to spoil this vacation for him. Only Junior in the room next door was enjoying the completely untroubled slumber of the truly innocent. By his side Lazarus Bear was lying face up, his eyes staring blankly into the ventilation grill.

Beyond that quiet cocoon, every inch of the city was seething with existence. Behind the grill, in the innermost shafts and recesses of the hotel, a sea of cockroaches picked at the leavings of the rats who, in turn, rummaged about in the garbage and gutters. And alongside the rats, on street corners, the gorgeous boy hookers would home in on their prey, taking their willing victims to the back seats of saloon cars or to out-of-town motels with coy names. In the menacing outer reaches of town in the northern flatlands, hired assassins stalked the night, picking off homeless minors one by one as casually as if they were clay ducks in a fairground gallery.

Above this scene stood the statue of Christ with his impossibly long torso and his arms outstretched. Christ the Redeemer tilted his head down towards the city of Rio de Janeiro in an attempt to protect and bless the city's assortment of waifs and strays.

Far below, on the Avenida Nossa Senhora de Copacabana, the two little ones were still very much awake, bedding down in the doorway of a vacant shop. They didn't always sleep here. Sometimes they chose the pavement by a bank or government building where there was no porter or nightwatchman. The reason for choosing a particular shelter was always the same: the need to be inconspicuous, the fear of being picked up, the fear of being moved on, beaten up, picked off, done in, strung up, gunned down. Unlike the cleverly camouflaged insects in the Tijuca Forest above them, these creatures stood out conspicuously, however still they lay. That is why, even during their deepest slumber at the dead of night, they were never at rest. They were always alert, afraid, ready to run for it.

The children of Maria das Graças Silva had different fathers. One glance would tell you that Cidinha was the descendant of plantation slaves and hunter-gatherers. Washington had more of the Portuguese colonizer in him. His genes were a salad made from the fruits of the Pancaruru and Kambiwa Indians of the São Francisco valley, from the Yoruba and Hausa tribes across the Atlantic, from frontier *bandeirantes* and Portuguese sailors, themselves descended from Moorish families in Lisbon and Jewish *conversos* in Spain.

It was unusual to see a sister and brother working as a team. Most of the bigger street children now went around in groups, sweeping down on the Southern zone, doing a trawl of well-to-do beaches like Ipanema and Leblon, taking whatever they could from the startled sunbathers. These children owed their loyalty to gangs who picked their young leaders according to who had the most nerve in thieving. Most of the street children were fugitives from the *favelas* and had no emotional ties. The Silva children were different. Washington still had strong recollections of life with their mother in a place called Bom Jesus de Lapa in the rural interior. The city had not yet obliterated this memory nor his notion of family.

When Mãe had first arrived in the city with her two children, they had begged as a threesome. Mãe would move from table to table with the baby Cidinha in her arms. With a blue bed-cover wrapped over her head they looked like a portrait of the Madonna and child. After a year or so, Mãe moved in with a man in the *favela* called Rocinha. This city within a city spilled lava-like down the slopes of a mountain. Mãe learned to call this vast, drainless slum her home. The man she lived with was called José. He stank and he drank and when he could stand upright he would knock them all about. He sent Mãe out to earn a little something and she would do whatever it took. José clouted her once too often and, in the end, she took flight with the kids. At night they would bed down in shop doorways and the blue shawl would be used as a cover to keep the two little ones warm. As Cidinha got older, she would playfully kick the cover off and Mãe would chide her.

Mãe would sometimes go off with someone at night. When she did this she would tell Washington to look after Cidinha and, as she left, she would always say, 'Don't forget to pray to Santo Onofre.' One night she went off with two men in a car. As she left she turned to Washington and smiled, 'Look after Cidinha and, *filho*, don't forget to pray to Santo Onofre.' Mãe looked deep into his eyes before turning her back.

Cidinha had been nothing but trouble that evening. She kept kicking off the blue shawl. She kept whining and complaining. It took hours to settle her and he knocked her about a bit to shut her up. Then, eventually, he nodded off and woke with a start the next morning. Mãe had not returned. Washington immediately knew what he'd done wrong: he had forgotten to pray.

Every night for weeks he prayed to Santo Onofre. He would sit there muttering until his head fell forward onto his chest. His prayers were never answered.

The American family woke early the next day. It was their last in Rio and they had a good deal to fit in. In the lobby on their way up from breakfast, they ordered a taxi to take them to the Sugar Loaf. The receptionist said he'd ring through when the car arrived.

Back in their room, Glen stood at the window once more, looking down on Avenida Atlantica. Joggers in colour-coordinated training outfits were pounding the Copacabana seafront. If you didn't look too carefully, you might think this was a Saturday morning in body-conscious California.

He tried to imagine the number of hours that had gone into laying the mosaic-work paving. Each stone was a tiny square, hardly bigger than the first joint of his thumb. He now realized it was just like everything else in this city. From close to, all you could see was a chaotic, incomprehensible jumble. Nothing made sense until you achieved the distance created by money. The superb abstract sweep of black, red and white could only properly be appreciated from a good height, from a roof-garden terrace or a penthouse duplex. These views-from-a-height had a sanitizing effect. No wonder tourism in Rio consisted of several long struggles to see the city from a distance. So far, the Morrison family had seen the Lagoon from the Corcovado, the Corcovado from the Lagoon, the city from the Vista Chinesa and a high view of Rio framed by foliage from the Mesa do Imperador.

Mother was trying to get Junior interested in the Sugar Loaf. She was doing her own children's version of the information in *Fodor's Guide*. 'Listen to this, Junior. Sugar Loaf gets its name from the Indians who called the mountain *Pau-nd-Acuguar* which means tall peak, but to the Portuguese it sounded just like their words for Sugar Loaf.'

Junior wasn't the slightest bit interested in the Indians Mom was talking about. He didn't care about the origins of the name and he was kicking up a fuss because his parents didn't want him to take Lazarus Bear.

'Listen Junior, he'll be much safer here in the hotel room. He'll be waiting for you when you get back.' There was no way Junior was going out without Lazarus Bear. 'OK, Junior, if you take the bear, you'll have to carry him all the way there and all the way back. We're not going to take him for you if you get tired, are we, Linda?'

'No way, honey. Junior will have to look after the bear like an adult.'

They finally reached agreement, just as the call came to say that the taxi was waiting outside.

Washington Silva was scratching his scalp and rubbing his eyes. The traffic ploughed by relentlessly, covering the little ones with a soft blanket of exhaust gases. There they lay, on their bed of newspaper, curled up like two little rodents in a ball.

Washington was thinking about that teddy bear, the *ursinho*. He had wanted to grab that bear for his sister. He sat up and stretched. Cidinha was still asleep. Her eye was getting infected again. This meant the gringos would shrink back if she got anywhere near them. Washington would have to do the begging today. Cidinha was becoming such a liability that sometimes he thought of running off and leaving her to fend for herself. There were moments when he liked to think about Cidinha playing in the road and how some great truck would flatten her. Washington thought about his mother. His waking was always haunted by a terrible longing for Mãe. He missed her smell and her touch. He missed the way she joked with him and said he was the man in the family. He loved to hear her call him, *'Meu filho'*. It was all his fault that Mãe had left them. She must have spoken to Santo Onofre. How else would she have known not to come back?

Cidinha was waking up now and stretching and yawning. Before she had even opened her eyes she began scratching furiously at her wrists and elbows. Washington looked down at her bony little form. Maybe if he managed to get her a teddy of her own then Mãe would forgive him and come home.

Glen and Linda had a map open and were trying to get their bearings. They were staring down on a breathtaking view of Guanabara Bay. The guide books said how, on a clear day, you could just see the jagged peaks of the Fluminense Mountains, but visibility from the Sugar Loaf was not wonderful this morning.

'What's that long bridge?' Linda asked.

'Hang on, lets take a look here. It goes from Rio to Niteroi on the other side of the Bay.' Glen enjoyed having all the answers.

'Junior, look down there sweetheart,' Mother called him over. 'You were on that beach yesterday. And look over there. That's the statue of Christ. We went there the day before yesterday, remember?'

'Mom, why are his arms always sticking out?'

'Well, it means that he's protecting all the people in the city.'

'Mom, does he protect all the bugs and killers and baddies, too?' She was just thinking of an answer when Glen came striding up.

'Now come on, you guys. Over here and line up for the photograph. Put your bear down for just one moment, will you Junior? He's not going to run away.'

Junior placed Lazarus Bear on a bench. The toy's bright blue eyes stared straight up into the bright blue sky.

'Move over, will you Linda, honey? I want to catch the view behind you. Junior, look up please. Look at me, straight into the camera. Come on, smile everyone, say "Cheese".'

Mid morning and the Ipanema sand was too hot to tread on unless, that is, you had lived most of your life barefoot.

Washington and Cidinha made their way slowly along the beach side of Ipanema's Avenida Viera Souto. They were two lean flesh eaters stalking the herd. It was hard work searching the crowd for their meagre piece of meat: a weak or inattentive sunbather who could be singled out and picked off.

At posto 9, without exchanging a word, they split up. This job was best done by Washington working alone. He moved on to posto 10 where the rich kids hung out. These bathers seemed to be less watchful than most, distracted by their cellular phones and the other trappings of their lifestyle. It was here that Washington at last found his mark. A group of young people sat around in a circle talking. A yard from the nearest of them, like a smooth speckled egg in an unattended nest, was a beach bag, perched on the corner of a velour towel. Nearby, two young men with perfectly defined muscles were taking a close look at a jet-ski.

Washington lay at the water's edge. His body sank into the wet sand and the waves broke over his shoulders.

The moment came. It was over in a second, in the blinking of an eye. It was a short sliding tackle which brought a sudden shower of sand. Washington pounced on the beach bag and then legged it, darting barefoot across the boiling sand. The jet-skiers, three times his age, three times his size, looked lamely on. Their beautiful, vast biceps and pectorals were strictly for show, not for confrontation. It was like taking candy from a baby.

Cidinha was waiting for him on the corner of Garcia D'Avila. Washington had long since dropped the bag but had kept the contents. Not much for a morning's work – just a pack of Hollywood cigarettes and a peach-coloured T-shirt. They continued to run, but slower now so that Cidinha could keep up. Washington could outrun anyone. One time, he was almost caught with a gold chain in his hand, but he had this way of changing direction and of accelerating at the last moment – just like Renato before he scored that goal for Flamengo. One day, Washington would duck and weave like this for Brazil. His mother would see him on the television. She would come to visit him after the big match at the Maracanã stadium. She would find her son. She would fold him in her arms and tell him how proud she was of him. She would say, '*Filho*, I always knew you'd make it big. I always knew it.' And she would look deep into his eyes in the way that he loved and she would not leave him again. One day, one day.

Meanwhile, a few miles away, the Americans were descending in the cable car, the picture-book view marred by the loss of Glen's wallet.

'Are you sure you had it with you when you left the hotel?' Linda was asking her husband. 'Sure, I had it right here in my sports-jacket pocket. I can't understand it.' The wallet had had a fair amount of cash in it, but the credit cards were in the hotel safe, thank God.

Back at the hotel, the receptionist explained to them how to get cash at short notice. They tried to take in what she was saying but it all sounded so complicated. The idea of not having currency made their blood run cold. It was like being a child again, like losing sight of your mother in a crowd. The hotel would make all the arrangements. A money changer called a *doleiro* would visit them in their hotel room. He offered a better rate of exchange than a bank, and it meant they wouldn't have to walk around the streets with large amounts of cash on them.

'But isn't that the black market?' Linda protested. Glen signalled to her to shut up. They were starting to argue now and, in the lift on the way up to their room, Linda started to complain about not coming to South America on a guided tour like most people.

Glen put on his patient voice and told her how, if you wanted to see the real country, really meet the people, then you shouldn't travel with the herd.

By the time they had changed their money, they'd lost a couple of hours. They had to change their plans. There wasn't any time to go to the beach, but that didn't matter because Linda's back was still stinging. Besides, it had clouded over and looked like it was going to rain. They still had time to visit Stern's, do a tour of their mineral workshops and then pick up a couple of nice gemstone souvenirs – nothing too glitzy. There'd just be time to get back to the hotel, take a shower, finish off packing and settle up.

Washington was doing well guiding cars in and out of their parking places. The drivers would hand him notes which he folded neatly lengthways and stuck in his pocket. Sometimes it was a lot, but never as much as the gringos were prepared to part with. He couldn't understand gringos. They were really crazy, really stupid.

Cidinha was wearing the newly acquired peach T-shirt and, on her, it was as long as a ball-gown. She was larking about. She never thought about where the cars were. He had to watch her like a hawk. Sometimes she really got on his nerves but then, at times like now, he liked having her around. Cidinha never turned on him like the other street kids and she was easy to impress. It had taken him a long time to perfect the art of blowing smoke rings and she giggled with delight when he got it right. You could do anything and she was impressed, like that time when he showed her how to sniff thinner.

He was showing off to her right now, telling her to point out any word and he would read it to her. Washington Silva, who had never once stepped inside a school-room, could read the following words, 'Coca Cola, Cruzeiros and Pepsi'. Cidinha pointed out a large ad for Varig Airlines. She gestured to the word Varig. 'Aeroplane,' Washington lied. She then pointed to the logo on the front of her new T-shirt. He looked carefully at the words 'Yves Saint Laurent' and then said, with confidence, 'It says, T-shirt.' Cidinha was clearly pleased with the answer and Washington glowed with satisfaction.

The Americans were wandering down Ipanema's main street. They had done their souvenir shopping and were taking a final walk down towards Copacabana. They had nearly come to grief on a plate-glass door in one of the shopping galerias. A sign on it said *puxar*. Glen made his wife wait while he looked it up in his pocket dictionary. She stood there uneasily while people walked past. 'Listen, honey,' he was really enthusiastic now,' '*puxar* doesn't mean push, it means pull. It's what they call a false friend.'

Glen was keen to break the codes around them, as if understanding were a key to controlling events. Linda just wanted to get the hell out. She could not remember what it was like to be illiterate and this new sensation filled her with foreboding. Her inability to read the hieroglyphs just made her aware of all the hidden signals she completely took for granted at home, like eye contact, body language, pace, dress and even choice of footwear. An abilty to decipher these messages was far more important than mere script. It was essential to their survival.

Like the passenger on a stagecoach gingerly making its way across the canyon floor, Linda could see the smoke signals, she could hear the distant beat of tom-toms. Her husband could not. Along with his wash bag, Glen Morrison had brought with him the idea that he was an intrepid traveller protected by the cloak of Uncle Sam.

As the couple walked along the crowded city pavement, they came upon something strange. A man sitting on a stool at the edge of the pavement was checking a list. At his side, a couple were talking excitedly and waving a piece of paper. Glen was immediately drawn to the scene. He guessed there was gambling going on, maybe something like 'Chase the Lady'. There was definitely money changing hands.

'Glen, I really don't think we wanna hang around here. Let's go. Really, I mean it.' She was tugging at his sleeve. Glen was stubborn. He wanted to know what was going on. He had his pocket dictionary out and was noting in the back what he couldn't translate. 'Honey, listen to this, *urso* means bear. They're shouting something about a bear.'

Linda flagged down an approaching taxi. As it drew up, she tugged hard at her husband's sleeve. At that moment it started to rain.

Back at the hotel, Glen asked the receptionist to explain it all. He tried to repeat the syllables exactly as he'd heard them, '*Nacab essa, nacab essa.*' The receptionist listened politely. It clearly wasn't ringing any bells. Glen tried again, this time with the help of his jottings.

'Ah, *urso na cabeça*,' the receptionist finally understood. 'That's from the Jogo do Bicho – it's the animal lottery and it means the bear has just won.' Glen was attentive now, excited by the prospect of having all the answers. 'The numbers-game bosses finance the Carnival parade. It's good public relations. They have a lot of power – they practically run the *favelas*.' The receptionist was explaining how each animal had a number – the bear, *the urso* was number 23. If you got two *desegnos* then it meant you'd won *na cabeça*, on the head. Glen was hopelessly confused now. He guessed it was a kind of gambling accumulator and that '*urso na cabeça* meant 'Bear wins all' or something like that. By the time the receptionist had fully explained the workings of the animal lottery, Glen had lost interest.

At 6pm in a Copacabana downpour the American family were speeding along in a taxi on their way to Galeão Airport.

'How much should we tip him?' Linda whispered to her husband. 'Don't worry about that now, honey. We've only just got in. Junior, will you stop playing with that window. You're letting the rain in.' Junior was playing with his teddy, winding the window up on the bear's neck so that its head stuck outside the car.

This type of rain was an efficient killer. It regularly sent orange-box homes careering down the mountains and turned the precarious hillside paths into gushing torrents. Occasionally, it sent tons of topsoil slipping over the coastal road, burying drivers alive in graves of rich red earth. Here, on the Copacabana street surface, the raindrops ricocheted fiercely in all directions. The windscreen wipers of the taxi jerked back and forth frantically.

In a shop doorway Washington and Cidinha stood waiting for the lights to change. They would approach the queueing drivers and ask for money but they would have to be quick because, when the lights turned green, the cars lurched forward like great stampeding beasts. Cidinha was never quite quick enough and got sprayed many times over as countless car wheels soaked her with the contents of the gutter.

Washington looked down at his sister. The droplets of rain on her thick black hair made him think of his mother. Sometimes, when his mother stood in the rain, it glistened on her hair like jewels, like Iemanjá's crown. Mãe had told him that Iemanjá was the Queen of the Sea and that, if you gave her a flower offering at New Year, she would grant your wishes. Next New Year, he would steal some flowers and ask Iemanjá to send him back his Mãe.

The lights changed and the two children returned to their doorway. A taxi was approaching at speed. Inside it the American couple were lost in their own anxieties. Suddenly, there was a howl from Junior. 'My bear, my bear!' His face was contorted with agony. He was practically climbing out of the open window. 'Junior, there's no way we can get it now.' Glen looked out of the back window. He could barely see past the water that was hitting the glass. He knew that Lazarus Bear would be unrecognizable after a few moments' punishment on a slushy three-lane highway. 'Junior,' he said gently, 'there's no way we can stop here. The traffic's far too dangerous. We can't just run into the road,' Junior was inconsolable. The taxi driver looked uncertainly around, but Glen waved at him to keep going. Linda took Junior's face in both her hands. 'Listen Junior, we can get you another bear just like Lazarus the moment we get home. Listen to me, sweetheart,' she looked deep into his eyes, 'There are plenty more bears where that one came from.'

In the doorway Washington was counting the cigarettes in the pack he'd got from that beach bag. He had to keep them dry or he wouldn't be able to sell them. Later, he'd smoke one, but he'd have to cadge a light off one of the peanut boys. He was studying the progress of a raindrop as it slid down the window pane. Any moment it would merge with the droplet below. He was chatting to Cidinha, boasting about his skilful beach theft. He turned around. She wasn't there. When would she learn that you stayed out of the rain until the lights changed?

He looked across to her. She was facing him, smiling broadly in the second of the three lanes of traffic. She was waving a squashed bit of nylon fur above her head. It was a victorious wave, like when Renato has just got the ball into the net for Flamengo. 'G-o-a-l!' the commentator would shout. Cidinha was looking directly at him, still waving the bear. It was like the slow-motion action replay he'd seen on the screens in bars and shops sometimes. He could barely hear Cidinha calling to him. '*Olha, meu ursinho*' – my bear, my bear, Washington look over here!' Washington saw the bus bearing down on her. It was the airconditioned *frescão*, upholstered, sumptuous, hermetically sealed from the elements. He heard its long futile blast on the horn. He watched the windows flicker past his vision. In that instant he understood, with absolute certainty, that he would never see his mother again. It was the kind of certainty that could never be erased, even for a few moments, by the strongest, most wistful fantasy. He screamed her name, not Cidinha's, but his mother's, 'Mãe, Mãe.'

Washington stood there sobbing. Cidinha faced him, suddenly frightened by the near miss. She had lowered her arm and the bear dripped limply by her side. She was hovering, not daring to move in the second lane, anxiously trying to make her break to the kerb. The traffic lights changed and the cars jerked abruptly to a halt. Washington wove his way between the revving cars and grabbed at her. They squeezed back between the bumpers just as the lights were turning. 'Look at my bear Washington! *Que bonitinho, que gracinha.*'

It was mid afternoon and the sun was slowly cooking the sticky tarmac of Avenida Atlantica's road surface. Washington Silva and his sister Cidinha were at the Hotel Meridien end of the beach. They had passed the Copacabana Palace and were planning to do the bars up as far as the Luxor Continental. Washington was kicking a stone along the mosaic pavement, showing off his nifty footwork and imagining a crowd of thousands cheering him on.

Cidinha's eye infection had not cleared up yet, but she had a new trick which got around the problem of approaching the tourists. It worked every time. She placed her *ursinho* so that his little teddy bear nose rested on the edge of the café table. What gringo could resist such a sight: a little waif holding up a damaged toy? The gringos would look from Cidinha to the bear: a little scrap of a thing in a designer T-shirt holding out a little scrap of yellow nylon. How could they fail to be moved? They would take one look at the bear's face and then feel for their wallets. There was something very appealing about the teddy's eyes, the way they looked straight at you.

Fit for a Princess

PAT RUSH

WHEN TEDDY bears are sold at auction, several factors can influence their price. Rarity is one, of course. But an interesting history can also boost the bids. When the two occur together, world records can be broken – as happened in May 1989 at Christie's in South Kensington.

Christie's had aroused plenty of interest in an unusual red bear by producing a special postcard of him to send to all their registered teddy buyers. His story was told in the press and on television so, by the time the auction began, tension was already beginning to mount. Bidding was fast and furious and, in little more than seconds, Alfonzo had a new home – for a then world-record price of £12,100.

Of course, it helped that he was such a rare bear. The button in his ear confirmed that he had been made by the renowned Steiff factory in Germany. But Steiff had no records of ever having produced such a range of red bears. They concluded that he was probably made in 1908 for Harrods department store in London which often ordered toys to be made specially for their best customers.

Perhaps even more important, however, was the identity of this particular customer. For the bear had been bought by George Mikhailovich, Grand Duke of Russia, as a present for his daughter, the Princess Xenia. After the Grand Duke was assassinated in 1919, the bear was to remain a treasured reminder of him until the Princess's own death in 1965.

Alfonzo spent much of his early life in a house called Horax, situated in the Crimea, almost next to the Tsar's own residence. He also probably travelled north from time to time, visiting the palace of the Princess's grandfather, the youngest son of Tsar Nicholas I.

In 1914, however, Alfonzo returned to London with the Princess Xenia and her mother for a visit to Buckingham Palace. They were still there when war broke out and, unable to return home, they became guests of Queen Alexandra at Marlborough House. Eventually they moved to a house of their own when it became obvious that their stay was to be a long one.

Alfonzo stayed with the Princess throughout all the upheavals and, after her father's death, she kept him near her always.

So it was that, in 1921, Alfonzo moved to America. The Princess had married William Leeds, heir to a tin fortune and whose father was popularly known as the 'Tin Croesus'. The couple set up home on Long Island and it was there that Alfonzo, too, was to remain for more than forty years. After the Princess's death, however, he moved to Connecticut. Four years later he found himself in Vermont where the real bears in the nearby mountains helped him to feel at home.

Finally, however, he arrived at Christie's in London and on 18 May 1989 he made his presence known by attracting that record-breaking bid. His new owner was Ian Pout, proprietor of a teddy bear shop in Witney, Oxfordshire. Alfonzo was to become the star of the shop's museum.

With his bright red fur and Russian-style tunic, he certainly made a distinctive addition to the collection. But his fame spread still further when Ian ordered 5000 replicas of the bear from his original maker, Steiff. Collectors rushed to buy them.

One, however, was sent as a gift to Alfonzo's previous owner, Princess Xenia's daughter Nancy, who was shocked by the similarity to her mother's old bear. Only one small difference could be seen. The replica's nose was in perfect condition, while the dearly loved Alfonzo's was almost bald from the many kisses he had received!

One Bear's War

ELISABETH
BERESFORD

*To Donner Underwriting Associates, without whom I shouldn't
have had to write this story.*

I WAS STILL a very young bear at the time. Some falling fur,
paws and nose showing a bit of wear, but looking forward
to an exciting, interesting life. And then it was nearly
snuffed out in a few seconds. That went for all of us. The whole
family on a perfectly normal summer afternoon. That, for me,
was when the war really started. Now I'm old I ramble on a little
and, strangely enough, I can recall my early days a great deal
more clearly than I can recall what happened yesterday.

Without wanting to show off I came from a very good background. One of the best really, Harrods, one guinea. That was a
great deal of money in 1938. And I was worth every penny of it.
A beautiful coat of glossy gold fur, blue eyes – unusual at that
time – velvet paw pads. I was much admired and I enjoyed
every minute of my working day. We were in a section of our
own and we rather tended to keep ourselves apart. Dolls are all
very well in their way, I daresay, and don't think for a moment
that I'm prejudiced, but you can hardly put them in the same
section as bears! Sometimes I had a fantasy in which I moved
into a Royal nursery, but it was not to be. This was just as well
as, the moment the family came into view, we only had to look
at each other to know. This is where I belonged and they
belonged to me.

It was sad to leave my companions at Harrods, but that part of my life was over. Time to move on. And, to be honest, things were very slightly going downhill in our section. They had started importing bears – I cannot call them teddy bears – from the Far East. Prickly, sparse fur, sharp noses, inferior eyes – price half-a-crown. Not at all what I was used to and they were embarrassingly friendly. I didn't care for it.

It was interesting to ride in a taxi and watch the world. The newspaper sellers were doing a good trade, persons were queuing up to buy and they looked anxious as they scanned the headlines. The name of Mr Chamberlain was everywhere, but – and I'm ashamed to admit it – it meant nothing to me. Then we went on an electric train and, finally, we reached our destination. It was a beautiful seaside town with tall, stately houses and a broad promenade. Two piers, sparkling with lights, stretched out into the dark sea.

Our house was right on the Front and I was in the day nursery, top floor front, with a splendid view over the seafront. There was quite a large staff, but the only one who closely concerned me was Nanny. She was quite young, rather plain, but nevertheless engaged to a baker. I came to know all this because Nanny often talked to me in the evening – I'm a good listener – curled up on the window seat and looking out over the promenade with its miles of sparkling lights. Impossible to imagine then how it was all going to change.

In fact the changes came so slowly one hardly noticed them. Strips of sticky tape across the windows, rolls of barbed wire stacked by the end of the groynes, hideous-looking gas masks in ugly cases hanging on the hooks in the hall. And one night, when none of us were expecting it, a call like a mad banshee echoed over the rooftops. When that happened everybody, including the cook, huddled together in the big pantry under the stairs.

We were told it was only a precaution, a practice, but it made my fur stand on end for a while. Not at all pleasant. And then the head of the family went away. Altogether it was as if the pattern of our lives, up till now so quiet and enjoyable and *ordered*, was breaking up. When he suddenly returned we hardly recognized him. He had become an officer in the Royal

Navy and I was proud of him. He looked every inch the best sort of sailor with his gold braid, polished shoes and immaculate uniform. For the first time I wanted to leave home and go with him, surging through the dark waters. But, of course, that was impossible although I did hear through 'channels' – my little joke – that a number of us did serve in the Royal Navy, even in submarines.

But I had to stay at home and do my best to keep up morale there. There was a long quiet patch, I recall, when nothing much seemed to happen although the barbed wire now stretched right along the promenade and there were no more twinkling lights. In fact, if there was so much as a glimmer from our windows a person on a bicycle would come peddling along the road and blow on his whistle and shout, 'Put that blinking light out!'

The Phoney War it was called and it ended quite suddenly with the banshee making its call up to six times a day. But we adapted to that quite quickly, not even bothering to go down to the pantry unless the call came at night. There were guns, big guns, along the Promenade now and the soldiers used to whistle and call out to Nanny. Privately, I think she rather enjoyed it; as I've said she was somewhat homely. But I looked straight ahead and kept my back straight.

Quite a lot of persons left the town and it no longer looked beautiful or elegant as the paint began to peel away and the windows were boarded up. Slowly, without realizing it, we started to become shabby. We were proud of it. It showed we were 'doing our bit'. And then it happened, the big change which nearly overwhelmed us.

It was a sunny Saturday afternoon in September. Four of us were having tea in the sitting-room on the first floor. There had been a banshee wail some time ago, but we had forgotten it although the heavy, orange velvet curtains were drawn across the long windows. Just as well. They saved our lives. One moment we were sitting there and the next – chaos! Personally I heard nothing, saw nothing. All I knew was that I was sailing across the room, hit the ceiling and ended up on top of a tall bookcase with plaster showering down on me. The great curtains were sliced to ribbons, there was a cloud of filthy dust and the sound of glass tinkling and smashing as it fell from windows all along the Promenade. Then there was machine-gun fire, persons running, the bell of an ambulance.

How long I lay up there, half expecting the rest of the ceiling to come down on me I don't know. Miraculously nobody was hurt, although the cook was buried in the basement. The bomb had hit us at a slant and blown the front off the house, leaving the back almost undamaged. Very strange. When the ambulance had taken off the cook the rest of the family tried to do some tidying up, but it was impossible. The house was ruined. Somebody remembered me and it was brave of them to venture across that shaking floor to rescue me. I was glad to get out into the street. We were all shocked and we looked like ghosts, covered as we were in white dust. There was glass and rubble everywhere and, in front of the remains of our steps, lay a still figure covered with a torn blanket. His postbag, intact, lay some distance away. He always delivered the afternoon post at 3.30 exactly. Never again.

Never again for a great many things. I was bundled away in a shopping bag which smelt of onions, but this was not the moment to worry about such trivia. What I wanted above all else was a good brush-down, but I had to wait for that. Some considerable time. Unfortunately, my fur never fully recovered. And so I became an evacuee. The people to whom we were sent were nice enough, retired doctor and his wife, but the house was small. Suburban if you understand me and not at all what I had become used to. However, I must give the doctor his due, he sewed up my two front paws – they were badly torn – quite beautifully. And Mrs doctor gave me a bath. I'd never had one before and I came out of it slightly lumpy, but extremely clean.

And so began another kind of war. Everything was in short supply. Petrol – so no car. I had to be carried everywhere. Food, severely rationed so everybody had to 'Dig for Victory'. Where there had once been a cricket pitch they had allotments where they grew beans and potatoes and those everlasting onions. I was sitting to one side of this one morning when that dreaded banshee wail started up again, but there was no pause this time. The plane came hurtling out of the sky within seconds and everybody ran in all directions.

'This is it,' I thought and closed my eyes. Nothing else I could do. The noise was amazing. A scream that went on and on, a second's pause and then a truly deafening blast as the plane hit the ground and exploded. There was a series of bangs and something extremely hot whistled past my ear. And, to crown it all, great clods of earth started to rain down. One hit me on the leg. Things quietened down after a while and I must have dozed off, shock I suppose, and when I came to I was propped up in bed with a bandage across one eye. For a while I didn't go out at all, but sat propped up looking out of the window as best I could with one eye and all that sticky brown paper across the window. There were quite a few raids, just sticks of bombs dropped at random, and all they ever seemed to hit were haystacks or old barns, although one did land in the duck pond. It was rumoured afterwards that quite a few persons had duck dinners, but nothing was ever proved, of course, because the evidence was – well – disposed of in a culinary manner.

Then, suddenly, it was all change again. I had become almost used to our suburban way of living and I always enjoyed listening to the vicar when he came in for a (rationed) glass of Bristol Cream. For a person of the cloth he had some very militant ideas and he would shake his fist at the planes and wish them a most unchristian end!

We were going home! With my sharp ears – nothing wrong with *them* – I soon caught the whispers and rumours. It seemed too good to be true and, suddenly, I realized how desperately homesick I had become. No car to take us this time, we travelled on a rickety old single-decker bus which was as shabby as we were. We were stopped just outside the town by soldiers. Quite cheery, but standing no nonsense. Everybody had to produce their identity cards. I had one too. Oh, yes. Stamped and official-looking with a photograph taken in my younger days and wearing a certain naval cap and a white silk scarf. Very dashing. Nationality British, of course, place of origin, Harrods.

When the sergeant saw that he banged his heels together and gave a very smart salute. We recognized each other. It was the baker! Everybody on the bus smiled and suddenly the day seemed less dark. Alas, not for long.

Stupidly I had supposed we would go back to the Promenade

and that somehow, in spite of the blackout and the banshee, life would be like it once was. Alas, it was quite, quite different. Two rooms and use of kitchen and bath in a back street. But there were thousands worse off than we were and we had to make the best of it. Which we did. I sat on the windowsill with a straight back and a paper Union Jack in my paw for all to see. Persons got used to me being there and they would often wave and smile as they passed. I felt I was doing my bit to raise morale and I was proud of it, especially on the day when the mine went up on the beach.

The authorities had been going round all day with loud-speakers warning everybody and all the windows were slightly open to counteract the blast when it came. And when it did come it was spectacular! It blew in not only the window, but the entire window frame as well. That's when I lost an ear! And I was a bit deaf in the other for a while. But, by the following morning, they had stuck some transparent paper stuff across the window and I was back at my post.

And then, suddenly, everything went quiet in our home. It was something to do with a telegram which had 'On His Majesty's Service' stamped on it. I thought it was splendid of King George VI to telegraph us when he must have had so much else on his mind. But I soon gathered that it was bad news. Very bad. I did what I could to be of comfort. Always upright, always smiling. It must have been about 2 o'clock in the morning – naturally, I never slept as somebody had to look after the household – that I heard a car draw up and voices. The car went off again and there was bang-bang-bang on the front door. Lights went on, running footsteps down the stairs and then a sudden cry which made my fur bristle. A few seconds of dreadful suspense and then there he was in the doorway. I nearly fell over. I've never seen such a sight. No smart uniform this time, but a dirty – very dirty – knitted cap, beard and oil all over his face, red eyes, a *soldier's* greatcoat and rubber boots covered in muck.

But who cares? He was back and that was all that mattered. He had a dreadful old cardboard suitcase and from it he produced a bottle of wine, a big cheese – the biggest cheese I'd seen in years – some pickled onions and chocolate. A feast. We all sat round and he talked and talked about his ship being torpedoed and how many had died from the blast and afterwards by drowning or cold. He had been three nights and four days on a raft, making everybody sing until they hated him. But he kept them alive until they were rescued by a neutral ship, Swedish, I think, from Malmö.

I was so proud of him and when, at last, I was left alone I kept thinking of how much he had been through . . . well, all the ship's crew. And then – then I felt a strange sensation in my bottom left paw. Something was creeping over it . . . and then there was more of it. It went on and on until all my fur was covered in whatever it was. It was the most hideous night and I thought dawn would never come and, when it did . . . the table was covered in cockroaches and so was I. They had hatched out in the suitcase. Of course they were dealt with. The room was scoured and dusted with insect powder, the suitcase and most of his clothes were burnt. But then it came to my turn.

My future hung in the balance. I, too, had become a casualty of the war. Would I survive it? The chances began to seem remote. But I hung on. I refused to give in. Tattered, minus this and that and now mutilated by cockroaches. Not a very rosy prospect. There was a lot of whispering and I caught the words . . .

'. . . try the hospital . . .'

Immediately my morale improved. They were going to send me to the King Edward VII Bear Hospital. The best hospital in the world! But no, the next time I heard the full news. I was to be sent to a *doll's* hospital! Me, a Harrods teddy bear! As I've said repeatedly, I have nothing against dolls in their place, I daresay they do a good job in their way, but to be sent to one of their hospitals . . . I very nearly threw in the towel, I can tell you. But the war was still dragging on and I had my duty to do. My duty to look after and guard the family. So I swallowed my pride and I went.

We will draw a veil over what they did to me. The ignominy of sharing crowded shelves with all kinds of dolls. I just had to grin and bear it – if you'll forgive the pun. There were even some of those bears from the Far East. One of them whispered to me one night that they had been 'set aside' for the duration. He was a seedy little fellow, minus a leg, and he clung to me rather. I tried to instill a little backbone into him, but it doesn't come naturally to that sort of bear.

The day of my release – I cannot describe it any other way – was one of the happiest of my life. My appearance by now was unusual. Fresh fur had been grafted on and one of my eyes was larger than the other. But we were so pleased to see each other. Tears were shed!

Then there was another surprise – we returned to our old home! But, oh, how it had changed. The shabbiness one could accept, that was now a daily way of life, but it was no longer a private house. We took in PGs, that is, short for Person Guests. Persons who paid us money to stay in the house. And what a strange but cheerful group we were. These were now our Allies. Polish airmen, Free French (I sometimes considered them to be a great deal *too* free), Australians, Canadians, New Zealanders from the Empire and Americans who, for some strange reason, were called GIs. I was living in the kitchen by now. On the top shelf of the dresser but still, I am glad to say, with my now somewhat tattered Union Jack. It was one of the GIs who, somewhat late one evening, insisted that I wear his cap. It was a kindly gesture and so I graciously accepted. From that moment on I was known as 'Hi there, Teddy'.

Our seaside town, which only a mere three years ago had become so empty, was now filling up rapidly. There were Allied and British and American troops everywhere. The side streets were full of strange small cars called Jeeps. I never did discover why. Further up the coast – I heard all the news in the kitchen but my mouth was sealed for security reasons at that time – there were landing craft in great numbers. By a strange quirk of fate I knew when Normandy was to be invaded before any person. A somewhat, shall we say, jolly General (American) came into the kitchen on his own and told me all about it. Times, places, landing plans. Everything. What with the accent and the malt he was carrying it was a little difficult to follow. But I must have been one of the first bears ever to have heard the entire plans for the D-Day Landings. (They were a day later than actually planned, but we won't go into that.) Naturally I never said a word.

They were very anxious, sometimes quite frightening, days which followed. Something called the V1 and then the V2 came into our lives. There were no banshee wails as far as they were concerned. They were not bombs, but rockets. There was little warning, just a ticking noise, silence and then an almighty explosion. And there were a great many of them. I just kept my back to the kitchen wall, held on to the flag and like everybody else hoped for the best. We had been at war for a long time by then and we were tired. Tired to the bone. But hanging on. Determined to see it through to the end.

There was that one last winter when everything seemed grey, almost hopeless, but we won't linger on that and then, suddenly, in the spring of 1945 grey struggle turned to sunny optimism. I picked up a rumour here, a half-told story there. The Master came back, no cockroachy suitcase this time I am pleased to say, and with much more gold braid on his jacket and cap. And when we were alone for a moment he took me off the shelf and we actually danced round the kitchen. I shall never forget what he said.

'We've done it Ted, you and me, all of us. The war will soon be over and there'll be peace in our time!'

It was a moment I shall always treasure. It made all those years of keeping my back straight, smiling and carrying the flag, worthwhile. I was not a Harrods bear for nothing! Unfortunately, after that small episode, matters became a little confused. The kitchen filled up, everybody was talking at once and I was kidnapped. There is no other word for it. I was snatched, rolled up and pushed into a kitbag. I was taken away for ever from the family. That's a bear's life.

When I recovered my senses I realized I was in the back of an army lorry full of soldiers. Some slept, some talked quietly, some sat silently. After the joyful time we'd had at home the atmosphere was definitely depressing. I had no notion how long I'd been unconscious so I have no idea how long the journey took, but it seemed interminable. We were forever being stopped at road blocks and, as the night faded into dawn, I was able to catch occasional glimpses of the road we were travelling.

It was something I never wish to see again. Ruined buildings scorched by fire, hanging shutters banging in the wind, whole floors exposed like one of those doll's houses. It was far, far worse than the damage I had seen at home. And it went on and on, mile after mile of it. Desolation. But worse than that was the never-ending line of persons, apparently carrying all their possessions, silent, ragged children at their heels. They walked without speaking, coming from nowhere, going nowhere, and then I saw a battered sign beside the road: Hamburg Strasse. I wished to know no more.

My wanderings during the next few years took me all over Europe. Sometimes I wore an American GI cap and became again 'Hi Ted,' or a Polish forage cap, 'Dzien Dobry'[1], and on one memorable occasion I was guest of honour to a number of Russian officers. I didn't care for them greatly until this Russian Colonel took me aside and told me, with tears in his eyes, that to him I was a symbol of his homeland. The great all-powerful red Russian bear! I must admit I was swayed for a moment, but then I thought of Harrods and home. It would never do.

Strangely enough, such are the quirks of fate, that a few days later a British Colonel came into our quarters during the Changing of the Guard – as I had come to call it in my own mind. The two Colonels talked and then the British one just happened to glance round and he saw me. I was quite a figure of fun by then, I'm the first to admit it. Fur all over the place, eyes of different sizes, ear missing, split paws. You name it, I had it! And besides that I had gathered a collection of flags and caps. Nevertheless, he instantly recognized me for what I was. His jaw dropped and he said one word, 'Teddy!'

And I knew from that moment that, no matter what problems, barriers or red tape lay ahead, that somehow he would get me home. Home to where I truly belonged. And he did. To what I believe is called 'The Imperial Bear Museum' in South London, although I may not have heard that totally correctly. I have my own show-case with my collection of caps and flags and every day persons come to look at me. The young ones smile and wave and we get on excellently as I pride myself that I have always remained young at heart. Some of the older ones become tearful, but I cannot imagine why. We have survived! I have a small private dream that one day a member of the family will chance by . . . we shall see.

I'm on the shelf now – another of my jokes! But I'm enjoying it. All person life is here and they stop and read the document entitled, 'One Bear's War'. I hope they learn from it! And as for me, 'sans paw, sans ear and sans quite a lot of fur, but *never* sans morale'. Goodnight.

Edward Bear (Harrods) OBBE [2]

NOTES

1. 'Good morning' in Polish.
2. Order of the British Bear Empire.

Confessions
of an Adult Bear
Collector

DAVID ELIAS

I'VE ALWAYS regretted not buying that astronaut teddy in a golden spacesuit, with his small furry face peering anxiously through a visor. He stood in a souvenir shop near the Kennedy Space Center in Florida and, though I found him appealing, my only thought at the time was that it was a pity I couldn't buy a spacesuit like that for my own teddy bear, back home in Nottingham. It never occurred to me to buy the bear and, at a stroke, to double my teddy bear collection.

Possibly my 'teddy blindness' stemmed from my childhood awe of my own teddy, a large Merrythought bear, bought for me by a kindly uncle who had generously picked out the largest bear in the shop. I called him 'Teddy' or, more probably, was firmly told what his name should be, and because I found him uncomfortably large I was more attached to a tiny black Scottie dog who leaked wood shavings from a hole in one stumpy leg until he wasted away. Teddy sat on a child-sized yellow chair, with a hinged seat under which a potty could be placed, and he perched on that slightly undignified roost for most of the next thirty years.

When I left home, Teddy stayed in South Wales with my mother who dressed him in an odd collection of garments rescued from the unsold pile at jumble sales – his legs were rammed so forcefully into a pair of child's ribbed tights that his left leg developed a warp which has never quite healed. On visits home, I occasionally noted his presence, but Teddy just glowered balefully at his uncaring absentee owner.

In fact, it wasn't until my mother died and my wife Gillian and I were sorting out which of her possessions we wanted to keep that we really thought about Teddy. We didn't dump him in the boot with the crockery and cutlery, but put him in the back seat of the car so that he had a chance of looking out of the window. As we left Wales on our way back to Nottingham, Gillian looked round and suddenly noticed a change in his appearance. 'Teddy's smiling! He didn't have a smile before, did he?' No, I seemed to remember a rather dour and slightly threatening Teddy, certainly no smile. We stopped and examined him more carefully.

Teddy's mouth was made from a stitched-on design of tough black thread, secured, we could now see, in the middle and at each end so that it was possible to brush against the thread and change his expression from solemn to smiling. In all the years I'd maintained a nodding acquaintance with Teddy, I'd not discovered this result of stroking his muzzle, but, as we had installed him in the car's back seat, one of us must have touched his face and made him grin. Either that, or he was expressing his own lightness of heart at the change of scene and the removal of his corseting tights.

Back in Nottingham, Teddy got more attention than he'd received for ages. Once his cast-off clothing was removed, we found his curly golden mohair fur beneath was still in remarkably good condition, almost pristine, and his slightly grubby face was soon sponged brighter to match his newly created smile. Eventually we bought him a blue tracksuit in a Mothercare sale and, with the addition of a badge or two, he happily adopted the persona of a 'Krypton Factor' bear, acting as my mascot in 1980 as I competed in the quiz and lumbered several times over the assault course.

Teddy had a busy time, appearing in press and magazine photographs, looking much slimmer and fitter than his owner; he proved to be a highly effective mascot – I got to the final, and was later asked to set the questions for the quiz for the next series, leading to a switch of career from lecturing to setting quiz questions. He remained my only bear for quite some time, however, and it was during this period that the purchase of the golden astronaut bear was missed – and regretted.

How did it come about, then, that from a reluctance to add to a bear collection of one, my wife and I are now custodians to a hug of some fifty or sixty bears? (We try counting occasionally, but they're all over the house and we keep adding to the collection, so all we know is that we have plenty of bears, but never quite enough.) I think the blame can be laid indirectly at the door of our great-niece, Rebecca. As our great-nieces and nephews came along, we bought each of them a teddy bear for their first Christmas. Katie, Sarah and Christopher each got locally bought bears but, soon after Rebecca was born, we were in Harrods and browsed around their toy department to audition likely bears for her. I was instantly smitten by a small plump bear who sat, arms outstretched in an appealing 'pick-me-up-NOW' pose, and who snuggled cosily against me as soon as I picked him up.

Like Teddy, this bear was a Merrythought, though over forty years younger, specially designed for Harrods, and we thought he'd make the perfect present. We took him home, looked into his large, deep eyes, and decided to christen him 'Max de Winter', as a literary joke. On one of the literature courses I was teaching at the time, Daphne du Maurier's romantic novel, *Rebecca*, was a set text, and we had a naughty vision of our great-niece, when twenty years later she read the book or saw the film, suddenly thinking, 'So THAT's why my teddy was called Max de Winter!'

We therefore found a little white vest that fitted the bear, had the name 'Max de Winter' embroidered across the front at a quick-stitch shop, and put him to sit on a bedroom chest to give us the pleasure of looking at him until he was called on to become Rebecca's Christmas present.

There was only one snag with that little plan – when he was packed up and sent off he left an accusatory gap on the bedroom chest, and we found we missed his wide-eyed, serious gaze. In fact, we missed him so much that we went on a special quest back to Harrods a few days before Christmas and, with a sigh of relief, bought one of the very few identical bears that remained. Well, almost identical – each looked very slightly different, and we chose one with a seriously contemplative expression. He settled comfortably into Max de Winter's gap, and we cast around for a suitably literary name to suit this appealingly podgy little bear. The right name came to us a few days later – both Gillian and I had lectured on the plays of Oscar Wilde, and *The Importance of Being Earnest* suggested that the perfect, the only, name for such a self-important furry newcomer was 'Ernest'.

After that, we began steadily to accumulate other teddies, and to spread the bear-collecting virus to other adult relatives by giving them as presents. Initially, Gillian's mother was startled and doubtful to be given a bear, but soon fell for its charms and now treasures a companionable hug of teddies that she reluctantly allows visiting great-grandchildren to play with, as long as they're careful.

Most of our early acquisitions were rather jokey – a flat-faced bear, whose green ribbon named him 'Albert', came from the V & A museum's Christmas catalogue, and a visit to the local AA office to research questions for 'Busman's Holiday' led to an impulse buy of a tiny patrolman bear in full AA uniform. We picked up bears almost incidentally, as long as they had some quirk that appealed, or showed some individuality of character. Only once did I buy a bear unseen, by mail order from Hamleys, and had nagging doubts until he arrived and turned out to have easily enough personality to make himself more than welcome.

Still acting on impulse, I bought the biggest bear of the lot whilst on a business trip to Kent; passing through a Canterbury department store I saw a child's pedal car with a huge silky furred bear in the driver's seat, the bear marked down to £25. Cash rescued him from his cramped position, but I then had the problem of how to get him home – progress through the crowded streets of Canterbury was a little embarrassing whilst lugging a 4'-tall bear in my arms, and I hadn't realized quite how far away my car was parked. He was christened 'Rochester' (partly geographical, partly another literary joke – remember *Jane Eyre*?) and he travelled home to Nottingham up the A1 with me, securely belted into the passenger seat, much to the astonishment of the children in a school minibus behind which I travelled for a few minutes before they identified the odd-shaped head they could see beside the driver.

But none of this was 'serious collecting', a quite different infection from the desultory accumulation of a few interesting but inexpensive bears. Except in the vaguest way, I'd not heard of the great German bear-makers like Steiff and Hermann, and when we'd browsed through the range of bears displayed in emporia like Harrods and Selfridges, a ticket showing a price much over £20 had immediately caused a sharp transference of attention to the next shelf. Why would anyone pay that much for a bear, when there were perfectly adequate and very lovable bears to be bought so much more cheaply?

It took a specialist teddy bear shop to open my eyes. One day, as we drove through a small village called Hathern, south of Nottingham, we saw a large white board at the roadside, advertising 'Teddy Bears', and pointing down a narrow lane. When we explored, we found The House of Bruin, a shop run by sisters Sue and Irene, themselves besotted with bears. They had the largest stock of bears we'd ever seen, neatly and invitingly set out on broad shelves, and the only question was, 'Which of these shall we have?'

Put the products of all the major and minor manufacturers of bears together and you soon realize why the well-made bears cost so much more – never mind the price tag, feel the personality! We bought, we came back and bought again, and learned from Sue and Irene which varieties were worth considering. The newly launched glossy journals, *Teddy Bear Times* and *Hugglets' Teddy Bear Magazine*, led us into the world of arctophilia and told us that useful collective noun, a 'hug' of teddies.

Our hug has grown steadily ever since. The House of Bruin moved from its original village shop to the centre of Loughborough, and now provides us with some of our choicest bears, like a replica of the world's most expensive (£55,000) bear, 'Happy', whom we christened 'The General' (because his original was made in 1926, the year of the General Strike), and a 1904 bear, bought from my winnings on the 1992 Epsom Derby, and naturally christened 'Dr Devious'.

Once we have the bears at home, they aren't allowed to loll about lazily, but are made to pose for photographs. They're arranged against interesting settings, and sometimes taken out to scenic locations that suit their characters. I've now had several batches of bear photographs published, and ideas for photographs often come from finding suitably sized props. In a sale, I picked up a model bicycle, so Gillian chose a bear of the right proportions to dress in Lycra shorts, gaudy singlet and peaked baseball cap. (We now call him 'Reg', after Reg Harris.) From a toyshop, a computer-shaped water-pistol and a pencil-sharpener fax machine led to a miniature office setting, complete with telephone, safe and filing cabinets, where bears can bustle and fuss. In photographs, our bears become animated and take on their own independent lives.

Now we've become enthusiastic collectors and look out for bears everywhere we go: from a holiday in New England we brought back a suitcase full of bears, a 'Southern Belle' from Mystic, a portly athlete from Salem whom we christened 'Streaker' (headband, running shoes and competitor's number, but no shorts), a fully-kitted tennis Paddington picked up for only $9, a Santa bear from Cape Cod, a surgeon bear from Harvard in green gown and face mask but, unfortunately, still no astronaut, still no bear in a golden spacesuit. Perhaps we collectors are always looking for the one bear we missed and can now never find, but the joy of the search, and of the company of our hug, is solace enough for me!

The Teddy Bears' Picnic

WILLIAM TREVOR

'I simply don't believe it,' Edwin said. 'Grown-up people?'

'Well, grown up now, darling. We weren't always grown up.'

'But *teddy bears*, Deborah?'

'I'm sure I've told you dozens of times before.'

Edwin shook his head, frowning and staring at his wife. They'd been married six months: he was twenty-nine, swiftly making his way in a stockbroker's office, Deborah was twenty-six and intended to continue being a secretary until a family began to come along. They lived in Wimbledon in a block of flats called The Zodiac. 23 The Zodiac their address was and friends thought the title amusing and lively, making jokes about Gemini and Taurus and Capricorn when they came to drinks. A Dane had designed The Zodiac in 1968.

'I'll absolutely tell you this,' Edwin said, 'I'm not attending this thing.'

'But darling –'

'Oh, don't be bloody silly, Deborah.'

Edwin's mother had called Deborah 'a pretty little thing', implying for those who cared to be perceptive a certain reservation. She'd been more direct with Edwin himself, in a private conversation they'd had after Edwin had said he and Deborah wanted to get married. 'Remember, dear,' was how Mrs Chalm had put it then, 'she's not always going to be a pretty little thing.

107

This really isn't a very sensible marriage, Edwin.' Mrs Chalm was known to be a woman who didn't go in for cant when dealing with the lives of the children she had borne and brought up; she made no bones about it and often said so. Her husband, on the other hand, kept out of things.

Yet, in the end, Edwin and Deborah had married, one Tuesday afternoon in December, and Mrs Chalm resolved to make the best of it. She advised Deborah about this and that, she gave her potted plants for 23 The Zodiac, and in fact was kind. If Deborah had known about her mother-in-law's doubts she'd have been surprised.

'But we've always done it, Edwin. All of us.'

'All of who, for heaven's sake?'

'Well, Angela for one. And Holly and Jeremy of course.'

'*Jeremy*? My God!'

'And Peter. And Enid and Charlotte and Harriet.'

'You've never told me a word about this, Deborah.'

'I'm really sure I have.'

The sitting-room, where this argument took place, had a single huge window with a distant view of Wimbledon Common. The walls were covered with rust-coloured hessian, the floor with a rust-coloured carpet. The Chalms were still acquiring furniture: what there was, reflecting the style of The Zodiac's architecture, was in bent steel and glass. There was a single picture, of a field of thistles, revealed to be a photo-graph on closer examination. Bottles of alcohol stood on a glass-topped table, their colourful labels cheering that corner up. Had the Chalms lived in a Victorian flat, or a cottage in a mews, their sitting-room would have been different, fussier and more ornate, dictated by the architectural environment. Their choice of decor and furniture was the choice of newly-weds who hadn't yet discovered a confidence of their own.

'You mean you all sit round with your teddies,' Edwin said, 'having a picnic? And you'll still be doing that at eighty?'

'What d'you mean, eighty?'

'When you're eighty years of age, for God's sake. You're trying to tell me you'll still be going to this garden when you're stumbling about and hard of hearing, a gang of OAPs squatting out on the grass with teddy bears?'

'I didn't say anything about when we're old.'

'You said it's a tradition, for God's sake.'

He poured some whisky into a glass and added a squirt of soda from a Sparklets syphon. Normally he would have poured a gin and dry vermouth for his wife, but this evening he felt too cross to bother. He hadn't had the easiest of days. There'd been an error in the office about the BAT shares a client had wished to buy, and he hadn't managed to have any lunch because, as soon as the BAT thing was sorted out, a crisis had blown up over sugar speculation. It was almost eight o'clock when he'd got back to The Zodiac and, instead of preparing a meal, Deborah had been on the telephone to her friend Angela, talking about teddy bears.

Edwin was an agile young man with shortish fair hair and a face that had a very slight look of a greyhound about it. He was vigorous and athletic, sound on the tennis court, fond of squash and recently of golf. His mother had once stated that Edwin could not bear to lose and would go to ruthless lengths to ensure that he never did. She had even remarked to her husband that she hoped this quality would not one day cause trouble, but her husband replied it was probably just what a stockbroker needed. Mrs Chalm had been thinking more of personal relationships where losing couldn't be avoided. It was that she'd had on her mind when she'd had doubts about the marriage, for the doubts were not there simply because Deborah was a pretty little thing; it was the conjunction Mrs Chalm was alarmed about.

'I didn't happen to get any lunch,' Edwin snappishly said now. 'I've had a long unpleasant day and when I get back here –'

'I'm sorry, dear.'

Deborah immediately rose from among the rust-coloured cushions of the sofa and went to the kitchen where she took two pork chops from a Marks and Spencer's carrier-bag and placed them under the grill of the electric cooker. She took a packet of frozen broccoli spears from the carrier-bag as well, and two Marks and Spencer's trifles. While typing letters that afternoon she'd planned to have fried noodles with the chops and the broccoli spears, just for a change. A week ago they'd had fried noodles in the new Mexican place they'd found and Edwin said they were lovely. Deborah had kicked off her shoes as soon as she'd come into the flat and hadn't put them on since. She was wearing a dress with scarlet petunias on it. Darkhaired, with a heart-shaped face and grey-blue eyes that occasionally acquired a puzzled look, she seemed several years younger than twenty-six, more like eighteen.

She put on water to boil for the broccoli spears even though the chops would not be ready for some time. She prepared a saucepan of oil for the noodles, hoping that this was the way to go about frying them. She couldn't understand why Edwin was making such a fuss just because Angela had telephoned, and put it down to his not having managed to get any lunch.

In the sitting-room Edwin stood by the huge window, survey-ing the tops of trees and, in the distance, Wimbledon Common. She must have been on the phone to Angela for an hour and a half, probably longer. He'd tried to ring himself to say he'd be late but each time the line had been engaged. He searched his mind carefully, going back through the three years he'd known Deborah, but no reference to a teddy bears' picnic came back to him. He'd said very positively that she had never mentioned it, but he'd said that in anger, just to make his point; reviewing their many conversations now he saw he had been right, and felt triumphant. Of course he'd have remembered such a thing, any man would.

Far down below, a car turned into the wide courtyard of The Zodiac, a Rover it looked like, a discreet shade of green. It wouldn't be all that long before they had a Rover themselves, even allowing for the fact that the children they hoped for would be coming along any time now. Edwin had not objected to Deborah continuing her work after their marriage, but their family life would naturally be much tidier when she no longer could, when the children were born. Eventually they'd have to move into a house with a garden because it was natural that Deborah would want that, and he had no intention of disagree-ing with her.

'Another thing is,' he said, moving from the window to the open doorway of the kitchen, 'how come you haven't had a reunion all the years I've known you? If it's an annual thing –'

'It isn't an annual thing, Edwin. We haven't had a picnic since

1975 and before that 1971. It's just when someone feels like it, I suppose. It's just a bit of fun, darling.'

'You call sitting down with teddy bears a bit of fun? Grown-up people?'

'I wish you wouldn't keep on about grown ups. I know we're grown ups. That's the whole point. When we were little we all vowed –'

'Jesus Christ!'

He turned and went to pour himself another drink. She'd never mentioned it because she knew it was silly. She was ashamed of it, which was something she would discover when she grew up a bit.

'You know I've got Binky,' she said, following him to where the drinks were and pouring herself some gin. 'I've told you hundreds of times how I took him everywhere. If you don't like him in the bedroom I'll put him away. I didn't know you didn't like him.'

'I didn't say that, Deborah. It's completely different, what you're saying. It's private for a start. I mean, it's your teddy bear and you've told me how fond you were of it. That's completely different from sitting down with a crowd of idiots –'

'They're not idiots, Edwin, actually.'

'Well, they certainly don't sound like anything else. D'you mean Jeremy and Peter are going to arrive clutching teddy bears and then sit down on the grass pretending to feed them biscuit crumbs? For God's sake, Jeremy's a medical *doctor*!'

'Actually, nobody'll sit on the grass because the grass will probably be damp. Everyone brought rugs last time. It's really because of the garden, you know. It's probably the nicest garden in South Bucks, and then there're the Ainley-Foxletons. I mean, they do so love it all.'

He'd actually been in the garden, and he'd once actually met the Ainley-Foxletons. One Saturday afternoon during his engagement to Deborah there had been tea on a raised lawn. Laburnam and broom were out, a mass of yellow everywhere. Quite pleasant old sticks the Ainley-Foxletons had been, but neither of them had mentioned a teddy bears' picnic.

'I think she did, as a matter of fact,' Deborah mildly insisted. 'I remember because I said it hadn't really been so long since the last one. Eighteen months ago would it be when I took you to see them? Well, 1975 wasn't all that long before that, and she said it seemed like aeons. I remember her saying that, I remember "aeons" and thinking it just like her to come out with a word people don't use any more.'

'And you never thought to point out the famous picnic site? For hours we walked round and round that garden and yet it never occurred to you –'

'We didn't walk round and round. I'm sorry you were bored, Edwin.'

'I didn't say I was bored.'

'I know the Ainley-Foxletons can't hear properly and it's a strain, but you said you wanted to meet them –'

'I didn't say anything of the kind. You kept telling me about these people and their house and garden, but I can assure you I wasn't crying out to meet them in any way whatsoever. In fact, I rather wanted to play tennis that afternoon.'

'You didn't say so at the time.'

'Of course I didn't say so.'

'Well then.'

'What I'm trying to get through to you is that we walked round and round that garden even though it had begun to rain. And not once did you say: "That's where we used to have our famous teddy bears' picnic." '

'As a matter of fact I think I did. And it isn't famous. I wish you wouldn't keep on about it being famous.'

Deborah poured herself more gin and added the same amount of dry vermouth to the glass. She considered it rude of Edwin to stalk about the room just because he'd had a bad day, drinking himself and not bothering about her. If he hadn't liked the poor old Ainley-Foxletons he should have said so. If he'd wanted to play tennis that afternoon he should have said so too.

'Well, be all that as it may,' he was saying now, rather pompously in Deborah's opinion, 'I do not intend to take part in any of this nonsense.'

'But everybody's husband will, and the wives too. It's only fun, darling.'

'Oh, do stop saying it's fun. You sound like a half-wit. And something's smelling in the kitchen.'

'I don't think that's very nice, Edwin. I don't see why you should call me a half-wit.'

'Listen, I've had an extremely unpleasant day –'

'Oh, do stop about your stupid old day.'

She carried her glass to the kitchen with her and removed the chops from beneath the grill. They were fairly black, and serve him right for upsetting her. Why on earth did he have to make such a fuss, why couldn't he be like everyone else? It was something to giggle over, not take so seriously, a single Sunday afternoon when they wouldn't be doing anything anyway. She dropped a handful of noodles into the hot oil, and then a second handful.

In the sitting-room the telephone rang just as Edwin was squirting soda into another drink. 'Yes?' he said, and Angela's voice came lilting over the line, saying she didn't want to bother Debbie but the date had just been fixed: 17 June. 'Honestly, you'll split your sides, Edwin.'

'Yes, all right, I'll tell her,' he said as coldly as he could. He replaced the receiver without saying goodbye. He'd never cared for Angela, patronizing kind of creature.

Deborah knew it had been Angela on the telephone and she knew she would have given Edwin the date she had arranged with Charlotte and Peter who'd been the doubtful ones about the first date, suggested by Jeremy. Angela had said she was going to ring back with this information, but when the Chalms sat down to their chops and broccoli spears and noodles Edwin hadn't yet passed the information on.

'Christ, what are these?' he said, poking at a brown noodle with his fork and then poking at the burnt chop.

'The little things are fried noodles, which you enjoyed so much the other night. The larger thing is a pork chop which wouldn't have got overcooked if you hadn't started an argument.'

'Oh, for God's sake!'

He pushed his chair back and stood up. He returned to the sitting-room and Deborah heard the squirting of the soda syphon. She stood up herself, followed him to the sitting-room and poured herself another gin and vermouth. Neither of them spoke. Deborah returned to the kitchen and ate her share of the broccoli spears. The sound of television came from the sitting-room. 'Listen, buster, you give this bread to the hit or don't you?' a voice demanded. 'OK, I give the bread,' a second voice replied.

They'd had quarrels before. They'd quarrelled on their honeymoon in Greece for no reason whatsoever. They'd quarrelled because she'd once left the ignition of the car turned on, causing a flat battery. They'd quarrelled because of Enid's boring party just before Christmas. The present quarrel was just the same kind of thing, Deborah knew: Edwin would sit and sulk, she'd wash the dishes up feeling miserable, and he'd probably eat the chop and the broccoli when they were cold. She couldn't blame him for not wanting the noodles because she didn't seem to have cooked them correctly. Then she thought: what if he doesn't come to the picnic, what if he just goes on being stubborn, which he could be when he wanted to? Everyone would know. 'Where's Edwin?' they would ask, and she'd tell some lie and everyone would know it was a lie, and everyone would know they weren't getting on. Only six months had passed, everyone would say, and he wouldn't join in a bit of fun.

But to Deborah's relief that didn't happen. Later that night Edwin ate the cold pork chop, eating it from his fingers because he couldn't manage to stick a fork into it. He ate the cold broccoli spears as well, but he left the noodles. She made him tea and gave him a Danish pastry and in the morning he said he was sorry.

'So, if we could, it would be lovely,' Deborah said on her office telephone. She'd told her mother there was to be another teddy bears' picnic, Angela and Jeremy had arranged it mainly, and the Ainley-Foxletons would love it, of course, possibly the last they'd see.

'My dear, you're always welcome, as you know.' The voice of Deborah's mother came all the way from South Bucks, from the village where the Ainley-Foxletons' house and garden were, where Deborah and Angela, Jeremy, Charlotte, Harriet, Enid, Peter and Holly had been children together. The plan was that Edwin and Deborah should spend the weekend of 17 June with Deborah's parents, and Deborah's mother had even promised to lay on some tennis for Edwin on the Saturday. Deborah herself wasn't much good at tennis.

'Thanks, Mummy,' Deborah managed to say just as Mr Harridance returned from lunch.

'No, spending the whole weekend actually,' Edwin informed his mother. 'There's this teddy bear thing Deborah has to go to.'

'What teddy bear thing?'

Edwin went into details, explaining how the children who'd been friends in a South Bucks village nearly twenty years ago met from time to time to have a teddy bears' picnic because that was what they'd done then.

'But they're adults, surely, now,' Mrs Chalm pointed out.

'Yes, I know.'

'Well, I hope you have a lovely time, dear.'

'Delightful, I'm sure.'

'It's odd when they're adults, I'd have thought.'

Between themselves, Edwin and Deborah did not again discuss the subject of the teddy bears' picnic. During the quarrel Edwin had felt bewildered, never quite knowing how to proceed, and he hoped that on some future occasion he would be better able to cope. It made him angry when he wasn't able to cope, and the anger still hung about him. On the other hand, six months wasn't long in a marriage which he hoped would go on for ever; the marriage hadn't had a chance to settle into the shape that suited it, any more than he and Deborah had had time to develop their own taste in furniture and decoration. It was only to be expected that there should be problems and uncertainty.

As for Deborah, she knew nothing about marriages settling into shape; she wasn't aware that rules and tacit understandings, arrangements of give and take, were what made marriage possible when the first gloss had worn off. Marriage for Deborah was the continuation of a love affair and, as yet, she had few complaints. She knew that, of course, they had to have quarrels.

They had met at a party. Edwin had left a group of people he was listening to and had crossed to the corner where she was being bored by a man in computers. 'Hullo,' Edwin just said. All three of them were eating plates of paella.

Finding a consideration of the past pleasanter than speculation about the future, Deborah often recalled that moment: Edwin's sharp face smiling at her, the computer man discomfited, a sour taste in the paella. 'You're not Fiona's sister?' Edwin said, and when ages afterwards she'd asked him who Fiona was he confessed he'd made her up. 'I shouldn't eat much more of this stuff,' he said, taking the paella away from her. Deborah had been impressed by that; she and the computer man had been fiddling at the paella with their forks, both of them too polite to say that there was something the matter with it. 'What do you do?' Edwin said a few minutes later, which was more than the computer man had asked.

In the weeks that followed they told one another all about themselves, about their parents and the houses they'd lived in as children, the schools they'd gone to, the friends they'd made. Edwin was a daring person, he was successful, he liked to be in charge of things. Without in any way sounding boastful, he told her of episodes in his childhood, of risks taken at school. Once he'd dismantled the elderly music master's bed, causing it to collapse when the music master later lay down on it. He'd removed the carburettor from some other master's car, he'd stolen an egg-beater from an ironmonger's shop. All of them were dares and, by the end of his schooldays, he had acquired the reputation of being fearless: there was nothing, people said, he wouldn't do.

It was easy for Deborah to love him, and everything he told her, self-deprecatingly couched, was clearly the truth. But Deborah in love naturally didn't wonder how this side of Edwin would seem in marriage, nor how it might develop as Edwin moved into middle age. She couldn't think of anything nicer than having him there every day, and in no way did she feel let down on their honeymoon in Greece or by the couple of false starts they made with flats before they eventually ended up in 23 The Zodiac. Edwin went to his office every day and Deborah went to hers. That he told her more about share prices than she told him about the letters she typed for Mr Harridance was because share prices were more important. It was true that she would often have quite liked to pass on details of this or that, for instance of the correspondence with Flitts, Hay and Co. concerning nearly 18,000 defective chair castors. The correspondence was interesting because it had continued for two years and had become vituperative. But when she mentioned it, Edwin just agreeably nodded. There was also the business about Miss Royal's scratches, which everyone in the office had been conjecturing about: how on earth had a woman like Miss Royal acquired four long scratches on her face and neck between 5.30 one Monday evening and 9.30 the following morning? 'Oh yes?' Edwin had said, and gone on to talk about the Mercantile Investment Trust.

Deborah did not recognize these tell-tale signs. She did not remember that, when first she and Edwin exchanged information about one another's childhoods, Edwin had sometimes just smiled as if his mind had drifted away. It was only a slight disappointment that he didn't wish to hear about Flitts, Hay and Co., and Miss Royal's scratches; no one could possibly get into a state about things like that. Deborah saw little significance in the silly quarrel they'd had about the teddy bears' picnic, which was silly itself, of course. She didn't see that it had had to do with friends who were hers and not Edwin's; nor did it occur to her that when they really began to think about the decoration of 23 The Zodiac it would be Edwin who would make the decisions. They shared things, Deborah would have said; after all, in spite of the quarrel they were going to go to the teddy bears' picnic. Edwin loved her and was kind and really rather marvellous. It was purely for her sake that he'd agreed to give up a whole weekend.

So on a warm Friday afternoon, as they drove from London in their Saab, Deborah was feeling happy. She listened while Edwin talked about a killing a man called Dupree had made by selling out his International Asphalt holding. 'James James Morrison Morrison Weatherby George Dupree,' she said.

'What on earth's that?'

'It's by A.A. Milne, the man who wrote Pooh Bear. Poor Pooh!'

Edwin didn't say anything.

'Jeremy's is called Pooh.'

'I see.'

In the back of the car, propped up in a corner, was the blue teddy bear called Binky which Deborah had had since she was one.

The rhododendrons were in bloom in the Ainley-Foxletons' garden, late that year because of the bad winter. So was the laburnam Edwin remembered, and the broom, and some yellow azaleas. 'My dear, we're so awfully glad,' old Mrs Ainley-Foxleton said, kissing him because she imagined he must be one of the children in her past. Her husband, tottering about on the raised lawn which Edwin also remembered from his previous visit, had developed the shakes. 'Darlings, Mrs Bright has ironed our tablecloth for us!' Mrs Ainley-Foxleton announced with a flourish.

She imparted this fact because Mrs Bright, the Ainley-Foxletons' charwoman, was emerging at that moment from the house with the ironed tablecloth over one arm. She carried a tray on which there were glass jugs of orange squash and lemon squash, a jug of milk, mugs with Beatrix Potter characters on them, and two plates of sandwiches that weren't much larger than postage stamps. She made her way down stone steps from the raised lawn, crossed a more extensive lawn and disappeared into a shrubbery. While everyone remained chatting to the Ainley-Foxletons – nobody helping to lay the picnic out because that had never been part of the proceedings – Mrs Bright reappeared from the shrubbery, returned to the house and then made a second journey, her tray laden this time with cakes and biscuits.

Before lunch Edwin had sat for a long time with Deborah's father in the summerhouse, drinking. This was something Deborah's father enjoyed on Sunday mornings, permitting himself a degree of dozy inebriation which only became noticeable when two bottles of claret were consumed at lunch. Today Edwin had followed his example, twice getting to his feet to refill their glasses and, during the course of lunch, managing to slip out to the summerhouse for a fairly heavy tot of whisky which mixed nicely with the claret. He could think of no other condition in which to present himself – with a teddy bear Deborah's mother had pressed upon him – in the Ainley-Foxletons' garden. 'Rather you than me, old chap,' Deborah's father had said after lunch, subsiding into an armchair with a gurgle. At the last moment Edwin had quickly returned to the summerhouse and had helped himself to a further intake of whisky, drinking from the cap of the Teacher's bottle because the glasses had been collected up. He reckoned that when Mrs Ainley-Foxleton had kissed him he must have smelt like a distillery, and he was glad of that.

'Well, here we are,' Jeremy said in the glade where the picnic had first taken place in 1957. He sat at the head of the tablecloth, cross-legged on a tartan rug. He had glasses and was stout. Peter at the other end of the tablecloth didn't seem to have grown much in the intervening years, but Angela had shot up like a hollyhock and in fact resembled one. Enid was dumpy, Charlotte almost beautiful, Harriet had protruding teeth, Holly was bouncy. Jeremy's wife and Peter's wife, and Charlotte's husband – a man in Shell – all entered into the spirit of the occasion. So did Angela's husband who came from Czechoslovakia and must have found the proceedings peculiar, everyone sitting there with a teddy bear that had a name. Angela put a record on Mrs Ainley-Foxleton's old wind-up gramophone. 'Oh, don't go down to the woods today,' a voice screeched, 'without consulting me.' Mr and Mrs Ainley-Foxleton were due to arrive at the scene later, as was the tradition. They came with chocolates apparently, and bunches of buttercups for the teddy bears.

'Thank you, Edwin,' Deborah whispered while the music and the song continued. She wanted him to remember the quarrel they'd had about the picnic; she wanted him to know that she now truly forgave him and appreciated that, in the end, he'd seen the fun of it all.

'Listen, I have to go to the lav,' Edwin said. 'Excuse me for a minute.' Nobody except Deborah seemed to notice when he ambled off because everyone was talking so, exchanging news.

The anger which had hung about Edwin after the quarrel had never evaporated. It was in anger that he had telephoned his mother, and further anger had smacked at him when she'd said she hoped he would have a lovely time. What she had meant was that she'd told him so: marry a pretty little thing and before you can blink you're sitting down to tea with teddy bears.

You're a fool to put up with rubbish like this was what Deborah's father had meant when he'd said, 'rather you than me.'

Edwin did not lack brains and he had always been aware of it. It was his cleverness that was still offended by what he considered to be an embarrassment, a kind of gooey awfulness in an elderly couple's garden. At school he had always hated anything to do with dressing up, he'd even felt awkward when he'd had to read poetry aloud. What Edwin admired was solidity: he liked Westminster and the City, he liked trains moving smoothly, suits and clean shirts. When he'd married Deborah he'd known – without having to be told by his mother – that she was not a clever person, but in Edwin's view a clever wife was far from necessary. He had seen a future in which children were born and educated; in which Deborah developed various cooking and housekeeping skills, in which together they gave nice dinner parties. Yet instead of that, after only six months, there was this grotesque absurdity. Getting drunk wasn't a regular occurrence with Edwin; he drank when he was angry, as he had on the night of the quarrel.

Mr Ainley-Foxleton was pottering about with his stick on the raised lawn, but Edwin took no notice of him. The old man appeared to be looking for something, his head poked forward on his scrawny neck, bespectacled eyes examining the grass. Edwin passed into the house. From behind a closed door he could hear the voices of Mrs Ainley-Foxleton and Mrs Bright, talking about buttercups. He opened another door and entered the Ainley-Foxletons' dining-room. On the sideboard there was a row of decanters.

Edwin discovered that it wasn't easy to drink from a decanter, but he managed it none the less. Anger spurted in him all over again. It seemed incredible that he had married a girl who hadn't properly grown up. None of them had grown up, none of them desired to belong in the adult world, not even the husbands and wives who hadn't been involved in the first place. If Deborah had told him about all this on that Saturday afternoon when they'd visited this house he even wondered if he would have married her.

Replacing the stopper of the decanter between mouthfuls in

case anyone came in, Edwin none the less found it impossible to admit that he had made a mistake in marrying Deborah; he loved her, he had never loved anyone else, and he doubted if he would ever love anyone else in the future. Often in an idle moment, between selling and buying in the office, he thought of her, seeing her in her different clothes and sometimes without any clothes at all. When he returned to 23 The Zodiac he sometimes put his arms around her and would not let her go until he had laid her gently down on their bed. Deborah thought the world of him, which was something she often said.

Yet, in spite of all that, it was extremely annoying that the quarrel had caused him to feel out of his depth. He should have been able to sort out such nonsense within a few minutes, he deserved his mother's jibe and his father-in-law's as well. Even though they'd only been married six months, it was absurd that, since Deborah loved him so, he hadn't been able to make her see how foolish she was being. It was absurd to be standing here drunk.

The Ainley-Foxletons' dining-room, full of silver and polished furniture and dim oil paintings, shifted out of focus. The row of decanters became two rows and then one again. The heavily carpeted floor tilted beneath him, falling away to the left and then to the right. Deborah had let him down. She had brought him here so that he could be displayed in front of Angela and Jeremy and Charlotte, Harriet, Holly, Enid, Peter, and the husbands and the wives. She was making the point that she had only to lift her little finger, that his cleverness was nothing compared with his love for her. The anger hammered at him now, hurting him almost. He wanted to walk away, to drive the Saab back to London and, when Deborah followed him, to state quite categorically that, if she intended to be a fool, there would have to be a divorce. But some part of Edwin's anger insisted that such a course of action would be an admission of failure and defeat. It was absurd that the marriage he had chosen to make should end before it had properly begun, due to silliness.

Edwin took a last mouthful of whisky and replaced the glass stopper. He remembered another social occasion, years ago, and he was struck by certain similarities with the present one. People had given a garden party in aid of some charity or other which his mother liked to support, to which Edwin and his brother and sister, and his father, had been dragged along. It had been an excruciatingly boring afternoon, in the middle of a heatwave. He'd had to wear his floppy cotton hat, which he hated, and an awful tan-coloured summer suit, made of cotton also. There had been hours and hours of just standing while his mother talked to people, sometimes slowly giving them recipes, which they wrote down. Edwin's brother and sister didn't seem to mind that; his father did as he was told. So Edwin had wandered off, into a house that was larger and more handsome than the Ainley-Foxletons'. He had poked about in the downstairs rooms, eaten some jam he found in the kitchen, and then gone upstairs to the bedrooms. He'd rooted around for a while, opening drawers and wardrobes, and then he'd climbed a flight of uncarpeted stairs to a loft. From here he'd made his way out on to the roof. Edwin had almost forgotten this incident and certainly never dwelt on it, but with a vividness that surprised him it now returned.

He left the dining-room. In the hall he could still hear the voices of Mrs Ainley-Foxleton and Mrs Bright. Nobody had bothered with him that day; his mother, whose favourite he had always been, was even impatient when he said he had a toothache; nobody had noticed when he'd slipped away. But from the parapet of the roof everything was different. The faces of the people were pale similar dots, all gazing up at him. The colours of the women's dresses were confused among the flowers. Arms waved frantically at him; someone shouted, ordering him to come down.

On the raised lawn the old man was still examining the grass, his head still poked down towards it, his stick prodding at it. From the glade where the picnic was taking place came a brief burst of applause, as if someone had just made a speech; '. . . today's the day the teddy bears have their picnic', sang the screeching voice, faintly.

A breeze had cooled Edwin's sunburnt arms as he crept along the parapet. He'd sensed his mother's first realization that it was he, his brother's and his sister's weeping. He saw his father summoned from the car where he'd been dozing. Edwin had stretched his arms out, balancing like a tightrope performer. All the boredom, the tiresome heat, the cotton hat and suit, were easily made up for. Within minutes it had become his day.

'Well, it's certainly the weather for it,' Edwin said to the old man.

'Eh?'

'The weather's nice,' he shouted. 'It's a fine day.'

'There's fungus in this lawn, you know. Eaten up with it.' Mr Ainley-Foxleton investigated small black patches with his stick. 'Never knew there was fungus here,' he said.

They were close to the edge of the lawn. Below them there was a rockery full of veronica and sea-pinks and saponaria. The rockery was arranged in a semi-circle, around a sundial.

'Looks like fungus there too,' Edwin said, pointing at the larger lawn that stretched away beyond this rockery.

'Eh?' The old man peered over the edge, not knowing what he was looking for because he hadn't properly heard. 'Eh?' he said again, and Edwin nudged him with his elbow. The stick went flying off at an angle, the old man's head struck the edge of the sundial with a sharp, clean crack. 'Oh, don't go down to the woods today', the voice began again, drifting through the sunshine over the scented garden. Edwin glanced quickly over the windows of the house in case there should be a face at one of them. Not that it would matter; at that distance no one could see such a slight movement of an elbow.

They ate banana sandwiches and egg sandwiches, and biscuits with icing on them, chocolate cake and coffee cake. The teddy bears' snouts were pressed over the Beatrix Potter mugs, each teddy bear addressed by name. Edwin's was called Tomkin.

'Remember the day of the thunderstorm?' Enid said, screwing up her features in a way she had, like a twitch really, Edwin considered. The day he had walked along the parapet might even have been the day of the thunderstorm, and he smiled because somehow that was amusing. Angela was smiling too, and so were Jeremy and Enid, Charlotte, Harriet and Holly, Peter and the husbands and the wives. Deborah in particular was smiling. When Edwin glanced from face to face he was reminded of the faces that had gazed up at him from so far below, except that there'd been panic instead of smiles.

'Remember the syrup?' Angela said. 'Poor Algernon had to be given a horrid bath.'

'Wasn't it Horatio, surely?' Deborah said.

'Yes, it was Horatio,' Enid confirmed, amusingly balancing Horatio on her shoulder.

'Today's the day the teddy bears have their picnic,' suddenly sang everyone, taking a lead from the voice on the gramophone. Edwin smiled and even began to sing himself. When they returned to Deborah's parents' house the atmosphere would be sombre. 'Poor old chap was overlooked,' he'd probably be the one to explain, 'due to all that fuss.' And in 23 The Zodiac the atmosphere would be sombre also. 'I'm afraid you should get rid of it,' he'd suggest, arguing that the blue teddy bear would be for ever a reminder. Grown up a bit because of what had happened, Deborah would of course agree. Like everything else, marriage had to settle into shape.

Charlotte told a story of an adventure her Mikey had had when she'd taken him back to boarding-school – how a repulsive girl called Agnes Thorpe had stuck a skewer in him. Holly told of how she'd had to rescue her Percival from drowning when he'd toppled out of a motor boat. Jeremy wound up the gramophone and the chatter jollily continued, the husbands and wives appearing to be as delighted as anyone. Harriet said how she'd only wanted to marry Peter and Peter how he'd determined to marry Deborah. 'Oh, don't go down to the woods today,' the voice began again, and then came Mrs Ainley-Foxleton's scream.

Everyone rushed, leaving the teddy bears just anywhere and the gramophone still playing. Edwin was the first to bend over the splayed figure of the old man. He declared that Mr Ainley-Foxleton was dead, and then took charge of the proceedings.

High-speed Ted

PAT RUSH

MR WHOPPIT first met Donald Campbell in 1957. Campbell was about to attempt yet another water-speed record in his hydroplane *Bluebird*, and his friend Peter Barker decided that it was time that he had a mascot. So saying, he tucked the little bear into the cockpit and soon Campbell and his new companion were racing across Coniston Water at 239.07 mph, to bring Campbell his fourth record on water.

From that day on, man and bear were inseparable. When Campbell went on holiday, Mr Whoppit went too. When he was given a Labrador dog one Christmas, the dog was named Whoppit as well. And when Campbell was rushed to hospital with a fractured skull after the fastest automobile crash in history, he insisted that someone went back to rescue his little friend who had been forgotten in all the confusion.

Campbell and Mr Whoppit went on to break several more records together – reaching 248.62 mph on Coniston Water in 1958, 260.33 mph there in 1959, and 276.33 mph in Australia in December 1964. Earlier that year, they had managed a record-breaking land speed of 403.1 mph at Australia's Lake Eyre.

On 4 January 1967 they were back on Coniston Water for yet another attempt at a water-speed record. With an outward run of 290 mph, success seemed imminent. But, on the return, disaster struck. At 300 mph, the nose of the jet-powered boat suddenly lifted out of the water. The vessel somersaulted and sank.

No trace of Donald Campbell was ever found. But Mr Whoppit was discovered floating on the surface of the lake, patiently waiting to be rescued.

For some months afterwards he lived quietly with Campbell's widow but, after about a year, he decided to take up residence with Campbell's daughter Gina.

'I think he decided he'd better stay with a Campbell,' she says.

Whether he was eventually to regret that decision, no one knows. But in due course he was again pressed into action as a mascot, this time for Gina herself who was out to break the women's power-boat record. He was with her when she succeeded, reaching 122.85 mph at Holme Pierrepont.

He was also with her when she, too, experienced a major accident. Gina herself quickly escaped from her sinking boat but the long-suffering bear was far less fortunate, having been firmly tied to the base of the steering wheel. Gina clearly remembers refusing to leave the water until divers had gone down to rescue the bear.

A little less traumatic were the three years or so that he spent touring schools in New Zealand, helping Gina to teach children all about water safety. She carried him around in a see-through bag, so that he could see what was going on, and he also had his own specially made lifejacket – identical to Gina's own except in size. A television commercial showed him falling into the water and floating happily in his jacket, and brought him so much fame that Gina had to resign herself to being known simply as the lady with the bear.

Later, however, he helped her take the limelight once more with a new women's water-speed record of 156.45 mph in New Zealand in April 1990.

Now he is enjoying a less hair-raising existence helping to run The Bluebird at Lentune coffee shop in Lymington, Hampshire. He even has a wife – found for him by Gina's mother to give him some stability in his life. But he has, apparently, remained a free spirit, and his lady bear is frequently left at home.

Mr Whoppit himself spends most of his days watching the comings and going in the restaurant from his vantage point in the kitchen where Gina is also generally to be found.

He still wears the little blue boots made for him by a friend of the Campbells after his feet were lost in one of his many accidents. And stitched to his red jacket is an embroidered bluebird, cut long ago from one of Donald Campbell's specially made silk shirts.

Embroidered bluebirds also adorn 5000 modern Mr Whoppit replicas, made by soft-toy makers Merrythought to commemorate the fastest bear on land and water. The original Mr Whoppit was made by them, too. He was based on a popular cartoon character and, of course, most of the bears bought in the 1950s were intended as children's toys. Today, however, it is collectors who are falling under his spell – as well as visitors to The Bluebird at Lentune who are often unable to resist taking a Mr Whoppit 'double' home with them as a souvenir.

Tedperfect

ALAN HACKNEY

ONCE AGAIN, Henry had brought some work home from the office. There was a note from Sylvia: 'Pizza ready for you to microwave. Gone to painting class.' So evidently it was a Tuesday when it all started.

When Henry had eaten, he sat down at his computer and leafed glumly through all the letters that ought to be done. He switched on and got into WordPerfect for his task. So, Franklin was bitching about some storage rates? Trying for a long period deal, apparently, without guaranteeing his stuff would even be stored next week. Well, reply to Franklin, for a start.

Then as Henry brought up his List of Files he spotted something a bit odd. Just before the one called Franklin.Ltr there was an unfamiliar file listed with the name Firstone.Ted. Henry retrieved this new file and on his screen was surprised to read:

> Well, you took your time. I've been looking over your company records for a couple of weeks and I can see it's about time you had a few bits of advice.

It was quite a small company that Henry owned. The grassy business park was all big buildings, but mostly small companies. Infant businesses in infant industries, a lot of them. And every now and then, a bit of infant mortality, too. There would

129

be faint sounds in the distance disturbing the hush that usually hung over the area, and from Henry's office window he would see the signmakers busy up their aluminium ladders, tossing down the grubby old plastic lettering and fixing up another bright new hopeful fascia name.

Henry's company offices were modest, though the warehouse they were tacked on to would be big enough to play football in, if it weren't full of other people's products. Or half full, to be honest, at the moment. A bit of advice might well come in handy.

On the screen it went on:

It comes free, but with two conditions. Never discuss it with anybody. And always delete these memoranda after reading.

Now delete this file, but check again in the morning. And don't wait up to try and catch me out.

Get a good sleep.

Ted

Who was this Ted? Henry thought, but couldn't remember knowing anyone called Ted. When had it got there? In the List, the filename showed last Thursday's date, and a time of 3am. Henry had definitely been asleep at that time, and the computer obviously switched off. A funny old business all right. Mystery.

The only Ted anywhere around was the teddy bear of Henry's boyhood, neglected for many years now, a bit faded and yellowish, sitting quite inertly several feet away on a bookshelf and clearly not responsible. Henry got up and examined him. He seemed much as usual, with one eye a bit loose, just as Henry had always remembered him. A little dusty, perhaps. Henry gave the bear a brief dusting over the wastebasket and set him back on his shelf.

Back at the computer, Henry read over the message again, and then routinely deleted it, the way he always did with stuff he had finished with, fearful of wasting disk space and suddenly getting the dreaded Disk Full message. Then he got on with the Franklin letter, and most of the others. As usual, it all took a good bit longer than planned. In the course of it Sylvia came back in from her class and was in bed and asleep before Henry packed up.

In the morning Sylvia said: 'Weetabix and juice. I'll pick some up on my way home.'

'OK,' said Henry.

'Otherwise we'll be out of it tomorrow,' said Sylvia.

'Can't have that,' said Henry.

He was shaving, but Sylvia came in, dressed to go, and pecked his ear.

'See you later, lovey,' said Sylvia, and she was off to her job with the doctors which she told everyone she enjoyed. There had been a time when she had enjoyed just keeping the house, but you can't expect that to last. And you could see she did at least still *think* about the housekeeping, which was all to the good.

Henry collected the correspondence from where he had left it, beside the computer, and stuffed it into his case. Then, on impulse, he switched the machine on and waited with curiosity while it booted up. He listed the WordPerfect files and scrolled through a good 200 names before he froze at the sight of a brand new one: a file dated 3am that morning, with the name Memo2.Ted.

Henry retrieved it to the screen, where he read:

What I'd like this evening is the latest lot of figures for the Croydon operation. I've a feeling your main weakness lies there. But I can tell better with the figures. I would remind you again: no discussions with anybody. Just enter the figures, with brief notes when you come home. Don't leave this on the machine: remember to delete the file before you go.

And thanks for the dusting, though a good vacuuming would in fact be preferable in future.

Have a nice day.

Ted

Henry sat down for a moment and stared at the screen. Other things being equal, which they were far from being, it all made sense. The Croydon warehouse was tedious to drive to but, having once expanded and acquired it, he should certainly be paying it closer attention – and more often. But who else knew about the dusting of the teddy bear?

Henry turned slowly to stare at the bear instead. It was certainly there, just where he had left it. But there was not the slightest indication of life in it as it sat impassively on the bookshelf, leaning up against two old *Good Food Guides*.

'Just what exactly are you up to, Ted?' asked Henry. But he said it in a low mutter, as if prepared to deny saying it if ever challenged.

Driving to the office he began thinking very seriously about Croydon. He thought about it during the morning, too, and in the afternoon drove over there for a visit.

In the evening Sylvia said: 'You're not going to be all evening at that computer again, are you?'

'Shouldn't think so,' said Henry, 'I'm just entering a few figures. Stuff on Croydon I need a bit urgently.'

In the end, it took him a good couple of hours, but Sylvia was quite used to that and was happy watching an old Jack Nicholson movie on the television. Henry finished in time to catch the end of it but his sharing of experiences stopped there. He didn't feel able to say much about Croydon yet.

Next morning Sylvia said: 'I'd better get going: Hoddinott's coming in early for once today.'

'So long as he doesn't make a habit of it,' said Henry. Early morning conversations in their house did not reach high on any scale of wit or brilliance. Still, a sort of even good temper usually prevailed which is more than you could say of some houses.

'See you sixish then,' said Sylvia. 'Bye for now.' Her mind was probably on something else. Henry's certainly was. He now stood impatiently in front of the computer, glancing a couple of times across to the bookshelf while it was booting up. The teddy bear was as impassive as ever.

'Been busy, have you?' muttered Henry, in a tone that was almost resentful for some reason he couldn't pin down. Stress, probably. Well, so what else was new? Run your own business and it comes with the territory.

He scrolled through the list of files – and there it was: Memo3.Ted. And at 3am again.

Henry brought it up on the screen. It said:

The Croydon numbers were very revealing. What is quite plain to me from them is that, for the last three months, you have been robbed blind. Look at the first quarter figures for Bays 3 and 4 and check against the invoices. Some customers have been having a free ride or else what they've been paying has not been put through the books. This alternative is inherently more likely, and I would therefore suggest an immediate audit at the Croydon warehouse. I wouldn't want to tell you your business but turning up today with your accountant to announce such an audit might well trigger a confession and save the effort of getting an actual audit done. I'd be glad to hear again when you get a result. Don't forget to delete all this straight away, including the data you entered yesterday evening.

And have a nice day.

Ted

Henry sat and thought long and hard. Then he made the deletions, switched off, called the accountant at home, and drove purposefully to the office.

In the evening Sylvia said: 'We ought to go out to a film, it's still early enough.'

'Is there anything on?' asked Henry. 'Local. I've done enough driving today.'

He did not elaborate. In one sense it would have been easy to run, blow by blow, through a day in which, startled by being faced by him for the second day running, both the Croydon manager McCarthy and his secretary Hilda had made a sudden clean breast of an operation that had started in a small way just before Christmas but had grown into the pillage of several thousands of pounds. There followed an instant dismissal and signed admissions. The police were not to be called in unless there was serious default in their repayments.

'In a way I'm glad you got on to this,' McCarthy had said, 'though I don't know how you did.'

That was the trouble for Henry. It raised an awkward issue. Any discussion of his sources was out. Equally, chatting to Sylvia about it was hardly a good idea either. A nice evening at the movies was a better bet. Took your mind off your work. And at the new multiplex you could get a drink in comfort and a meal if you were really pushed.

Henry was sorry about Hilda. She had once been his secretary and, when he opened up in Croydon, he had transferred her there to help McCarthy get started smoothly. He had given her a raise for good measure. Nonetheless, it had been Hilda who had been at the bottom of this swindle; she had kept the books smoothly, with no trace of it showing.

When he and Sylvia got back home, Henry took a couple of minutes off to enter:

Croydon is now under new management. Many thanks for what you were able to tell me. My accountant was amazed, though he tried to conceal it. The new people I have promoted seem likely to play it straight – they have seen what happens when you don't! I am very grateful. Hope this doesn't sound too much like a solicited testimonial.

H.

As he saved this and switched off Henry was thinking: 'What am I actually doing here? Leaving a message for a teddy bear, that's what. And tomorrow morning I shall come here again and switch on, and expect to find a reply. Maybe. We'll see. This can't really be happening. On the other hand it hasn't done any harm, so far. Quite the reverse, actually.'

'So much for Croydon for the moment,' he said aloud.

'Problems?' said Sylvia.

'Not really,' said Henry. 'I'm just coming to bed.'

In the morning Sylvia said: 'Can you put the bin bag out for the dustmen before you go?'

'Right,' said Henry.

'I'll have a quick go-round with the vacuum when I get in this evening,' said Sylvia, glancing round the place from the doorway. 'Bye.'

Henry was just about to make a small cleaning request but bit it back just in time. When Sylvia had driven off he picked the teddy bear off the bookshelf.

'I suppose the small brush end would do you,' he said. 'And then the nozzle.'

Vacuuming the bear was pretty straightforward, though the small brush end was not really stiff-bristled enough. The fierce intensity of the narrow nozzle however, seemed just right for a deep-seated cleansing of the skin and the surface of the stuffing below. A quick ruffle of the fur, and back on the shelf. And the vacuum cleaner back in the cupboard ready for Sylvia.

On the computer was a new file, Memo4.Ted. Henry retrieved it, almost without a second thought, and on the screen he read:

Glad you acted immediately; that was what was needed. Good work. It may be the time has come to think about a replacement for Croydon, but let's get it running properly first. That should be quite quick now. Then you might well get some takers for it, and switch to somewhere more convenient. Slough might suit as a better location for a second warehouse for several of your customers, but keep in mind possible future expansion to a third site at a sensible distance.

This was impressive thinking, and beyond what Henry had allowed himself to plan for. With the financial drain at Croydon stopped, however, it didn't seem by any means too forward-looking.

The next sentence stopped his thinking in its tracks:

For some time now I have been reflecting on a more personal matter. The affair you have been conducting with the girl, Chloe Duckworth, is going nowhere and is, in any case, bad for your marriage. You should seriously consider dropping it.

Ted

Henry turned towards the bookshelf and raised his voice in some heat.

'That's my damn business,' he said, 'and no business of yours. And, my God, haven't you got a pompous, pedantic way of phrasing things, like some bloody schoolmaster!'

It had startled him for a moment. He didn't think anybody knew about Chloe Duckworth. He deleted the message indignantly, shut his briefcase, and went off very crossly to the office. As he drove, he turned over Chloe Duckworth in his mind. She was a subject that often came up there for contemplation. He had made a number ' of in-depth examinations of Chloe Duckworth in several motels. She travelled in stationery supplies and did pretty well at it. If you took into account the other skills she had you could definitely say she was a good allrounder.

Now the question had arisen about whether it was all going anywhere. Henry gave it some thought. Was it? Did it *have* to be going somewhere? Did he *want* it to be going anywhere? If he did, where to? If he didn't, what was the point of it really? Applying logic to things like this was a change for Henry, and he found it quite liberating. By contrast, his normal policy of masterly drift in these matters seemed both inadequate and likely to tie him into situations he did not actually want.

By the time he arrived at the office he was quite clear in his mind what to do. He would phone Chloe. He could still get the stationery from her, but his call would include two elements:

1. a substantially increased order for stationery;

2. a sensible, though warmhearted, suggestion that it was probably time they stopped seeing each other socially, for both their sakes really. It had been a lovely trip but the train had now reached Chicago, and Chicago was where he got off.

The only uncertainty in Henry's mind was in which order to present these two elements. Stop seeing first, then stationery order? No, that wasn't as good as the other way round. The bigger order just seemed like something thrown in to make up for the other thing. Certainly, that's what it was, but that way round made it so much more pointed.

So, in the end, he did it in the 1,2 order as originally planned. And, in the event, he didn't even have to bring up the Chicago analogy because the conversation skewed off into a couple of amusing reminiscences and didn't even take all that long. Henry was not sorry to lose the Chicago reference which had suddenly started to sound insincere and awkward. Anyway, he couldn't think where it had come from. Something he must have read somewhere, but it didn't sound right. Better than Euston, or King's Cross certainly, but not up to much really.

One thing that nettled him slightly was that, when he thought about it, Chloe had sounded not so much hurt as relieved. Wistful he would have been content with. Relieved, on the other hand, hurt *him*. Not very much, it was true. A pinprick, but unexpected.

'Don't go worrying about it, Henry love,' Chloe had said, and it was plain she wasn't either.

Still, it was a task done, an advance made, a step in the right direction. Coming back to thinking about it in mid afternoon, Henry had almost convinced himself that he had made a pretty good move, all of his own devising. 'And it'll be good for my marriage,' he told himself. At this point he recollected the wording of the message he had read that morning. All right, he had been well advised – but he had taken the advice and the initiative. As to the rest of the message, well, Slough was a place he had considered before now. Time to have a drive over there, perhaps? No harm in a scout around.

In the evening Sylvia said: 'Place look a bit better now?' She was just winding up the vacuum-cleaner cord.

'Wonderful,' said Henry. 'Not that I was complaining. Look, rather than mess it up again, should we go out to that new Chinese, or the old Italian? We could ask Jane and Nick.'

'Sam and Monica would be better,' said Sylvia. 'I think it's next week he's away, not this.'

'OK, but he's not into pasta,' said Henry. 'So Chinese.'

They were late back and he didn't, for once, leave any comment on the computer.

In the morning, Sylvia said: 'He's put on a lot of weight, Sam. Not that I'd dream of telling him.'

'I expect he knows anyway,' said Henry.

'Witty for the time of day, dear,' said Sylvia, and she was off.

Despite having left nothing on the computer, Henry switched it on. It was getting to be automatic. Not compulsive, exactly. Obsessive, maybe. Still, perhaps there wouldn't be anything. There was, quite a lot. Memo5.Ted read:

First, I must convey my thanks for a splendid vacuum cleaning which did me a power of good. Much appreciated. Weekly would be nice. I note that you left no report yesterday evening, which is fine. I'm here when you're ready. Incidentally, you should be aware that communication between us cannot be direct. I think you have already found that speaking will elicit no response. It is really only through the computer that we can make contact and progress things. Response to what you enter, or to any queries you may have, will come overnight, which allows time for both mature consideration and for the subconscious to tackle deep-rooted problems directly.

Take your time over Slough. I don't see any hurry just yet. As to Croydon, is the new man reporting just weekly? Would daily perhaps be better until he's got his eye in?

So have a nice day.

Ted

There was, Henry noticed, no mention of Chloe Duckworth, though in a way this did not surprise him. There seemed, instead, to be an assumption that any little hint dropped was going to be picked up and acted on, which seemed a touch arrogant though quite in keeping with the general stance adopted by Ted, that of a very senior partner. The linguistic style was certainly something from former days. Fogeyish. Like some old buffer of his father's age. When Henry thought about that, it struck him as quite appropriate. If Ted was already grown up and mature when Henry was a small boy, it would figure.

As to whether Morton, newly promoted at Croydon, should report to him *daily*, no. Henry felt that was a touch too heavy. Twice a week, though, that was more like it. Yes, twice a week. At the office he telephoned Croydon and was pleased when Morton himself suggested he should fax reports to Henry twice during the week, for a start anyway. Morton seemed like a good man for the job: keen to be in full charge, yet anxious enough to show his dependence by reporting often. An excellent start.

A month later, Sylvia said in the morning: 'Are you going to buy that Slough place?'

'If I get a decent deal,' said Henry.

'And you'll sell Croydon?' asked Sylvia.

'Like a shot. I've had a couple of good bids in. Let's have a couple more, then we'll see.'

'You are going to sell it first, before you buy Slough?' asked Sylvia. 'You'll do it that way, won't you?'

'You're describing the ideal way to do things,' Henry told her. 'Let's see how it goes. Well, nearly time I went.'

'Just don't go overreaching yourself,' said Sylvia. 'I'd best be off.'

When she had gone Henry switched on the computer, anxious to see what solution would come through for a problem on fork-lift–truck costs he had put into the machine the night before. It was getting to be second nature to him by now. Rather like a procedure in medical practice: list the symptoms one evening, find out next morning what the consultant proposed.

On the screen Memo29.Ted was ready to be read. It began:

Forklift costs should not be a major concern provided you do not extend the racking upwards to an extra level.

It went on to explain the received wisdom: historically, fork-lift truck costs should sit comfortably among costs borne by any capacity over 50 per cent occupied. Only well below that level were you likely to be in trouble, though there were several other variables. It began to get a little technical, but then abruptly set all this aside:

There is little advantage to be gained pursuing all this.

What I would recommend instead is something of a new departure.

You may remember my earlier comments on Miss Duckworth. These remain valid, as I hope you will recognize. She was a lady of limited possibilities, confined essentially to the small world of stationery supply. Situated as you presently are, I see a number of advantages open to you if you became acquainted with someone I could recommend highly. Her name is Sophie Cooper. She is married but separated, and has a wide range of contacts in both manufacturing and information technology. Mrs Cooper's phone number is . . .

Henry read this with mounting consternation. Just what was Ted up to, giving him women's phone numbers? A bit of a change from his former sniffy, moralizing tone when he was disapproving about Chloe Duckworth. A really fundamental change by the look of it, which made Henry deeply uneasy for a moment. But, it has to be said, not for much more than a moment.

To be frank, he did not find it too difficult to adjust to this new, expansionist attitude on the part of his adviser. Not that he was free of doubts about it. In the main, Henry was too cautious to be really greedy but, still, something useful might come out of contacting this Sophie Cooper who came so highly recommended. There would be a small problem of how to introduce himself. But apparently not:

You should say that several people had spoken of her at the Institute of Directors, praising her efforts for Famine Relief. Your own interests of course will be more in the business connections she has developed both in her own career and through her husband.
Have a nice day.

Ted

At this time Henry was in something of a dilemma over the Slough warehouse. The price they were asking was low enough to tempt him to buy, but he was hesitant because only half the space in it was occupied and had remained stubbornly like that for the past year or so. Hence the low price – but, if he bought it, would he ever be able to fill it? Even so, to be safe, he probably needed to sell off Croydon first, as Sylvia had just pointed out.

Henry drove to his office thinking deeply, and went on thinking till the early afternoon when he called the number of Mrs Cooper. He got her machine and left a carefully phrased message.

It was the next day before she called him back.

'People don't usually call me out of the blue,' said Sophie Cooper. 'But you're lucky, you've caught me at a spare moment. You say there are five things you want to ask me about when we meet. *If* we meet, there's one thing I'm going to ask you: how did you get this number?'

But, in the end, she didn't ask that and, instead, they asked each other a number of other questions which laid the foundations of a blossoming, then remarkably fruitful, working relationship that was to transform Henry's business.

During the next six months the firm switched on to a very positive track, and stayed right on track. The problem about Slough seemed simply to evaporate. Henry bought it cheap and was able to fill it right up with storage contracts put his way by Sophie Cooper. There was no longer the need to sell Croydon which was well run now, profitable and well filled.

What had been a medium-term dream of expanding into Bracknell became something urgently accomplished as orders came flooding steadily in. On top of all this, Sophie Cooper was very good in bed.

After a week in Barbados, Sylvia said: 'Now we're back I still want to do my job with the doctors. It gets me out, it's a real job, and I don't see all that much of you these days.'

'Fair enough,' said Henry, 'I don't want to stop mine either.'

'Shall I see you sixish?' asked Sylvia.

'Eightish,' said Henry, 'I have to nip in for a London meeting.'

He pecked Sylvia and she went.

Henry switched the computer on and collected his briefcase

contents while it warmed up. In the List Of Files was
Memo226.Ted.

Henry was surprised to read:

OK, now it's time for presents. I've never asked you for
anything before, but I think you can easily afford it now.
What I'd dearly love is a pair of good gold ear-clips. They
have some decent ones in Asprey's.

                                                                  Ted

Looking over towards the bear on his shelf, Henry could see
they would have to be quite a fair size to look like anything,
clipped to those prominent round ears. Well, he happened to be
going into London, so why not?

'It shall be done,' said Henry aloud, but the bear sat there
impassively.

The clips were very expensive, indeed, but as nothing compared to the business which had been put his way. There was a
moment when he nearly gave way to an impulse to present
them to Sophie Cooper whom he was seeing that afternoon, but
he didn't give way and, from that evening, Ted sat arrayed in
them on his bookshelf, looking quietly confident.

Three days later, Sylvia said absolutely nothing in the morning,
which wasn't like her, but Henry presumed it was some kind of
headache and didn't pester her for conversation.

She drifted silently through to the next room and then Henry
heard a startled noise. A second later Sylvia came prancing in
again with glad cries, wearing the ear-clips.

'How sweet of you, love, I'm so grateful!' she chirped, her
mood quite changed. 'I knew you couldn't have *really* forgotten
my birthday. How funny to put them on Ted for me to find!'

'Many happy returns, darling,' said Henry, 'and I'm booking a
table at Le Gavroche tonight.'

On the other hand, Ted was furious. The next morning a file
had been added to the List with the name: Lastone. Ted. It said
simply:

This is an act of gross betrayal. How could you let that

woman get away with it? Are wives the only people who get bought earrings? You won't hear from me again. You've let me down very badly.

                                                                    Ted

And, as the days passed, no more messages came. Every morning Henry anxiously scrolled through his List Of Files. Nothing. Sometimes he would himself enter a request, and wait. There was never any reply.

Though work went well, and Sophie Cooper was as stimulating as ever, Henry began to develop a most uneasy feeling. The more he thought it over, the more he began to see there was one person with the opportunity to sneak out of bed at 3am to leave all those messages. Who else but Sylvia? She had some knowledge of his business and could apply a little common-sense to problems. And the motive? Simple: the rewards that would come her way. That *had* come: a very solid share in his growing prosperity; the trip to Barbados; and, finally, those incredibly expensive ear-clips. What a manipulative creature! Well, the woman obviously had hidden depths. You'd never think it, dealing with her on an everyday basis.

Then his blood ran cold. So she had known about Chloe Duckworth, and now she knew about Sophie Cooper into whose arms she had cynically nudged him. A bold, realistic move, that. So the message was clear: Sophie was no threat because she had been chosen. The calculation evidently was that he was to be allowed Sophie provided Sylvia still got her very large share of goods and remained in the driving seat. Well! It certainly showed a sophisticated degree of self-confidence. The manipulations of women fair took his breath away.

Obviously, Henry could not discuss all this with Sylvia. Instead, he took to treating her a little more attentively – and with great caution.

Then one weekend when Sylvia was away for two nights in Paris with her painting class – and wearing the ear-clips for the trip, of course – Henry came in from a lunchtime drink at the pub with Sam and heard a familiar humming noise. Was his computer switched on? He went through and saw the blue glow of the WordPerfect screen. And there, on the screen, it said:

> I made all that effort, you reaped the benefit, and bloody Sylvia got what I worked for. On me they looked fine, but they don't suit her one bit. Well, the hell with both of you. I have not decided yet what I will do about it all, but I'm putting you on notice: watch out.
>
> T

Henry swung round and stared at Ted, earclipless on his bookshelf. But he was just sitting there, inert as usual, strictly in position, totally in character. But this was not 3am, this was broad daylight, and never in the hours of daylight had it ever been known that a teddy bear . . .

Henry slowly sat down, slowly turned round and read the message on the screen again, then switched the computer off.

Then he drove shakily in his new Mercedes to the airport to meet Sylvia's plane.

The Servant Problem

DAVID ROBERTS

I SUPPOSE, LOOKING back on it, I made rather an ass of myself. Miles says I 'over-reacted', but then he would. I think what upset me most was Albert breaking the rules in the way he did. After all, there is a code between master and manservant which is all the stronger for being unwritten.

Albert had come to me from the agency when I was at a low ebb and he seemed like a gift from heaven. My previous man-servant had worn large boots and clumped about the flat even when he was supposed to be off-duty. Then again, he had smelt. I had spent the last two weeks of his employment with me trying to identify the odour. It was somewhere between boiled cabbage and over-ripe bananas and, frankly, it got on my nerves.

When at last I summoned up the courage to get rid of him I thought there might be a bit of a row so I arranged for Miles, who has the flat directly above mine and has claims to being my oldest friend, to wait with his door open in case I shouted for help. As it turned out the fellow took his dismissal quite calmly and left within the hour. I discovered afterwards that he had taken a good deal of my property with him. I kept on idly asking myself where was the silver jug which stood on the mantelpiece next to the porcelain shepherdess or that ivory paper-cutter that I always had on my desk, and so on, until it dawned on me that they were gone for ever. Still, I was so relieved to be shot of the man I did not call the police which is what Miles said I ought to have done.

For a day or two I even considered doing without a servant but, really, it wasn't on. I needed to be woken in the morning with a cup of Lapsang Souchong. I wanted my bath run for me, my breakfast prepared, my shoes cleaned and my clothes laid out for the day. In particular, when I got home from the club, I wanted someone there to bring me a whisky and soda before I dressed for the evening.

The night before Albert arrived I had been out with a party of Americans and though, normally, I am not a heavy drinker, under their influence I had imbibed more than was good for me. I did not get back to the flat before three in the morning. A year or two before, this would have had no effect on me the morning after. I would have been up with the lark, bright-eyed and bushy-tailed, ready for a convivial lunch with some of the gayer element at the club. Miles said I was getting old and 'could not stand the pace'. He has such a vulgar way of putting things sometimes.

Anyway, when the doorbell rang I almost did not answer it. I had forgotten that the agency chap had said he was sending someone round for me to interview. When I did drag myself to the door I saw this short, hirsute, rather severe-looking creature who announced himself as having come to fill the vacant situation.

'Oh yes?' I said, groping for a beam of understanding in the fog that was cluttering up my usually razor-sharp mind.

'My name is Albert, sir. I believe, sir,' continued Albert, 'you are seeking a servant.'

'Ah, yes!' I cried, light dawning. 'Come in.' There were some basic questions I knew I ought to ask but I simply did not feel up to it. 'Can you cook?' I asked weakly.

'I am a superb cook,' answered the tubby little chap in tones that would have been convincing in a bishop. 'Do the ironing?' I tried hopefully. 'My ironing is impeccable,' said Albert firmly. Then, as I seemed incapable of saying anything else, he added: 'I have been trained to be a gentleman's personal servant at the Harrogate Academy.'

'The what?' I parried.

'The Harrogate Academy for Performing Bears.'

Now, as I say, I had not woken up feeling at my best but there had been something niggling at the back of my mind ever since I had opened the door and, with the word 'bear', I knew what it was.

'You're a teddy bear, aren't you?'

Albert bowed his head gracefully.

'But teddy bears don't speak, do they? I mean, I've never seen a talking bear.'

'No sir?' said Albert, with polite surprise in his voice. I tried again. 'Are you human?'

'Certainly not, sir!' responded Albert, sounding rather shocked. 'Excuse me one minute, sir.'

Albert went through the swing door into the kitchen and I heard him turning on the gas and soon there was the hiss of the kettle coming to the boil. I lay back in my chair trying to come to terms with Albert not being a man but, instead, being a bear, and not a real one at that, when my eyes closed and I must have dropped off.

I awoke to find Albert standing respectfully at my elbow with a steaming cup of something that smelled refreshing on a silver tray, one of the few portable silver items that the previous fellow had not taken with him. I took the cup, sniffed it and looked at Albert questioningly.

'Honey, sir, and lemon with a few herbs. I think you will find it to your taste.'

I sipped at it and, whatever it was, it certainly did wonders for my hangover. I began to feel clear-headed. Bear or no bear, Albert was what I needed.

I showed Albert where his quarters were but he came back in a couple of minutes carrying what looked like the corpse of a decomposing rat.

'Is it your wish, sir, that I share my room with this . . . animal?'

Albert looked so censorious and I was so concerned that he might leave on the spot that I grabbed the thing and threw it out of the window, narrowly missing a policeman patrolling on the street below.

'Good heavens, no, Albert! I had no idea that was what the smell was.' And I told him about his predecessor's unpleasant personal habits. Albert seemed mollified and I decided to escape to the club while the going was good.

'Will you be dining in, sir?' asked Albert as he passed me my hat.

'Ah, yes, Albert. I shall be dining in. I may have a friend with me. Shall we say dinner at eight? I shall return at six. Goodbye Albert. Um . . . glad to have you on board and so forth.'

At the club I downed a couple of martinis and tried to decide if I had been wise to take on a teddy bear. Miles came about one. He pretended to do some sort of a job in the morning – advertising, I remember him telling me. It can't have been very time-consuming because he spent every afternoon in the club and most evenings out with me.

Miles quickly spotted that I wasn't my usual ebullient self. 'So what's up, old cock?' he said loudly, patting me on the back so I almost choked on my martini.

'I'll tell you over lunch,' I replied.

'In that case it had better be on you, old sport.'

I don't know how often I have asked him not to address me as old cock or old sport. He once spent three months in Australia and I really believe he has not spoken proper English since. Today, I wasn't in the mood to remonstrate with him though. I needed the advice of a friend and Miles *was* a friend but not one whose advice I would normally have taken on which brand of cigarette to smoke, let alone whether I should allow myself to be looked after by a teddy bear.

The funny thing was that it wasn't until we were having coffee in the smoking-room that I was able to find the words in which to describe to Miles the events of the morning. Even to me it seemed unbelievable, so what would it sound to Miles who was always so cynical? I knew he thought I was mentally deficient and if I started on about teddy bears he would accuse me of hitting the bottle before breakfast. No, the thing to do was to break it to Miles gently. Or, better still, not actually say the word teddy bear. Wait until this evening and then Miles could judge for himself.

My musing was interrupted by Miles. 'Now then, old cock. If I didn't know you better I would say you were thinking. Tell all to Uncle Miles. I know, you have asked a girl to marry you and she has said yes.'

'Oh, no!' I said, pulling myself together. 'Nothing like that. No, it's my man, don't you know. Or rather not my *man*. You see I employed a new servant today, from the agency . . . he came from the agency.'

'That's where I would have expected him to come from. What is it you are wittering on about, old chap? What about this new man?'

'Well, you see Miles . . . I don't quite know how to put this but . . . he's hairy.'

'Hairy?'

'Yes, hairy . . . and chubby,' I said warming to my description. It was good to get it out in the open.

'So? *I'm* hairy and rather chubby.'

'No, Miles, I mean hairy all over and he sort of growls.'

'You mean, he turns into a bear when the lights are out?' said Miles, laughing loudly.

'Not when the lights go out, no,' I said gravely. 'He says he's a very good cook,' I went on more cheerfully. 'I say Miles, are you doing anything tonight?'

'Nothing that I wouldn't give up to meet your hairy manservant,' answered Miles. 'You really have intrigued me this time. Did this hairy person who looks like a bear give you references?'

'No, I don't think so. No, I am sure I would have remembered if he had.'

'You should have asked for references, old chap. I mean, you left him in the flat without knowing anything about him. I dare say he has stripped the place by now.'

'Oh, I say! Do you really think so?'

'Well, let's walk back to the flat now and see.'

'All right,' I said, 'but if everything is as it should be don't come in. I would rather you came down just before seven and met him then. I wouldn't like him to think he was being inspected, like in a zoo, you know. It wouldn't be polite.'

At the flat, I sent Miles up to his flat saying I would call out if there were a problem. Otherwise, I would see him for dinner. The first thing I noticed as I came in was that everything was so tidy. And it smelt better too, fresh or even better than fresh.

'I'm sorry sir,' said a voice. 'I did not think you were returning until later.'

'Oh . . . ah . . . yes, Albert,' I burbled. 'I'm home early. Felt a bit jaded, you know.'

'I'm sorry to hear that, sir. Can I get you a refreshing cup of tea?'

He spoke in a respectful but kindly sort of way. It was very soothing. I accepted his offer of tea. He went off to put on the kettle and I followed him into the pantry. I noticed it at once. The pantry had been in a terrible mess when the other fellow left. Now it was spick and span. Everything looked as though it had been washed. The china had lost its grey look. The sink was shining and Albert seemed only this minute to have finished cleaning the knives and forks.

'I say, Albert!' I cried appreciatively. 'You have been working hard. And it all smells so good, too.'

'You are very kind, sir. Honey and lemon, honey and lemon. That is my secret,' and Albert almost seemed to smile. I realized that Albert's rather severe expression masked a genial character and I began to relax. Albert might have his funny ways and he was distinctly hairy . . . no, not hairy . . . of course, furry!

I glanced at his hands. They were paws. There could be no doubt about it. I was being offered a cup of tea by a teddy bear. True, this was a teddy bear in a suit and tie who I knew sported a bowler but, indubitably, he was a teddy bear.

Miles was prompt. It was only just seven when the doorbell rang and I heard Albert opening the door. He ushered in Miles and I was rather pleased to see that Miles was looking perplexed. It was difficult to talk with Albert in earshot but Miles, in stage whispers, drew my attention to the fur on, or rather all over, Albert's ears and the glassy expression in his eyes. We talked loudly during dinner of neutral topics – the failure of the Prime Minister's talks with the German Chancellor, the test-match ruined by unseasonable rain and so on and, of course, the food we were eating. Albert had not deceived me; he was a quite remarkable cook. We began with an artichoke soup of exceptional delicacy, the fish was a sole lightly grilled and served with a honey-and-lemon salad unique in my experience. The *canard pressé* was the best I had eaten outside the Tour D'Argent and that was followed by a cassis sorbet that could only have been made by a master-chef. The feast culminated in a soufflé of such airiness it seemed to have nothing to do with the sordid reality of everyday life.

When Albert had at last retreated behind the green-baize door, after being showered with compliments by Miles and myself, we retreated to what I called my snuggery for brandy and cigars. I said nothing, waiting for Miles to comment, but it was a full five minutes before he regained his habitual, not to say often annoying, loquacity.

Pulling on one of my finest Havanas, Miles stroked his stomach thoughtfully and offered the irrefutable judgement that we had just partaken of a meal fit for the gods.

'And Albert?' I could not resist prompting.

'Albert,' said Miles consideringly, 'is a marvel.' He spoke slowly without any of the heartiness which so often made his conversation tiresome.

'And would you agree that, to all appearances, he is a teddy bear?'

'I would,' answered Miles wonderingly, 'though I would never have believed I could be saying so. When you told me about Albert at lunch I must confess, dear boy, and for this you really must forgive me,' I waved a cigar in the air as a token of my pardon, 'I thought you had finally gone off your head.'

I was wounded, and said so, but I could see that he was penitent so I did not rub it in as I might have done. Miles was always too ready to see me as a buffoon and it did him no harm to find out just how wrong he was.

Oddly enough, and rather to my disappointment, Miles did not stay to have a second cigar and talk the thing over. He seemed preoccupied, almost shocked, as though the whole basis on which he had, up until this moment, viewed the world had been shaken. I, on the other hand, was getting used to the idea of having the perfect servant, furry all over and glassy-eyed though he might be.

It would be tedious to go over in any detail the days that followed. The fact was that Albert was the perfect person to have about the home. He never intruded, never spoke unless required to do so. He did more than meet all my needs, he anticipated them so that if, say, I was on the point of asking him for *The Times* there it was ironed and ready for my perusal. I only had to lick my lips and a whisky and soda or a cup of tea, depending on the time of day, was there on the table beside my chair. Always there was in the air a delicate scent of lemon and honey.

I hardly ever went out now but I noticed that more and more people dropped in on me. Some were friends I had not seen for months who just happened to be in the neighbourhood. Some were acquaintances with only the flimsiest shreds of an excuse for barging in, while a few were complete strangers. In fact, it was beginning to be rather a bore and spoiling what might otherwise have been defined as domestic bliss. I mean, I am as convivial as the next man but when a perfect stranger knocks on the door and demands to see 'that bear', without even a 'please', you can see I had reason to be a bit fed-up.

The funny thing was that Miles seemed to be the only one of my friends who was conspicuously *not* begging for invitations to breakfast, lunch and tea. Still, one evening about a week after our dinner I looked out of the window and I thought I saw him deep in conversation with a plump figure who could have been Albert. There was one other rather rummy thing. I got a phone call from the employment agency apologizing for not having sent me anyone to interview for the post of manservant. I said, of course they *had* sent someone, and that I was more than satisfied and was expecting their bill. But the girl on the phone was adamant that there had been a mixup and they had not sent anyone for me to interview.

I suppose I was a fool not to have foreseen what was to come. Somehow, though, Albert gave the impression of being so completely reliable that I was lulled into a false sense of peace and harmony. I know what it was about Albert: he had perfect manners. I don't mean just that he opened the door for me and was always deferential. I mean that, without being subservient, he put me at my ease. When I was in his presence everything was as it was meant to be.

I knew he was gone the moment I walked through the door. It was the smell, or rather the absence of that pervasive lemon-and-honey scent, which I now needed if I was to feel truly content. Not a thing was out of place; my clothes were laid out for the evening and even my bath had been run. I felt the water with my finger. It was precisely the temperature I liked. I guessed that Albert could not have been gone long and I looked out of the window as though he might be in the street below. I did not really think he would be there. I knew for a certainty that Albert would only be found if he wished it. I did knock on Miles's door a couple of times but there was no one at home.

The next few days were sad ones for me. I can't explain the depression I suffered in any other words than to say it was as though I was mourning a lost love. Ridiculous, I know, to feel that way about losing a servant, however good, but that was the way I felt at the time.

It must have been about a week later that I was having breakfast, a very poor affair compared with what I had got used to under Albert's regime, and was disconsolately leafing through the paper when this headline caught my eye. It wasn't a big headline – those were all taken up with stories of approaching war – and there was only a short report beneath the words that had caught my eye. 'Bear's big break,' I read.

'News just in confirms that the talented teddy bear that has been the surprise sensation of this year's social scene has clinched a five-figure deal to promote French fashion house Maison Rêve's new scent. Called simply "Albert's air", the new fragrance is tipped to be a winner on both sides of the Atlantic. The bear's agent, Miles Codrot, said in New York: "I first spotted Albert when he was an unknown, cooking in an apartment of a friend of mine in London. I immediately recognized him as an exceptional talent and I predict a great future for the bear."'

I put down my paper with a thump, upsetting the coffee. That rat! I might have guessed it. Miles was the wretch who had stolen my teddy. I have to admit it; I put my head in my hands and wept. The tears rolled down my face as they had not done since my old nanny died.

And that was the end of it. Except, of course, that war broke out three weeks later and Albert's scent went down along with a host of other peacetime projects. I did not gloat and I was sad that I never heard from Albert again. Miles said he had gone to California. Miles was infuriatingly insouciant about the whole affair. He soon went into PR for the armed services where he made quite a name for himself.

Salute to a
Military Bear

MARY ROSS

IT WAS a very hot day towards the end of July 1950 when young Officer Cadet Edward Bear arrived from Abingdon, complete with Army Pay Book and smart new combat suit from Moss Bros, to begin his career at the Royal Military Academy at Sandhurst – one of the world's most famous training schools for army officers.

The formal training of British army officers goes back more than 250 years, and Queen Charlotte – wife of George III – presented Colours to the Royal Military College at Sandhurst in 1813, a year after what is now called 'Old College' was opened. Since that date, many famous people have gone through the excellent regime and training of Sandhurst, including the soldier/states-man Winston Spencer Churchill whose time there is commemorated by a building which seats 1200 – the Churchill Hall.

But the most colourful career must be that of Senior Under-Officer Edward Bear, who – after more than forty years of gallant service – has now officially retired and is permanently domiciled on the main corridor of Old College in the Sandhurst Museum.

Few people who were there on that day in 1950 realized that this was a bear who would not only become the official symbol of the RMAS Parachuting organization, but would also be the longest serving cadet ever to pass through the RMAS.

When Edward Bear first joined Sandhurst, circumstances were very different from those of today.

One of the most startling differences was that the Academy was solely a male preserve; it was not until May 1981 that the training of officers for the Women's Royal Army Corps was transferred to Sandhurst.

Today, RMAS trains all officers for the British Army – men and women – with the exception of the Queen Alexandra's Royal Army Nursing Corps and Army late entry officers. SUO Edward Bear had no comment to make on the inclusion of women cadets to Sandhurst, but it is understood that there has been no move towards allowing female bears to be admitted to the Academy.

From the beginning, Edward Bear showed a particular aptitude for parachute jumping, always being the first 'man' out of the plane. Soon after his arrival, in 1950, the Edward Bear Parachute Club was formed; he jumped regularly with the club during the short parachuting courses organized for the cadets during their recess period.

The Edward Bear parachute course was voluntary, but in the fifties so many cadets volunteered for the course that only a small percentage were able to secure a place at the RAF's Parachute School at Abingdon. At Abingdon they had to make eight jumps in order to qualify; then they could wear the parachute emblem on the left sleeve of their service uniform and be entitled to the Edward Bear Club insignia – a green tie, emblazoned with silver filigree teddy bears suspended from parachutes.

In 1972 the course at Sandhurst was shortened. Consequently, there was no recess when parachute training would be possible. This made the continuation of the Edward Bear Club impractical, though officer cadets who were already qualified parachutists continued to jump and become members of the club. In 1975 the club was disbanded and the officer in charge took club records into his personal keeping.

But this was by no means the end of Bear's career. And, indeed, Edward still has his own personal scrapbook in which the whole of his career has been meticulously recorded from Day One right up to the present day. It is held on Edward's behalf by Dr Tony Heathcote, curator of the RMAS museum.

From early days, Edward Bear has very proudly worn the white parachute on his left sleeve to denote the successful completion of the course. This emblem is often jokingly called the 'light bulb', though Edward Bear has never been heard to refer to it as such.

In his youth, Cadet Officer Edward Bear was perhaps a little unconventional and a certain mystery hangs over the first two years. Some people have even insinuated that Edward deserted during this period and that the bear that General Sir Richard Worsley GCB, OBE – then Captain Worsley – officially presented to the Edward Bear Club in 1952 was an impostor. But whether it was the original, or only a look-alike, from then onwards Edward's career went from strength to strength.

Senior Officer Cadet Bear, at only 18" tall, is the shortest cadet ever to have been accepted by the Academy, yet his rise to glory has been spectacular. By 1959 he had successfully completed 120 descents and, in addition to his own personal parachute made for him by the RAF Parachute School, he had been decorated for his daring parachute descents by military academies in Britain, France and Iraq. It is even rumoured that he has, once or twice, jumped without a parachute, with no apparent serious injuries. A charmed life indeed – though it must be admitted that he has occasionally been photographed wearing a bandage round his head, perhaps due to these unscheduled landings.

In 1957 our military equivalent in France – Saint Cyr Military Academy – decided to compete with Sandhurst in a series of exercises. Capitaine Tuttu of the French Foreign Legion and former instructor at the French academy, along with Captain Hobkirk of the 15/19th King's Royal Hussars, organized suitable competitive manouevres and, when official sanction had been received by both countries, the Edward Bear Club was parachuted into Brittany where cadets of the Saint Cyr French Military Academy were waiting to defend their positions. Needless to say, Sandhurst won.

Two further exercises were held – one in 1958 and one early in 1959 – with similar results. On one of these exercises in Brittany, Edward Bear became detached from the main party and was assumed to have been taken prisoner. In a conference held after the exercise Saint Cyr was cleared of the offence and, after a newspaper report of the incident, Bear reappeared. He was unable to give a satisfactory account of himself, but the matter was overlooked on this occasion.

The same could not be said of an event later that year when the Saint Cyr cadets dropped on Salisbury Plain in a subsequent exercise during which they did manage to take Edward Bear prisoner, much to his chagrin. The British contingent fought bravely on, but without Edward Bear I regret to say that victory, that time, went to the French.

Bear has been taken prisoner on several occasions. He was kidnapped by Guy's Hospital rugby team, then later by the RAF Technical College at Henlow, and later still by the RAF College, Cranwell. Fortunately, he has always managed to return to base unscathed.

It was while he was at the Royal Air Force College, Cranwell, that he went on an official service pilot's course, but this hardly qualifies as one of his successes.

His progress was said to be 'unusual, but interesting', and it was felt that he was not at ease in an aircraft cockpit. He seemed to have difficulty in coordinating the actions of his hands and boots when flying, and it was said that he had a 'marked desire to abandon aircraft at 800''. Not, perhaps, the best of recommendations for a pilot!

In August 1959 a reporter from the military magazine, *Soldier*, watched Edward Bear on his 120th successful parachute jump when he dropped from a Beverley aircraft at a height of 1000'. As usual, Edward was the first man out of the advance guard of thirty-five cadet parachutists who fought a pitched battle until midnight when the exercise was abandoned. It was then discovered that Officer Cadet Bear had landed in a tree and had to be rescued.

Bear jumped regularly until 1975 by which time, having been gradually promoted through the ranks, he was now Senior Under-Officer.

He never quite reached the status of Second Lieutenant, perhaps because of the period spent Absent Without Leave – AWOL. He was court-martialled for the offence in 1980, escaping the more serious offence of desertion by a whisker. He was sentenced to indefinite detention in the 'glass-house'. In his case – pardon the pun – a glass case in Sandhurst Museum, but he has since been released on parole for various jumps and sponsored events.

In the course of his career Edward Bear has had a catalogue of injuries, but bears them all with dignity and courage. He lost his left eye in a jump some years ago, and now wears a patch which – it has been said – only adds to his air of battered rakishness. He has also lost the end of his nose, and has had to have various limbs replaced by skilful surgery.

Even with these appalling injuries he is still very fit, and was photographed in 1971 doing weight-lifting and a spot of practice jumping in the Sandhurst gym.

This was in January of that year, immediately prior to being honoured by his fellow officers for completing his 400th jump to celebrate the twenty-first anniversary of the club named after him. Officers spoke with awe of a time when his parachute failed to open during a jump and he fell on his head, but SUO Bear, with his usual stiff upper lip, refused to comment on the incident.

It was a matter of tradition that Edward always ignored the safety count when jumping. This safety count is important in allowing the parachutist to get rid of excess adrenalin before checking whether his parachute has opened properly, and taking remedial measures if not. Edward Bear has never been heard to make the required count and, even after this terrifying incident, still does not do so.

I can report on good authority, however, that, in spite of this, he has been honoured by no fewer than five countries. Major Watson, who was putting him through his paces in the gym at the time, said that Edward Bear was in good shape and that he 'helped to bring the academy closer to the general public'. An indication of the esteem with which he is held by the public, and by other bears, was revealed on the occasion of his twenty-first birthday when Sandhurst was flooded with birthday cards. One hundred and two bears congratulated him from Somerset alone!

Edward's last official event was a low-altitude jump from 200' on 26 September 1984. His jump book records a 'good exit and position. No count. Canopy control good all the way.'

But there were other unofficial jumps. On 17 March 1989 a further kidnapping took place – this time by the Royal Marines at Lympstone.

To be frank, Edward Bear was bored – otherwise, there was no other reason for his leaving his post at the museum and taking part in such an exercise without permission.

But the Royal Marines can be very persuasive – and it was, after all, a sponsored jump for a very worthy cause. The jump was from the top of London's Hilton Hotel in Park Lane. Edward did a base jump off the roof in tandem with one of the Royal Marines. There was a free fall for two seconds from 350', then a pilot 'chute of 220 sq. ft opened and he cleared the front of the building, landing on a patch of grass in front of the hotel.

Although it had been some time since Edward's last previous jump he had lost none of his skill and, afterwards, he and the lads went and had a much-needed beer in Covent Garden.

He was later awarded the Globe and Laurel badge of the Marines and, in fact, enjoyed himself so much that he stayed with them for two days before returning to Sandhurst.

But, after more than 400 jumps, it was time to hang up his parachute and call it quits. He was – and is – the longest serving graduate ever at the Royal Military Academy at Sandhurst. But the gap left by his retirement could not be left unoccupied for long. There had to be someone, somewhere, who could follow on such a long and famous career. After careful consideration it was decided to groom another bear to take his place.

It would be a hard act to follow but, in 1991, Harrods were approached to see if they could provide a suitable bear to take over and, in June 1992, Officer Cadet Bear Jnr arrived.

Edward Bear Jnr's pedigree is impeccable. He is from the Merrythought Limited Edition Yes/No line of bears, produced to mark the sixtieth birthday of Merrythought Ltd, one of the oldest surviving British soft-toy manufacturers. The Merrythought line of bears came into being in 1930 at Ironbridge in Shropshire.

Edward Jnr's first ancestors from the 1930s were known as Chummy and were filled with kapok and wood-wool instead of today's wood-wool and polyester. The family resemblance is plain to see, but Edward Jnr is far more handsome and has just a hint of a hump. He has large, flat, rounded ears and a pointed, clipped muzzle like Chummy. His eyes are a similar colour – brown, with black pupils – but perhaps rather smaller than his ancestors'. He is 18" tall and has a limited edition tag, signed by the grandson of the firm's founder on his left side. He is already more advanced than his predecessor in that, with some encouragement – and judicious use of a small lever – he can shake or nod his head to signify positive or negative replies to any question.

Edward Jnr is, of course, in uniform – but he is not the first of the Merrythought bears to wear uniform. In the 1970s and 80s there were Merrythought policemen, Beefeaters, Guardsmen and Highlanders. But none were kitted out in quite such a special fashion.

Edward Jnr's uniform was made by the leading military tailors, Gieves and Hawkes. Their Head Cutter, Ted Bailey, cut, made and fitted the uniform and beret in three days and, as a special device to aid Jnr's parachuting expertise, he has been fitted with a zip and weights (lorrybolts). This should prevent him drifting off course and falling on his head quite as often as did Edward Snr.

Like his predecessor, Edward Jnr also has his own personal parachute. This time it was made by Aldershot's Red Devils freefall team.

Edward Bear Snr welcomed his replacement to Sandhurst after the newcomer's parachuting debut in aid of the Karim Centre for Meningitis. This took place at Netheravon, in a static jump from 2000', and, in the true tradition, Edward Jnr was first man out, followed by twenty other Officer Cadets.

Again, in true tradition, Edward Jnr did not give a safety count on exit. It seems that this recklessness is hereditary.

The course was run by the Flying Dragons, the Queen's Regiment Freefall Display team; their jump master, Corporal Vince Brierley, recorded in Edward Jnr's jump record that he did a 'loop on exit'. Nice one, Edward!

The first five weeks at Sandhurst are perhaps the most traumatic for cadets as they face the transition from civilians to soldiers. One of the traditional things one has to do is to visit the barber, for – as it is called – 'a thirty-second cosmetic sheep-shearing'. Edward Jnr has not had to face this ordeal, and it is thought that there will be a special dispensation in his case.

One thing he has done within those first five weeks is to jump from an Army Lynx helicopter at 1000' during a final exercise in France on 14 July, Bastille Day. Captain Harry Bucknall of the Coldstream Guards, who is in charge of young Edward, and Major David Parkinson of the Parachute Regiment – his jump master and despatcher – noted that he 'performed a diverse exit, failed to correct twists in his rigging lines and drifted off into the distance'.

The exercise for OC Bear was not an unqualified success. Edward – perhaps in imitation of his more famous predecessor – drifted off-course into a tree in a French farmyard where he hung for the rest of the morning. The search party who found him reported that he had narrowly missed falling into a well and was besieged by several ferocious dogs who had to be driven off before Edward could be rescued.

Forty years previously, when Edward Bear Snr had met a similar fate, it had taken Major-General Charles Gordon-Lennox to save him. This time, young Bear Jnr was not such a prized prisoner for the French who were quite unaware of the future importance of their guest.

Later, in spite of the somewhat inauspicious beginning to young Edward's career at Sandhurst, the Commandant, Major-General Tim Toyne-Sewell, presented him with his parachute badge.

Both Edward Snr and Edward Jnr now have their official club wings, and one can be sure that, with the tips that Edward Snr is bound to pass on, young Bear will soon improve. After all, Captain Harry Bucknall, who has carefully updated all Edward Snr's records, reported that an entry recording the older bear's first jump said that he 'displayed a complete indifference to instructions'. Who would have known from that report that he would go on to become so famous and well loved?

Dr Tony Heathcote, curator of the RMAS Museum where SUO Edward Bear Snr now lives, agrees that the older Bear has a few black marks on his career, but says that it has been 'long and distinguished' and that he would be missed. Perhaps in another forty years we will have even more to say about 1992's new recruit.

Worth a Bash

REBECCA FRASER

THE TEDDY bear is rather forlorn-looking now. Its fur is greyish, its eyes are dull. It really ought to be put away somewhere. People must wonder why a grown woman, yes, almost a middle-aged woman like myself, has it on her bed. But, to me, it's a symbol of what I believe is nowadays called assertiveness, self-expression really (and they're very keen on that here). I suppose I keep it because it is a justification of my behaviour many, many years ago, and it is one of the few things that remain to me from that time, one of the few things that remain to me at all.

My sister Alethea was born five years after me. I can now see that she was, she *was*, everything that I was not. She was placid and smiley and dimpled. I see, looking back, a thoroughly *baby* baby, whereas I – well, I think that you could read a little of my character in my face which, as a child, was dark with a hidden look to it, 'secretive' my nanny used to say, shaking her head; though, of course, what *I* say is that I only became secretive when Alethea was born.

Everyone tried to persuade me that nothing would change, that I was still my mother's baby, but the fact was, as I viewed it, that there just wasn't room, or even time, for me any more. They tried to pretend that everything was the same, but when you aren't picked up by your mother, not even when you are unhappy, because she'd rather pick up someone else – that

165

stupid Alethea – well it begins to get to you.

I remember all the things that started to arrive for the baby, that were brought round by people 'dying to see the baby' as they said again and again, but no one was dying to see me and there were no presents for me. And I remember saying to my mother when someone at last sent something for me, 'It's for the baby', with a sort of dull acceptance. Then there were tears shining in her eyes. And she said loudly to my Daddy, 'Poor little thing, she thinks everything is for the baby,' which was typically stupid of her because, of course, when you came down to it, everything was really.

It became clear to me, I suppose quite soon, that I was going to have to take steps to put an end to my nursery being disturbed by the baby. If I wasn't careful she would overrun my life. I put a stop to the grown ups' silly idea of us ever sharing a room by just screaming and screaming as loudly as I could when we were on holiday in Cornwall, and I think that that taught them a bit of a lesson, particularly that stupid woman my mother with her bleating ideas about being *friends* with the baby. Yes, I think that Cornwall was really the turning point.

You see, we used to go to the beach a lot, that uncharacteristically hot, tedious summer. We'd lie there in a rather pointless way, the baby accompanied by a long procession of grown ups fussing over it and putting umbrellas over it and getting bottles for it, which made me want to *scream*. I suppose that I used to wander along the shore a lot, picking up sticks, trying to find things, always on my own. My Daddy, who was always slightly more reasonable than my mother, used to pretend that he wanted to come, but then my mother would always shriek at him that Alethea needed something and then he'd be off again. I can see them still, my father in his dark-blue towelling robe, and my mother behaving as if the baby was the infant Jesus, staring at it with that sickly sort of adoration I used to see in church paintings, and the baby herself, totally unaware of the trouble she caused, and how unhappy she made me.

Up till Cornwall I had sort of believed that the baby would go away somehow, and that then it would be back to the happy relationship we all used to have, me on my mother's lap, sitting in the back of a taxi always off somewhere, just the three of us, a close, happy little entity. But I think that, after about six months, I suddenly realized that things were never going to go back to what they once were, that I was just going to go on being left out and miserable. It's a funny thing, what happened next, what I remember my Sunday school teacher called 'God working in wondrous and unexpected ways'. Because one day when, as usual, I was wandering by the seashore not talking to my family I happened to come upon a man with a net. He was taking fish out of the sea, and then knocking their heads against a big stone he had, so they looked all funny and broken and wet and red. They lay there and didn't move. But when they had come out of the sea they had been snapping and twisting and moving, and quite scary, but now he'd hit their heads they were all still and not frightening or annoying at all. And I remember thinking I wonder whether I could do something to Alethea that would make her stop gurgling and wriggling, and stop annoying me, and make her go away. For ever.

Well, while we were in Cornwall my sister, that is, the baby (I don't like to call her sister, because I like the sister here and I don't feel the same way at all towards *her*), started to yell a lot. My mother said in her soppy way, again almost with tears in her eyes (she had tears in her eyes about anything to do with the baby), that she was teething. She used to give it things to chew, not my things because she didn't dare, but old bits of leather or carrots. Anyway, one day the baby managed in her grasping way to get hold of my teddy, and was chewing it.

Now you young people won't realize what teddies meant to us then in the late fifties. It was really quite soon after the War and there weren't the soft toys then like there are now – oh, I can see quite a lot about modern life on my television, 'Playschool' and other programmes which are really my favourites, so well done I always think, full of very *nice* people who actually like children, but I digress. As I said, the baby had got hold of *my* teddy which was the one thing that really belonged to me, and wouldn't give it back. And it was such a beautiful teddy, with its honey-coloured hair, and I felt that it was the one thing in the whole horrible household who understood me, who never yelled at me for fiddling with things on my mother's dressing-table, and didn't tell me to 'Stop crying for

God's sake,' when the baby was always crying and getting on my nerves. And when I snatched it from the horrible baby but was then told to give it back so she could slobber all over its beautiful fur, well, then I knew what had to be done.

I'm not quite sure how I got the stone back home. I think I must have put it in the green bucket which a grown up had bought for me near the hot-dog stall. No one paid much attention to me nowadays, anyway, so I got quietly into the back of the car, with all the confusion and shouting about who was going to sit where, and what we'd do about lunch. I stroked that smooth heavy black stone in the back of the car as the sun blazed down and the grown ups argued, and I looked at Baby Alethea and I felt a lot better. Calm. Powerful, like the stone.

My mother was always saying to me, 'Will you look after the baby, darling?' with her big idea that we were going to be friends, and she said the same this lunch time. 'I'm just going upstairs to the loo,' she said, 'you'll look after her, won't you darling?' And she smiled her weak and soppy smile, but not for me as it once had been, but for the baby. And this time, for once, I smiled and said yes.

I did it quite quickly. The baby was on the floor, like the fish had been, and I just picked up the stone and dropped it on her head.

There was a lot of fuss, and then I think that my Mummy and Daddy went away and they never took me away with them again. In fact, quite soon after I started to live in this place. I suppose I knew that things never would be the same as before that baby, and that they never really wanted *me* once they saw *her*, but I thought it was worth a bash, as you might say.

Cuddles

MARIE MACNEILL

I SHOULD HAVE known from the start, when she told me her code name was Mule, that there was no way I'd end up any where except on the butt end of nowhere. She had those big blue baby eyes that guys from my walk of life only dream about, and when she fluttered those long brown eyelashes I knew, instantly, I was in love, forever. Forever turned out to be a short time, but forever always does and, what the hell, it was a terrific bumpy ride on a brightly coloured carousel. I'm paying for it now, maybe society is better off, but I need to set the record straight: I am innocent. All I did wrong was to behave like a goof and fall in love. And now I've got plenty of time to reflect about how things might have been, could have been, and should have been. In my head I kick a tin down the pavement, shrug my shoulders *hasta la vista*, and tell myself to forget her, there are plenty more canapés on the party plate. Further down my torso, my heart is pumping real tears for the baby broad they took from me just before they knocked the stuffing from my soul.

I remember that first night, she held me in her arms, pursed her lips close to my face and whispered, 'I think I'll call you Cuddles.' I'm no putz; what she was offering I couldn't refuse, so I took it with good grace. Sure she dated other Balonys: Big Ted; Jack from the Bronx would spring up from time to time; and the Worm from Brooklyn would keep her occupied for hours, but she always came back to me in the end and, after all,

I was the only dude she ever took on the long trips. Besides, what would you do? The shelf life of a toy-boy is notoriously short-lived so I put her fooling around down to natural curiosity, and a thirst for knowledge and experiences, and decided to live it up. Besides, she always paid the bills.

It was one of those clear bright mornings that make even ugly people feel good about the way they look. The sun was so hot we could have run a short-order griddle on the manhole cover outside the apartment. I was lounging on the bed when she rushed into the bedroom, plucked a vanity case from her wardrobe, and announced, 'It's raining in London, I'd better find your mac.' A half hour later Big G and the Missus, otherwise known as the Godparents, were bashing the bell with pudgy, greedy fingers. Big G was a slight oily rag with pearly pointed teeth that would put a shark's nose out of joint. The Missus reminded me of a stranded lump of lard left at low tide to flounder. Her eyes were mean, small and blazed like cut diamonds under bushy black brows. Her smile was calculating and rationed – I was nobody so I never saw her gold incisors full frontal, but I did get a glimpse of the dark yellow beauties from the side when she flashed charm at others who I called the Unfortunates. The air was thick and expectant. Mule fussed and asked questions we all knew wouldn't be answered.

I was sitting feeling foolish in a pair of wellingtons, my thoughts circulating around the fact that I didn't want to bump into Big Ted or Jack on my way out for fear of being saddled with some new nickname like Grand Central or Pennsylvania. The matching red hat didn't help either. They went into the bedroom to get the bags, and I heard their voices bouncing off the walls. Big G was angry, but Mule was giving as good as she got. She ran back into the living-room and grabbed me by the arm. Big G was hot on her heels. He threw her to one side, and I felt helpless as the beached whale held me down and Big G pumped something into my arm. I could hear Mule screaming through an anaesthetic haze but, before I knew what had hit me, my life was plunged into darkness.

It must have been several hours later when I woke up; my head felt like a practice ball before the World Series, and a dull pain ticked over one eye. As I tried to move my legs I realized

I'd been stitched up. Mule and I were sitting in the back of a car. She was looking out of the window, her soft blonde locks dancing like Ginger Rogers's feathered frock in *Top Hat*. I tried to speak but no sound came – maybe I was literally paralyzed with fear, I dunno, but nothing moved.

The scenery was changing, we had left the city and were climbing towards the outskirts and a faceless collection of warehouses and factories. The Missus manoeuvred a flabby mottled forearm and the indicator ticked monotonously in rhythm with my spinning head until we turned left at a sign marked 'Airport'.

Mule cradled my head and whispered sympathy as the Godparents retrieved the bags from the boot. Soon we were waiting in the departure lounge, staring into styrofoam cups of lukewarm coffee. Big G was busting out of his belt with indignation, and I didn't feel it was the right time to challenge him with my annoyance at the previous incident. Mule and I had sailed through Customs but Big G, now safely chewing a nicotine butt, was black affronted with his ordeal at Security. They finally declared him clean although, at the time, I didn't understand why, even Noddy would have spotted he hadn't had a bath in at least a month.

On the plane the Missus settled comfortably across a bank of seats with a box of chocolates and a 'Does Your Partner have Sex Appeal' questionnaire in some cheap rag. I could have told her the short answer to that one. Big G occasionally patted Mule paternally as she restlessly tickled the palms of my hands, round-the-garden style. We must have looked like a typical on-holiday family, and even if we didn't we were trying. Not so, an hour later, when Mule went to the bathroom without me. Big G hissed and spat and I finally realized the importance of the load I was carrying.

Mule sported a pristine Heidi hairdo as we walked towards the Customs desk at London Airport. We chose the green channel but they stopped us anyway. A grisly grey officer yawned his way through our belongings. The Missus had stashed away a couple of hundred cigarettes but apparently that was allowed. Then it came to me. I didn't stand a chance, they tore me to shreds, and I thought this is the end of the road, I'll never see Mule again. All I can remember is her screaming 'Cuddles' as they took me away.

That was six months ago. Today I'm being moved to another cell, and they still refuse to move the tag from my heel. If I don't get out of this hothouse soon I'll sprout wings. I guess I'm still weak from the ordeal, as the policeman had to carry me down the corridor and now I'm here. There's a lot of people looking down at me. But wait, listen, I didn't do anything, all I did was to love . . . I look up and there she is, my Mule, gingham dress and pigtails. They parade me, a dozen strangers peer at my unhealed scars but it's worth it, I got to see Mule again. The tag on my foot is biting into my fur, I can see the label through tears and polythene; it reads, 'Exhibit A'. Mule looks at me with disinheriting eyes and says in a loud clear whisper, 'But that's not my bear.'

Of Monks and
Teddy Bears

GILLIAN ELIAS

THERE IS something resolute and 'important' about a
teddy bear dressed up as a monk. As soon as he dons the
habit he is invested with a sense of purpose and a consciousness of the need for discretion, propriety and serenity. He
acquires, at a stroke, a whole operational dimension of his own,
particularly if he wears gold-rimmed spectacles. He becomes a
grown-up bear, and he does not need you any more – you have
to let him get on with his vocation in the monastery of his
choice. Believe me – I know this, having placed several teddies
in religious life.

The first was Brother Theodore, a Cistercian bear now living
as a member of the Community of Mount Saint Bernard Abbey
in Leicestershire. Father Abbot had remarked casually in conversation that he was rather fond of teddies, and I was struck
instantly with a powerful image – the neat black-and-white
dress of the Trappists on the rotund, furry form of a teddy bear.
I said nothing then but hastened home in a fever of creative
excitement.

Once I had started on the project, it was clear that the teddy's
clothes had to be accurate. A bear dressed vaguely like any old
monk would not do at all. I had just finished writing a book on
Cistercian life, so I knew exactly what elements of sartorial cor-
rectness to provide: the white habit and the black hooded apron
or scapular with its black leather belt, the long white stockings

and obligatory sandals, and, over all, the voluminous white cowl with its wide sleeves which originally gave the Cistercians their popular name of 'White Monks' in the Middle Ages. When all these garments were completed, the anonymous little bear stood transformed before my eyes. He became Brother Theodore at once, and his first loyalties belonged to the Abbot, not to me, from the moment I finished his habiting.

I composed a carefully worded letter of introduction ('raised in the best Ursine traditions, obedient, disinclined to growl . . .') and took him to the Abbey where he left me without a backward glance, absorbed instantly into the fraternity of his fellow Cistercians. I am told that he meets (and charms) selected visitors on occasion, but otherwise leads a life of seclusion in which I have no further place. Fortunately, I did foresee the wrench that parting with Theodore would bring, and I also habited Brother Edward, my own Cistercian teddy, at the same time. I say 'my own', but he is faintly reproachful, a monk out of his cloister and, although he once won a prize in a competition for 'the cuddliest teddy bear', he felt it was rather beneath his dignity.

Theodore is no longer the only teddy monk of Mount Saint Bernard, however. I dressed another of similar height and colouring, but of greater amplitude of figure, for my friend Brother Jonathan, the Abbey Archivist, who decided to name his ursine companion 'Brother Basil'. Basil's monastic trousseau incorporated some minor improvements. I had not given poor Theodore any pockets in his habit, a defect the Abbot immediately noticed, but Basil could boast not only two ample pockets but a monogrammed handkerchief and a plain but serviceable black-and-silver rosary to go in them. Such refinements of detail are very important to an ecclesiastical outfitter to the undersized, for the pursuit of accuracy becomes a benign obsession and, because of the Cistercian teddies, I was destined to find a monastic arctophile who shares that enthusiasm in full measure.

The winter issue of *Teddy Bear Times* in 1991 included a short piece about Brothers Theodore and Edward, illustrated with photographs by my husband, David. Soon after the publication of the magazine, Father Anthony, a Benedictine monk from a monastery in the Scottish Highlands, wrote to Mount Saint

Bernard hoping to contact the ursine tailor, and my Cistercian friends were happy to put him in touch. Here was a monk who was actively seeking a monastic teddy, and there was I, dying for another excuse to make a habit for one! Neither of us could believe our good fortune.

The new Benedictine bear's all-black outfit (habit and hooded scapular) was a simple matter to design after my Cistercian experience, and I decided to send him off to Father Anthony in Scotland sensibly equipped with a set of thermal underwear and a pair of thick black stockings, as well as the (by now) standard pristine white handkerchief and black-beaded rosary.

Before he made the journey north, however, David and I wanted some photographs as a souvenir and record of the little Benedictine, and we took him with Brother Edward to a beautiful local deer-park on a 'location shoot'. The new teddy monk was already exhibiting signs of his individual personality, cheerful and alert, with a strong practical bent. I couldn't help seeing him as 'Brother Cadfael', the hero of the famous series of mystery novels by Ellis Peters. Cadfael is a twelfth-century Benedictine monk herbalist, so we posed the teddy with a tiny wicker basket filled with plants, as if he were busily collecting 'simples' to use in his various potions. A selection of the resulting photographs accompanied the teddy to Scotland where Father Anthony decided that the name 'Brother Cadfael' suited him admirably.

This medieval dimension to Cadfael's character was productive of much further inspiration. As far as I was concerned, the Benedictine bear was 'gone, but not forgotten', and I felt he needed some specialist equipment to help him settle in his new home. I made a miniature medical kit for him, complete with tiny spatulas, knives, spoons, mortar and pestle, phials of pills, rolls of bandages, and other necessities that a twelfth-century medical monk might be expected to carry, neatly enclosed in a soft fabric roll. A stout leather satchel on a shoulder strap, the medieval equivalent of the doctor's bag, left him free to stride out unhampered on his herb-gathering expeditions.

Now, Father Anthony is a man who is seriously interested in bears, and Cadfael had rapidly become his companion and alter ego. We agreed that to achieve the authentic scholarly

demeanour of a genuine ecclesiastic, every teddy monk worth
the name needs a decent pair of spectacles. Brother Edward
looks down his slightly disapproving furry nose at me through
his gold-rimmed glasses, and I really couldn't deprive Cadfael
of a similar adornment, particularly as his owner confided that
he wore such spectacles himself. But might specs of this kind be
an anachronism for a twelfth-century monk? We reasoned eventually that teddy Cadfael had a dual role as a modern
Benedictine and a medieval herbalist, and this allowed a com-
promise solution: I fashioned an embroidered case for the specs,
shaped like a medieval 'scrip' or purse, that could be slotted on
to his belt. Monks used to be issued with such purses when they
went on long journeys, and Cadfael has adopted the accessory
quite contentedly, Father Anthony tells me. The colourful
embroidery is discreetly hidden under the folds of his black
scapular for, unlike Cistercians, Benedictine monks wear their
belts beneath, not over, the shoulder-apron.

Theodore, Basil, Edward and Cadfael are all 12" bears but,
when I found some appealing little 5" teddies, I became interested in the possibilities suggested by 'mini-monks'. Brother
Poverello (Franciscan) and Brother Angelo (Cistercian) joined
Father Anthony in Scotland to form the nucleus of a select
ecclesiastical 'hug', and tiny Brother Benet (3½"), a Benedictine
teddy intended for Cadfael himself, but a vigorous personality
in his own right, soon followed.

These small teddies could be posed to advantage in a variety
of photographic scenarios, and we began to collect and make
'props' for them, amassing a series of photographs showing
monk teddies going about their daily lives – gathering apples,
tending sheep, illuminating manuscripts. But modern monks
use modern technology, so a recent set of photographs reflected
this by revealing miniature habited teddies in an office setting,
coping rather anxiously with the complications of their computer and fax machines. Ursine monks, like real ones, always find
plenty to do and lead a well-regulated life. Their industrious
bustle is the source of much amusement among our monastic
friends, and now we have two teams of 5" bears, Benedictine
and Cistercian, to pose against various backgrounds. One indis-
pensable attribute in the cloistered life is a well-maintained

sense of humour, and our friends at Mount Saint Bernard are always tolerant and kind in their reactions to our picture essays, even if they suspect we are slightly unhinged.

A monk's habit is of necessity always 'sober and demure', however, and after my prolonged period of plain tailoring I began to hanker after the unashamedly sumptuous in ecclesiastical attire for bears. The idea of a cardinal in full fig appealed to me as a project, and Father Anthony's approaching birthday seemed a good excuse to venture into the more elaborate mysteries of ursine clerical outfitting. I selected a portly 9" bear with a suitably amiable expression, procured a quantity of scarlet felt and Nottingham lace, and started work on the complicated Victorian vestments of Cardinal John Henry Newbear.

How shall I describe the blissful self-indulgence of creating the red robe with its train (not too long, as it would make him tumble over backwards), the hooded shoulder-cape, the rich lace cotta, the skull cap and the scarlet slippers, after the rigorous austerity of all those monastic habits? Cardinal Newbear's ensemble was based as accurately as I could make it on the superb Millais portrait of Newman and on contemporary photographs, but of course the ascetic leanness of the original luminary of the Oxford Movement formed a ludicrous contrast with the dumpy self-importance of the little bear whose figure bore witness to a diet of pasta rather than one of piety.

Constructing the essential red biretta hat, with its pom-pom, was a tricky exercise in the art of miniature millinery, but it was tremendous, exhilarating fun – the point of the whole project. Once the hat was finished, there had to be a glossy red hatbox bearing the real name of the Pope's robemaker on a gold label and, by this stage, the little Cardinal had taken over my life. He began to gather a collection of tiny possessions – his gold pectoral cross, his ornate rosary, his worn (pre-stressed) leather monogrammed briefcase crammed with necessities such as his writing case, spectacles, a copy of his own spiritual autobiography, and a miniature birthday card for his new owner.

Father Anthony, faced with the delicate diplomatic problem of easing this 9" cleric of vastly exalted rank into the environs of his humble monastic cell and the company of the incumbent ecclesiastical 'hug', was serenely equal to the situation, and the

Cardinal, an unassuming character, is now perfectly at home, presiding with a natural air of quiet authority. He has, more importantly, encouraged his resourceful host to try his hand at the craft of clerical outfitting on his own account.

The everyday dress of a Benedictine priest is sober black but, at the altar, his vestments are rich with colour and texture. Father Anthony happens to be skilled in cross-stitch embroidery, a style suited to the making of miniature vestments. An examination of the Cardinal's robes showed Father Anthony that there was nothing particularly difficult about their design or construction, and he is presently at work on a magnificent set of priestly vestments, embroidered with original designs, for a 1909 Steiff replica bear (Father Bruin), a gift from his family.

As a priest himself, Father Anthony is obviously far more knowledgeable about vestments and their decoration than any lay ursine outfitter could possibly be, and Father Bruin is to have robes historically appropriate to the turn of the century. I hear in fascination, but bewilderment, of albs, chasubles, maniples, orphreys and cinctures, for Father Anthony has taken to ecclesiastical tailoring as one born to it, in the limited recreation time available to a busy and dedicated monk. So the costuming of Father Bruin proceeds quietly, with plans for future projects in the same line. I may be out of my depth here with the authenticity of the details, but I have an active and enjoyable part to play, by making Father Bruin's black biretta along the same lines as the Cardinal's. I also have the fun of finding the various trimmings, since a monk can hardly go out and browse round the shops for himself. Armed with a tactfully worded list of esoteric requirements, I have chosen among silk cords and satin ribbons, woven braid, lamé and lace, selecting items to be transformed into something rich and strange.

So this story of monks for teddies and teddies for monks continues to unfold and to develop. It is easier to perceive the appeal of ecclesiastically garbed bears than to define it, but it has something to do with the basic incongruity between the dignity of office, symbolized by clerical dress, and its short, fat, furry wearers. For Father Anthony, a genuine arctophile, teddies have a true spiritual dimension – they represent innocence and the childlike (but not childish) acceptance that is part of his fundamental belief, while, for the other monks, their liking for bears is not so deep-seated. They see teddies as funny, self-important and harmless, perhaps valued as a keepsake from a friend, a token of affection, but essentially nothing more than 'a source of innocent merriment' in an austere way of life.

But accuracy of detail never fails to fascinate even the most detached observer and, to get full entertainment value from a teddy monk, you need to know exactly how his human counter-part should be dressed. They are almost three-dimensional cartoons in which the very miniaturization is ironic in itself, although the irony is loving, not cruel. I sketch teddy monks constantly, because they are 'real' to me, inside my head, and perhaps to be a teddy enthusiast you have to be in the habit of imagining a world in which they live, move and have their being. That cast of mind has nothing to do with chronological age, of course. I have known children who were completely indifferent to teddies and elderly gentlemen who loved them. Among the monks of my acquaintance there are fellow arc-tophiles, and there are those who find my preoccupation a mystery, but none who rejected out of hand the products of an enthusiasm they could not fully comprehend or share. One monastic friend, a classical scholar, was prepared to translate into twelfth-century Latin the text of an illuminated address to accompany the gift of a monk teddy I had habited for a famous writer; his contribution added tremendously to the general effect, but his efforts were an act of kindness, not of devotion to arctophilia. Monasteries are full of very nice people.

The Bard

JANE BEESON

I MUST CONFESS to having been a far from perfect mother. This is a bold confession because I have observed, amongst my friends, that a lack of mothering ability is considered the equivalent of a man who can't drive a car.

Perhaps due to this lack I particularly dreaded bedtime – by which I mean the bedtime of Ben, Robbie and Felix – aged seven, six and four respectively and commonly known as 'the boys'. All day long I could manage, *cope* as the counsellor at the clinic put it, but as six o'clock – the hour of the bath – drew near, I could feel myself begin to tense. I would start planning how to manoeuvre the situation to avoid a head-on clash. On the face of it, it should have been easy enough; it was, after all, no more than a change from standing upright to lying flat, eyes open to eyes shut. Yet more often than not this natural transition resulted in myself hot and red-faced, pleading in an unattractive and humiliating fashion, my children eying me curiously as I transformed myself from Caring-mother to Wicked-witch and back again for the final act – that tucking up and kissing bit. 'Avoid confrontations,' said my shelf of books on child care. Yes, but how? What I needed, I decided, was not a book on *care* but one on management – *Child Management*. I visualized the title.

I accepted that to get my children into bed would take the best part of two hours, but if I could see my way clear by eight

181

o'clock – by which I mean the unsightly scattering of portions of toys concealed in the cupboard, the door wedged shut, the boys bathed and in bed – then I could take a deep breath, sink into the armchair, relax, even think, vaguely I admit, or talk to Simon if he was back from work.

Since our family had increased to three, Simon seemed to need longer hours in the laboratory. It made sense, with three children we would need more money, Simon had explained.

'Is the overtime much more?' I asked him the night he shuffled in around 10 pm.

'Overtime?' he said, staring. 'What overtime?'

'For staying late. The extra pay?'

'I don't get overtime, not for research. It's up to me what hours I put in.'

I absorbed this. 'So, then, is it the children?' I asked. 'Do you find them tiring?'

'No. But I don't see much of you if I *am* home. Putting them to bed seems to take up the entire evening.'

It's me, I thought. I'm not up to it. Out loud I said, 'I just wondered.'

Privately I planned that, starting from tomorrow, I would get myself together, start earlier, be rigorously organized and cut down on the lengthy process of bedtime. It all seemed easy enough as I lay in bed beside Simon, thinking about it.

Morning dawned, Ben and Robbie went off on the school bus as usual, Simon went to work, I took Felix to the supermarket, sat him in the trolley, pushed him round helping myself to this and that – an uneventful and even soothing beginning to the day had not Felix toppled fifty cans of Campbells soup as I waited at the cash desk. I helped pick them up, apologized, managed to lose my purse, found it again, paid, pretended not to be aware of the row of angry customers behind me, plopped Felix in his carseat and went home. That seemed to take all morning, no worse than usual really.

After lunch Felix angelically slept, so I cleared up, did the washing and some ironing, prepared in my mind for the improved evening ahead of me, and met Ben and Robbie off the bus at 3.30. Actually the bus was late because it was a new driver who went round the wrong way so Felix and I waited, trying to find blackberries for forty minutes, and, just as the bus did arrive, Felix swallowed one the wrong way and choked, so I was in no position to complain to the driver as I was trying to hold Felix upside down and pat him on the back with only two hands. Ben and Robbie helped, patted Felix on the back, the blackberry dropped out and we all went in for tea. Even as far ahead as this I was already bracing myself in anticipation of bedtime.

Accordingly, at six o'clock on the dot, I began in a carefully casual tone, 'Let's clear up, shall we – put your toys away?' This meant that Ben curled himself more securely in the armchair, sucking his thumb and looking resentful; Robbie assumed a belligerent expression while idly kicking down a tower of bricks; and Felix sat observing his two elder brother, anxious at all costs to be 'one of the boys'.

'Felix has to go first – Felix is a baby.' Tears filled Felix's eyes.

'I'm not going till Ben goes,' Robbie stated unequivocally.

'Why should I go the same time as Robbie, I'm older.' Ben removed his thumb from his mouth for this well-worn statement.

I picked up Felix. 'Felix and I will go up first,' I said, 'then you two can come up in five minutes and have a play until Felix is out of the bath. If we hurry,' I went on all in the same breath, 'there should be time for a read.'

This was greeted by a temporary lull in the noise. I congratulated myself on having instilled a love of literature in my children at an early age, for naturally I chose from *good* books, preferably classic stories.

What followed was my 'improved' version of a basic ritual – Felix in the bath, a short play with the plastic ducks, Ben and Robbie entering, grumbling that there wasn't enough water in the bath and that Felix had made it 'dirty'. They then ran too much water until it almost flooded, and got in. It did flood. I put Felix in his bed and returned to sop up the bathroom while Ben and Robbie romped about naked, destroying the bedroom. When I entered the room they leapt into bed guiltily, their eyes large with anxiety that my disapproval might curtail the length of 'the read'. I sat down in stately silence and began.

Yes, I did know the books by heart and, yes, they were dead boring to me, but I had developed the facility of reading with suitable expression while thinking about something entirely different. Fifteen minutes reading – it was closer to twenty – was a cheap price to pay for those few golden hours ahead of me by the living-room fire . . .

But the distressing, the wholly depressing thing was that, in spite of my early start followed by my organized procedure, I had not cut down on time. Not at all. It was all too clear that what had seemed so easy in the abstract had failed in practice. When I finally went downstairs at 8.15, Simon was in the kitchen looking hungry with the door of the fridge open.

'You're late,' he said. 'What have you been doing up there?'

'What do you think?' I replied tartly, unwilling to admit my failure. 'Reading to them, of course.'

'I could put them to bed tomorrow if you want?' he offered pleasantly. Tomorrow was Saturday.

'All right,' I said. 'You can try.'

'Try? I did it the weekend you were away. No problem.'

'Without bribing them with a read?' I asked.

'Yes.'

'How?'

'I told them it was bedtime, got them into bed and put out the light. Left the one on in the passage,' he added, as though he was telling me how to do it. 'You've got to be firm, speak as though you mean it.'

The next night I spoke as though I meant it. Actually, I shouted. Ben and Robbie regarded me with expressions of shock, Felix began crying. 'For God's sake,' I said. 'I've asked you four times to clear up and go to bed and nothing happens, absolutely nothing happens. You ignore me. You're old enough, all of you,' I went on, glaring at poor little Felix, 'to understand what I'm asking.'

Ben's thumb automatically went in his mouth; Robbie, after the first shock of my raised voice, went on round the room on hands and knees, pushing his transport carrier, known from his earlier years as a Long-along. Felix's tears ceased but his breath continued to catch in a gulp every few seconds.

'Simon,' I yelled, 'will you come and help?'

Simon appeared. 'They won't go to bed,' I said resentfully. 'Can you tell them they are wearing me out?'

'Do you hear what your mother says?' he said obediently. 'You're wearing her out.'

It was rather parrot-like of him, I'd given him the lines. But it worked. Very subdued they allowed me to put them to bed, even getting out of the bath to allow themselves to be wrapped in oversize towels at my first request. Simon went back to his laboratory to check out his maturing experiment, or whatever, and I was left feeling contrite and humiliated. It seemed feeble that I couldn't manage my own children without help, although it did seem that the rest of the evening might have gone ahead smoothly, and in a shorter space of time than usual, had not the book Robbie had set his heart on my reading to him, disappeared.

We searched upstairs and down, under the bath, under cushions, down the sides of the sofa and armchairs, in the garden. I even went through the dustbins. Robbie settled for lying on the floor, kicking at anything his leg would reach, to the accompaniment of a persistent moaning whimper; Ben's thumb revealed a raw red patch from sucking; even Felix, sensing the full import of the tragedy, sat in unusual silence. Bedtime showed every sign of stretching till midnight, and it was no exaggeration to say I was at my wits' end. There was a radio play at 9 pm; if I wanted to hear it something had to be done – and quickly.

Apprehensive that Simon would come in at any moment to find I had achieved almost nothing since he left, I had an idea. The whole point was that it was *not* planned; had it been, I might have been more wary after my previous failure. On the contrary, it came to me in an instant, in the same way, I imagine, as it had to Rousseau on his walk to Vincennes – I think it was Vincennes – in a flash that I mistakenly took for inspiration. But while mine did not mark the way to Revolution, it did have a marked effect on the next months of my life. I said, fool that I was, 'I'll *tell* you a story.'

Three pairs of brown eyes transferred themselves to my face.

'What about?' asked Ben.

Robbie still kicked and whimpered, but at a lower level.

'About . . .' I said helplessly, casting my eyes round the room until they alighted on the shelf above the cupboard, '. . . about Yellow Teddy, Pink Teddy and Black-and-White Teddy,' for those were the unimaginative if appropriate names allotted to the tatty trio who sat gazing back at me with brown beady eyes. Yes, fortunately, they had still got eyes.

It worked like magic. Robbie got up in silence and he and Ben followed Felix and me upstairs. I congratulated myself inwardly, I was 'coping' well; in no time at all three glowing eager faces were lined up in our big bed for the story.

'One day,' I began, with no idea whatsoever what was coming next, 'Pink Teddy, Yellow Teddy and Black-and-White Teddy were going for a walk' – a dull enough beginning of no possible originality, but my audience was captured.

'Go on,' they said, jerking their bodies vigorously as though they meant it.

I did. It took an absolute age, the teddies had to be set up: Pink Teddy was comic, did and said funny things; fell into traps, got his paw stuck in jamjars (I stole unashamedly from Milne and Kipling, no one cared, art lives on art, I reminded myself. Art?). Yellow Teddy instigated adventurous exploits and was brave to the point of foolhardiness; Black-and-White Teddy was always half asleep and never recognized danger even under his nose – oh yes, there had to be plenty of danger!

My story easily assumed what I can see now to be the classic structure of a soap – an amusing start with clearly defined behavioural patterns, each episode building to a crescendo of excitement, i.e., Pink and Yellow Teddies under a rock with Jaguar overhead about to pounce, and Black-and-White Teddy seeing Jaguar but too goofy to realize the danger and give warning until exactly the moment when Jaguar gathered himself to spring. Then Black-and-White Teddy yelled and Yellow and Pink Teddies dashed off, saved in the teeth of death or from deathly teeth. I excused my alarming lack of imagination to myself by it being the end of a long and, I hoped, *caring* day with my children.

During this creation my children sat, never taking their gaze from my face, the silence absolute as they absorbed every appallingly contrived situation. Ben's thumb had slipped from his mouth and lay on the sheet; the moment I stopped, it was replaced. Docile as well-nursed kittens they curled to sleep that night, leaving me dizzy with success.

When I went downstairs, Simon had just got home. He remarked on the unusual quiet up above.

'I told them a story,' I explained, proud of my new-found ability. I refrained from saying 'talent'. 'It seems to have worked,' I added modestly.

Simon looked less impressed than I had thought he would. 'Watch out,' he said, 'they'll never let you off the hook.'

I laughed. 'It's worth it,' I said, 'for peace and quiet. Much better than having them running around half the night like most of our friends' children.'

'Yes,' he agreed, without conviction. I felt a bit miffed, it was all very well for him spending those long, relaxing hours in his laboratory.

'Felix will be at school this time next year,' I pointed out to give myself courage. 'Mrs Baker told me she often uses oral story-telling – at primary-school age children assimilate the information better than by having it read to them.'

'Yes,' said Simon. Then, 'It won't alter his bedtime . . .'

'Not their *bedtime*, no. But during the day . . .'

'. . . you'll get a lot more time to yourself.'

I immediately felt guilty. Why should I want time to myself? Hadn't I had the children because I wanted them? Yes, more or less. And, once they arrived, I adored them. Ben's birth was the most exciting thing of my life – and Robbie's, and Felix's. As those older and wiser told me, I must make the most of them now as they wouldn't be this age for long!

'Perhaps you could tell them a story tomorrow night,' I said.

'No.' Simon was definite. 'I'm prepared for the odd read but I'm not a story-teller.'

'I didn't think I was until tonight,' I said, still inflated by suc- cess, 'but I may not be able to think of another.'

'Agreed,' said Simon, 'you may dry.'

It was almost a challenge. 'I'll probably manage one more night,' I said loftily. 'After that, they'll be fed up, want to get back to a book.'

'Don't be too sure.' His tone disconcerted me, I didn't like the prophetic ring it was apt to have when he felt confident in his truisms. Rather smug. In these instances he refused to elaborate or explain.

'I can't believe,' I said, 'that you are incapable of thinking of *any* story to tell them.'

'They're happy with yours,' he said. 'That's good. Keep it up.'

'Simon, it doesn't seem to occur to you it may be exhausting for me – having to wrack my brains at the end of a long day.'

'It does occur to me. That's why I suggested you didn't let yourself in for it.'

'Well, I've done it now,' I said. 'It's too late. I've promised them another tomorrow.'

'Tomorrow and tomorrow and tomorrow . . .' quoted Simon.

I switched on the play, tried to concentrate, feeling anything but calm. Actually, it was rather boring. I switched it off and said, 'It's not fair.'

'Look,' said Simon, standing up so all his papers fell off his knees – he does have a quick temper on occasion – 'if you want to tell them a story, fine. But don't expect me to. Right?'

I decided that his day at the laboratory hadn't been quite as relaxing as I had imagined. He went in the kitchen and I heard him uncorking a bottle of wine. I relaxed. Simon might not be good at saying the right things but, at least, he did them. Well, on occasion.

Needless to say, Robbie returned from school the next day with the lost book in his rucksack. I seized upon it eagerly, 'Look, Robbie, isn't it lucky we wrote your name in it otherwise Miss Baker wouldn't have known whose it was? We can read it tonight. If we go up a little earlier I might even be able to finish it.'

This was poorly received; disappointment was never better mirrored by three faces. 'After all that fuss, don't you want it?' I asked.

Ben took out his raw thumb. 'We want a teddy story, like last night.'

'Oh . . .' My mind revolved vacantly under my lowish brow, 'Oh, but . . .'

'You promised,' they accused.

Bedtime was no problem, even clearing up the toys was a cinch. In no time at all their scrubbed faces were once again before me, shining with anticipation for my mouth to open, pearls to drop. Such is the power of projection!

'Does it *have* to be about teddies?' I asked tentatively, hopefully.

'Yes,' they chorused.

'All right,' I conceded, murmured a rapid invocation to a nameless muse, and began. I assured myself that, in two or three days, they would be fed up, I trusted their natural taste I had so carefully fostered. Halfway through, episode 2 seemed to me so vapid, so lacking in even a good storyline, that I asked them if they would rather I stopped and read Robbie's book?

'No,' their eyes looked fiercely at me.

'You can't stop in the middle.'

'Go on.'

I now began to comprehend the problem of ancient bards; the necessity to keep going at all costs. If I even paused there was trouble, words had to pour forth, if not like an unquenchable fountain then at least like a garden hose. I could understand the bards' fear of being eaten should they fail to deliver. And as the days – or rather nights – passed, and I continued to trade my paltry creations for a speedy and non-confrontational bedtime, I soon grew to understand the formula; if I strayed from it I was brought up short, put right in no uncertain terms.

Each episode must, but *must*, contain the three main characters, comedy, and a brush with death. Nothing else was acceptable. And each character must stay true to himself (they were all male, no doubt if I had had girls they would all have been female – identification was important). If I stepped out of character, let Yellow Teddy clown about, for instance, instead of Pink Teddy, or, worse still, made Pink Teddy sleepy like Black-and-White Teddy, I was instantly corrected. Felix was clearly not allowed, apropos Black-and-White Teddy, to offer any competition. Felix never complained, he didn't understand, I told myself with a shaming lack of perception.

As the tension, the pressure mounted, evening by evening, I tried to take avoiding measures. I pleaded tiredness, a headache, a sore throat. They would unwillingly hand me an agreed book, accepting my disability without believing in it for one moment, but hesitating to doubt my word. The following aura of dissatisfaction they managed to evoke was as startling as it was depressing; as I closed the book they would chorus, 'When will you tell us another teddy story?'

'When I can think of one,' I was deceitfully evasive. But that was not the end of it; the evenings after I had read were neither tranquil nor uninterrupted. Ben, Robbie and even Felix would find it necessary to come downstairs two or three times for drinks of orange juice, or simply because they 'couldn't sleep'.

'When will you tell us another Teddy story?' they would sidle up individually to convey in my ear, afraid if Simon heard he might shout.

'Tomorrow,' I procrastinated, gambling on us being out and having a baby-sitter for the evening.

But I didn't win. The following morning, at *7am*, three small bodies landed on my bed for a teddy story.

'I'm too tired, too sleepy, I can't think,' I rolled over, pulled the sheet up over my head. Simon pretended to be asleep. Excuses were ignored, they sat there like See-no-evil, Speak-no-evil and Hear-no-evil, sucking their thumbs and waiting. It was like being haunted. Finally, I raised myself on one elbow, demanded they bring me a drink to lubricate my dry throat, and began in a tranced stupor: 'One day Pink Teddy, Yellow Teddy and Black-and-White Teddy . . .'

I was an unwilling horse reversed between shafts and when, finally, after six weeks I put my leaden hoof down and said I was too old for work, I found myself guiltily avoiding their eyes as I kissed them good night.

'You've got a bard's block,' said Simon comfortably, 'they will just have to accept it.'

'They don't,' I said, 'and anyway I'm not a bard. I'm just a very bad story-teller.'

I studied my predicament from their point of view, something at which I was particularly adept. 'What they see,' I said, speaking carefully because I was thinking hard, 'is a mean mother who doesn't love them enough to tell them a story about teddy bears. That's how they see it.'

'If it makes you feel better, less mean, keep right on telling!' Simon laughed. I really hated him.

'You don't seem to understand,' I said patiently, 'my imagination has evaporated – poof, like that, like a whiff of dung – into thin air. I simply haven't another story in me.'

I wasn't quite sure that this was true. I suspected stories were rather like magicians' handkerchiefs that come from up their sleeves – the more you pull the more they come. If this was the case then what the children thought about me was true, my 'block' was just laziness, I *was* a mean mother who couldn't be bothered to tell her children stories. Should I then give in, perform night after night, not let up as Simon suggested? I switched the image of myself from a horse to the figure of Liberty, subjected to the pleasure of three rapidly growing tyrants. I said as much to Simon who grinned evilly, 'If you see yourself that way, far be it for me to destroy your illusion. I think you secretly *like* telling stories,' he said.

'I don't' I denied absolutely, mortified by his implication of my hypocrisy. 'Like!' I exclaimed, 'What do you mean, "like"? I dread every evening now because of the bloody stories.'

'I hope not,' he said.

'What?'

'I hope they're not bloody.'

'You're a fool!' I said, but I did find it in me to laugh.

It reached the point when I nursed dreams of putting Pink Teddy, Yellow Teddy and Black-and-White Teddy in the incinerator . . . But that was too cruel, even for me. Amazingly, and incredibly, they never did tire of my stories, however bad (perhaps that says something about soaps, too), neither did they give up requesting further episodes. I was harried as a celebrity before the press, even blackmailed into further eloquence when one or another was ill. But I took care to keep those occasions as one-offs and didn't use the teddies. I sensed their unspoken disappointment but hardened my steely heart.

Surprisingly, it was Felix who broke through my 'block', made me burst forth in a new series. It came about when he went into hospital to be operated on for a squint. It was the first time anything like this had happened to one of our children so there was a general flap, signalled by apparent outward calm, carefully controlled voices, that sort of thing. Felix was instantly the centre of attention, even Robbie seized his toys less frequently than usual.

When the momentous day came and we drove Felix into hospital, we stopped off in the main street to buy him a compensatory present – a magnificent, brown teddy bear. Felix smiled. Ben and Robbie eyed Brown Teddy.

'Let's have a look?' said Ben.

'Can I see?' Robbie's hand grasped Brown Teddy's woollen arm.

Felix proudly handed over Brown Teddy who was duly handed back after examination. I knew Robbie was itching to point out the defects, but his normally all-too-well-concealed nobility of spirit triumphed and he remained silent. At that moment, at any rate, Felix was happy.

When he returned from the hospital five days later, patched but clutching Brown Teddy, his poor eyes hurt a lot. But Felix's upbringing by his brothers hadn't allowed him to fuss. What, I whispered into his small, transparent rose ear as he lay face down on the pillow, could I do to make him better?

'Tell a teddy story,' he muttered, 'with Brown Teddy in it.'

So I did. I didn't take any notice of the rules and, in spite of the look of consternation that passed across Robbie's, if not Ben's, face, I made Brown Teddy into the hero, brave, clever and funny – the lot. Definitely not sleepy. Felix loved it. He was no fool, every evening at bed time his eyes hurt so much that he had to have a Brown Teddy story to make them better. And, before I knew it, I was into a brand-new series that ran even longer than the first. In fact, it finished me off.

'Simon,' I said, 'I've had it. I can't. I promise you – I just can't.'

So Simon, because he suspected it might be an inherited squint from his side of the family, took over. It transpired that he could tell stories perfectly well, it was just a matter of trying. But after a bit he gave up, too. He suggested, yes, suggested, we advertise for a 'Help' – apparently those hours of unpaid overtime had paid off, if you understand me, he had got promotion.

Bliss! I auditioned 'Helps' and asked the applicants to improvise a teddy story. Remarkably, only one of them even attempted it; she was called Miranda and got the job. Her imagination easily surpassed mine, if not Simon's, her humour was modern and inclined to bawdiness; the boys followed her up at night like imprinted ducklings. Ben even stopped sucking his thumb.

I said to Simon, 'They are a bit older now, anyway, aren't they?'

'What are you getting at?' he asked.

'I mean, we have made the most of them,' I said.

'Yes, I'm absolutely in agreement with you there!'

We were munching our Sainsbury's salad in front of the television as we talked. Upstairs, we could just hear the sound of Miranda's voice and the boys' delighted chortles. Peace. Well, for a while at least.

A Symbol of Unloneliness

PAT RUSH

H E STANDS a mere 4" tall. But it could be said that little Theodore is responsible for much of the current popularity of the teddy bear on both sides of the Atlantic. For Theodore was the 'number one' bear of actor and arctophile extraordinaire – Peter Bull.

Peter's books introduced thousands to the teddy bear world. Secret teddy lovers suddenly discovered that they were not alone, that there were others just as 'dotty' as they were – or, frequently, far more so. Many wrote to Peter to tell him about their own bears. But many others wrote to the little bear that travelled everywhere with him, causing Peter to bemoan the fact that he sometimes felt he was just Theodore's secretary.

According to his birth chart, Theodore was born on 28 April 1948, so we can assume that he joined Peter either on that date or soon afterwards. Peter could still vividly remember the trauma of being told by his mother that his childhood teddy had been given to a jumble sale. So Theodore's arrival – as a first-night gift from a friend – was warmly welcomed.

For more than thirty-five years the two were inseparable. If Peter went away for a night, Theodore had to go too, for, if Theodore was there, even the most miserable of theatrical digs would soon feel like home. He was, said his owner, 'a symbol of unloneliness'.

For the first twenty years of their time together, it was Peter who enjoyed the limelight as he pursued his acting career. Little Theodore was simply there to give moral support. But all that was to change when Peter decided to write a book about bears. His idea was simply to gather together people's teddy bear memories – happy or sad – and share them with other bear lovers.

An advertisement was duly placed in the Personal Columns of *The Times*. It brought so many letters that he was forced to employ a secretary to cope with them. Appearances on television and radio brought still more reminiscences, while an appearance on the American *To-day* programme resulted in so much mail that Peter found himself with a second full-time job answering it all.

Things became even more hectic when Theodore made another American television appearance with Peter, this time on Johnny Carson's *To-Night* show. Not only did more letters flood in for Peter, there was also a mass of fan mail for his bear. Since Theodore was unable to reply himself, Peter had to respond to all these letters too.

By the time *Bear with Me* was published in 1969, Theodore had acquired a large number of penpals. He had been deluged with offers of marriage, not to mention all sorts of gifts, and one anonymous correspondent had even sent him a tiny companion in the post – all of 1½″ inches tall.

Well-wishers had sent him a sword and a revolver in case he had to go into Central Park after dark. There was a set of matching luggage to take with him on his travels, not to mention his own passport, and a brush to keep his fur in tip-top condition. There was even a tiny Greek dictionary to help him feel more at home when he visited the house Peter owned on a remote Greek island.

Needless to say, the publication of the book led to still more fan mail for both man and bear. Further books brought even more fame. Theodore found himself cast in the role of agony uncle of the teddy bear world – no doubt helped by the fact that he was such a sensible, serious-looking little fellow. He was also often invited to parties and, in due course, there were guest appearances at teddy bear picnics and rallies, as teddy lovers started to get together with fellow arctophiles and their bears.

Peter Bull was always much in demand as a guest at these events, and it was unthinkable that Theodore should be left behind – even after two of Peter's other bears found their way into the limelight. Delicatessen, for instance, was selected to play the role of Aloysius in *Brideshead Revisited*, while a more recent arrival, Bully Bear, became the subject of a whole series of little books.

Sadly, Peter died in 1984 but Theodore and many of his belongings found a new home with Peter's friend, Enid Irving, who had collaborated with him on his final book of bears and had also provided the illustrations for the Bully Bear stories.

These days the little bear leads a much quieter life, away from the limelight, but few would dispute that his retirement is a well-earned one. As Peter himself said in his book, *A Hug of Teddy Bears*, Theodore was for him the 'embodiment of loyalty, friendship and complete understanding'. And who could ask more from a bear than that?

Ted and Angeline

DINAH LAMPITT

TED SAID: "'Ere, what's your game?'

'Are you addressing me?' replied Angeline in a high, reedy and exceptionally irritating voice.

'Well, I'm not addressing the chair,' Ted answered, and guffawed loudly.

'Then, in that case, please be so kind as to speak correctly. To what game do you refer?'

'Your staring, that's what. 'As anyone ever told you that your eyes are glassy?'

'And has anyone ever told you you have a *ridiculous* mouth. It's just like a moustache. And if you only knew what you looked like in that tie. You're just a common teddy boy.'

And with that Angeline pealed with such a fit of tinkling laughter that her hat slipped down over one eye.

'Blimey O'Reilly, talk about the pot calling the kettle black. You're stuck up, Angeline, that's your trouble.'

'End of round one,' commented the clown, and banged his cymbals.

There was silence during which the distant noises of the world outside could be heard through the nursery window: the mowing of a lawn and the deep, sweet voices of the prize dairy herd.

'I never thought I'd get to like the country,' Ted observed reflectively. 'It was so flipping quiet I couldn't get to sleep at first.'

'*He* used to say that,' Angeline replied tartly. 'That's where you got it from. Nothing original comes out of you.'

'And that's what *she* used to say. She used to tell him he was too common to be clever.'

'Well, he was,' Angeline answered.

But Ted was no longer listening – he was reminiscing now: the crowded railway station, the children with labels tied to their coats, the bustle of wartime London and himself clutched frantically beneath his owner's arm.

'I don't want to go, Mum,' Jimmy had cried, and buried his face in his mother's lap.

'But you'll be happy in the country, luv. Away from all those nasty bombs. Anyway, you've got Ted. He's going with you.'

'I hate Ted,' Jimmy had lied, wretched at leaving behind him all the warmth, the colours and characters of the East End, including Mr Bloom the tailor who sat cross-legged in his shop window stitching garments with his long-nailed hands, busy yet always ready for a chat.

'Mr Bloom,' said Ted now. "E made me, you know.'

'What are you rambling on about?' asked Angeline crossly.

'Mr Bloom of Whitechapel, 'e made me and gave me to Jimmy one Christmas – not that he celebrated it 'isself, mind.'

'It all sounds very tawdry to me. *I* come from France, *I* am a Jumeau fashion doll.'

'Pity you're fadin', ain't it?' And Ted guffawed again, slapping his solid thigh with a paw which had once been covered by Mr Bloom's finest velvet.

'I remember the day Jimmy came here,' Angeline said sharply. 'I thought Betty would never stop crying at having such a horrid little evacuee in her home.'

'She was a silly little snob. But, mind you, I felt sorry for Mrs Lewin, 'er mum. "Oh, my dear," she used to say to the vicar's wife, "I don't know what I'm going to do. He didn't even have a bathroom at home. It's a nightmare." But 'e soon come round, did Jimmy. Do you remember how 'e took to the animals on the farm?'

'Yes,' answered Angeline softly, her voice taking on a pleasanter tone. 'He tried hard, poor little blighter.'

"Ere, that's one of my words!'

'End of round two,' said the clown and clashed his cymbals again.

'The Christmasses and the fun,' remembered Ted. "'Ow many did Jimmy 'ave 'ere?'

'Three. They gave him the train set the first time.'

'Yes,' Ted answered, watching as the train on hearing its name did a lap of honour round its circular track. 'And then come the news that 'is dad 'ad been killed at the Front. Do you remember that?'

'How could I ever forget? Jimmy ran away for two days, taking you, and it was Betty and myself who found the pair of you.'

'She cuddled 'im like a little mother. I reckon it all started then.'

'What?'

'Jimmy loving 'er. 'E said, "When I grow up I'm going to marry you, Betty."'

'It was she who cried when he left her at the end of the war. The whole village turned out to see the evacuees off and Jimmy waved and waved until the train was nothing but a little blob. And then she went home and wrote to tell him he'd left you behind by mistake.'

'And 'e wrote back to say she could keep me to remember 'im by. Blimey, there's gratitude for you.'

'Don't be silly. You'd got to like the country by then. You said you didn't want to go back to smelly old London.'

'Nah, you're right. But I had a yearning to see old Bloom again. 'E was my dad, see. I'd 'ave liked to cast me old glass eyes on 'im one more time.'

'They've sounded the Last Post,' said the wooden soldier, whose arm was held permanently aloft in a waving attitude.

Angeline ignored him. 'How old was Jimmy when he came back?'

'Nineteen, and 'andsome as 'andsome though I do say it who was 'is best bear.'

'Well, my Betty was considered a beauty. All the young farmers were fighting one another to go out with her.'

'But Jimmy kissed 'er, up 'ere in the nursery when they came to look at us. Do you remember?'

Angeline blinked her fine lustrous eyes. 'It was a love kiss, not a children's one.'

'Not 'arf,' said Ted, remembering.

'Of course Major and Mrs Lewin weren't very pleased about it, fond though they were of Jimmy. I mean his mother worked in a shoe shop and lived in a council flat.'

'And they was the owners of The Grange.'

'I could hear the Major shouting at Jimmy from up here. He said, "You've got to make something of yourself, young man, before you can come courting my daughter".'

'But Jimmy done it. Went to agricultural college and all, then got a job in farm management just outside Tewkesbury.'

'Do you remember the wedding, Ted? You had a white bow tie and Betty, who liked to be called Elizabeth by that stage, made me a white cape and hat, for fun.'

'I thought me 'eart would burst with pride at seeing my Jimmy all dressed up like a toff. Then Lupin and Charles come along and we was called back into active service.'

'Attention!' said the soldier.

'Elizabeth wouldn't let them play with me too much because she said she had a feeling I was rather rare and precious. And of course I was. As you know, Jumeau fashion dolls are collectors' items these days. Unlike human beings, my value increases with age.'

'Mine, too. Or have you conveniently forgotten?'

'What?'

'You know what.'

Banging his cymbals once more, the clown said: 'Final round.'

'If you are referring to "The Antiques Road Show" why don't you come out and say so?'

'All right, I will. It was a bit of triumph, like, wasn't it. I'll never forget the look on that geezer's face when he says, "Blimey, this bear appears to be a Bloom," and Elizabeth says, "It *is* a Bloom. It was made by him for my husband. But I never knew there were any more." "Well, there was," the geezer answers. "Only about six. Well, now, they've become 'ighly collectable. 'Ave you any idea 'ow much this would fetch at auction?" "No," says Elizabeth . . .'

Angeline gave a delicate cough. 'As I recall, the expert was bowled over by me, said I was an exquisite example of Jumeau's work.'

'Elizabeth come 'ome all of a dither and says to James, "Lawks, you'll never guess what – Ted and Angeline are *valuable*." The thing is, they didn't sell either of us. Even though I am worth £2000 and you 500 less.'

The clown banged his cymbals and said, 'A points victory to Ted. I formally declare the bear, champion.'

'Oh, shut up, you horrible little freak,' Angeline answered crossly.

'Shut up all,' ordered the soldier. 'I detect action.'

Instantly there was silence as the nursery door opened and Elizabeth came in, looking over her shoulder to check she was alone.

'Oh, I can't believe it,' she said, hugging herself before turning slowly in a circle. 'I can't believe it.'

'Gawn orff 'er 'ead,' mouthed Ted at Angeline.

'At last, at last,' Elizabeth went on. 'And I thought Lupin was only interested in acting.'

She turned to the toys, who sat absolutely still in their respective places. 'Well, you'll have to be spruced up even if you are too valuable to play with.'

One of Ted's eyes flashed beadily but Elizabeth did not notice. 'Lupin's going to have a baby,' she said. 'I'm going to be a granny. And you shall be head of the nursery even though new toys will be coming.'

'Head of the nursery,' said Angeline as the door closed. 'Yes, I think that role will suit me very nicely. After all, I *am* a fashion doll.'

But Ted did not answer and when Angeline turned her beautifully articulated neck to look at him she saw that he was asleep. After a few moments she, too, lowered her elegant lids and slept. And, while she dreamed of Monsieur Jumeau who had made her with so much love that a little of his own soul had gone into her, Ted dreamed of a Jewish tailor who had sat cross-legged in the window of his shop and made with his long-nailed hands a teddy bear to which he, also, had given his heart.

Stuff and Sawdust

*A dramatized account of
teddy bear history (1880–1903)*

VALERIE THAME

MARGARETE EDGED her wheelchair nearer the window. The winter daylight of 1880 would not last much longer and she wanted to finish her sewing before the lamps were lit. She was a cheerful and spirited young woman who, though crippled by polio since early childhood, refused to accept her disability as a handicap. She knew she would never be able to walk again and that she would always be dependent upon others, especially upon her family, but she was determined to keep that dependence to a minimum.

She lived in Geingen an der Brenz, a rural village in southern Germany, where her family owned a felt-making factory. Margarete had already taken a course in dressmaking and the ready supply of material from the factory gave her the idea of starting her own business – making and selling ready-made clothes. Her mail-order company was set up in a downstairs room and the warm and comfortable garments, especially the new felt underskirts, sold extremely well during the crisp Bavarian winters.

Margarete shivered. The fire, it seemed, was fading with the light and there were no spare logs in the hearth. She would have to wait until somebody came to make it up but, until then, she would carry on sewing. Her work table was set directly in the window overlooking the street, mainly for light but, also, so that she could see the passers by and they could see her. Some school children, anxious to get home before dark, ran past. They waved and she waved cheerfully back. Everybody in the village knew Margarete Steiff and the house was always full of visitors, especially young ones. Margarete enjoyed the company of children.

Her sewing complete, and with still a little light left, she began trimming the seams of a felt jacket. Snippets of material fell to the floor and nestled comfortably with the left-over scraps from other garments. So intent was she on her work that she did not hear the door of the drawing-room open. Her brother Fritz came in with an armful of logs.

'You'll hurt your eyes working in this light.' He made up the fire and lit the lamps. The room began to glow comfortably, looking less like a workroom and more like a living-room.

'Look at you,' he said, fussing round, 'almost knee-deep in cuttings. Stop working now, Gretel. That's enough for today.'

Reluctantly, Margarete put down the scissors and wheeled her chair over to the welcoming fire. She brushed some scraps of felt from her lap.

'So much waste,' she said. 'I don't like to throw it away, Fritz. There must be something I can do with all these pieces.'

Fritz, considering the question, picked up a handful of snippets and a dropped pin, of which there were many, pricked his finger.

'How about a pincushion?' he said.

Margarete laughed. Her brother's remark may have been flippant but, nonetheless, it made her think and the following day, before she started work, she made herself a pincushion – but not an ordinary one. Always inventive, Margarete used a model elephant as her pattern, cutting the shape out of some grey felt scraps, stitching it and stuffing it with sawdust. The elephant pincushion sat on her sewing table in the window and when the village children saw it they fell in love with it.

'Will you make us one, Fraulein Steiff. Please?'

How could she refuse? So, in between making dresses, Margarete made little felt elephants and gave them away. But word, like the elephants, quickly got round the village and, to her surprise, orders started to come in. News of the new toy quickly spread to surrounding villages and, eventually, came to the notice of some dealers who placed quite substantial orders.

She was so busy making elephants there was little time left for dressmaking and, before she knew what was happening, the Felt Mail-Order Company had become a toy factory and Margarete had become the creator of the world's first soft toy.

Fritz, although a master builder and married with a large and growing family, was full of encouragement and enthusiasm for his sister's new success; he could see great possibilities in the manufacture of these toys. He and Margarete had always been very close and now, as the business grew, he became more and more involved. Orders for the toys continued to arrive daily and, to the amazement of them both, by the end of the year 600 elephants had been sold. In fact, the soft toys had become so popular that customers began asking for other animals – monkeys, horses, rabbits. Margarete, enjoying the challenge of something new, was more than willing and ordered new material especially for the toys.

Fritz persuaded his sister to let him take some to sell at a local market. He marched off with a sackful and sold them all. The toys began to overtake the sales of ready-made clothes and the time came when Margarete simply could not cope with the demand. But there was no question of giving up. She and Fritz took on extra help and, by the end of their sixth year, had four regular employees, ten home workers, and were producing over 5000 assorted soft toys.

The business was taking up more and more space in the house and so, against all the odds, and with health which continued to be troublesome, the intrepid Margarete Steiff moved her company to larger premises. She bought a big house in the village, with a corner shop, and on the side of the house she had painted the words 'Felt Toy Factory'.

The business continued to flourish and all sorts of new animals were developed, including miniature mice, plush pigs and velvet cats. But, never satisfied, she and Fritz were constantly adding to, or adapting, the range. Sometimes they fitted wheels to some of the animals so that they could be pushed along, or they made them with strong internal frames so that children could ride on them. Then, in 1893, some thirteen years after making the elephant pin cushion, Margarete felt confident enough to register her business with the local Chamber of

Commerce and to produce the first Steiff catalogue. She was very fond of her brother's children and, now that the company was more firmly established, she was able to invite one of her nephews, Richard Steiff, to join the family firm; it was not long before two of his younger brothers, Paul and Franz, were also included.

Richard, who had been trained at art school in Stuttgart and studied in England, had a passion for drawing animals, especially bears, and he suggested they make one.

'Make a bear?' said a surprised Margarete. 'But why? They are so ugly.'

'No, they're not,' said Richard. 'Let me show you.'

His sketchbook was full of bears he had seen at the Stuttgart Zoo and, from these sketches, he prepared a design-drawing for a toy. Margarete, who had designed many of the new toys herself, studied the drawing critically. She was very fussy about her toys.

'Hmm, it might work,' she said. 'Perhaps if I made the body in brown tweed . . . and added plain felt patches for paws . . . and boot buttons for eyes . . .'

The two of them discussed the new bear at great length and, when she was satisfied it would work, Margarete agreed to make it and was unexpectedly pleased with the result. But Richard was not.

'It isn't real enough,' he said.

'Not real enough? I don't understand.'

'Well, it's just stuff and sawdust, like all our other toys.'

'It certainly is not,' said an indignant Margarete. 'I use only the finest woodshavings.'

'Yes, yes,' said Richard, 'but you know what I mean. I want this bear to be different. The brown tweed body is wrong. We should use something like – mohair plush.'

'Mohair plush?' gasped Margarete. 'But that's so expensive. It's made from goat's hair and it has to be specially treated and woven on special looms. Really, Richard! Mohair plush for a toy?'

'Why not? Mohair looks like real fur and that's what's needed. And,' he began sketching again, 'to make the bear even more realistic, he should have movable limbs.'

Margarete watched in amazement. A bear made out of mohair plush *and* with movable limbs? That would be much too costly and it would never sell. But Richard's enthusiasm was contagious and, before long, Margarete was once again caught up in the excitement of a new venture. She began work immediately on the revolutionary design. The new bear had a sad but beguiling face with bright, boot-button eyes. He was furry and cuddly with large, padded paws, stitched woollen claws and an embroidered woollen nose. He could stand up on his hind legs, sit down or walk on all fours – and the whole family loved him.

'He is so good, and so different, he must go to the Leipzig Toy Fair,' said a joyous Fritz.

'Oh dear, such a big exhibition for such a small bear,' said Margarete, doubtfully, although she knew, as well as any, that the trade fair was an important event in any toy manufacturer's calendar.

'But we must show our new bear,' said Fritz. 'Buyers from all over the world will be there. It'll be a golden opportunity.'

In fact, Margarete needed little encouragement. She, too, thought the bear was wonderful and so plans were made for it to be exhibited at the 1903 Leipzig Toy Fair along with all their other animals. But, as she waved her family goodbye, she could not help thinking that perhaps the new bear, exciting though it was, might be just a little too expensive.

The toy fair was well attended, and Fritz and his two sons quickly set up their stall, eager to demonstrate their new product.

'See here, gentlemen,' said Fritz, holding up the bear. 'See how lifelike this bear is, and how furry. See how the limbs move. He can stand up. He can sit down. I can assure you, gentlemen, that this bear is like no other toy you'll see here today. Can I interest you in taking half a dozen?'

But to their surprise, and disappointment, nobody was interested and the first day ended without a single order. Fritz caught sight of Richard's long face and clapped him on the back.

'Don't worry, my son,' he said. 'Tomorrow we will do better.'

But tomorrow was just the same. Nobody wanted to buy. The Steiffs began to think they had made a dreadful mistake. There was nothing wrong with the product, of that they had no doubt. It was very well made, as good, if not better, than any of their other toys. So why didn't it sell? Slowly, Fritz was coming to the conclusion that people simply did not want a toy *bear*, however well made it might be. Bears were ugly. They had long snouts, dangerous claws and humps on their backs. They had bad breath, bad temper and in all the story books, what did they do? They ate little children. Was it any wonder parents would not buy a bear? Perhaps Richard's idea was not such a good one, after all.

The last day of the fair came round and they still had not got a single order. Fritz was now impatient to be gone. He had no stomach for telling his sister how badly they had done but neither could he wait for the end of this disappointing fair.

'That's enough, boys,' he said, halfway through the day. 'Let's go home.'

Then, as they were packing up and feeling just about as miserable as could be, a 'one in a million' chance occurred. A buyer, representing an American toy company, walked by their stall and saw the bear partly hidden in a packing case.

'Excuse me,' he said, 'but bears are big in the States right now. D'you mind if I take a look?'

'Not at all, sir. Not at all.'

Richard unpacked the bear. He demonstrated the movable limbs and made much of the mohair plush body.

'It's extremely durable. Will take any amount of cuddle and should last a lifetime.'

The buyer was impressed.

'Fine. I'll take 3000.'

So the journey back to Geingen turned out to be a happy one. Margarete was delighted with the massive order but, as she pointed out, they would need more help and even more space. Those were anxious and exciting times for the Steiff family and plans to enlarge the factory were drawn up.

Eventually, the new bear went into production and 3000 were duly packed and dispatched from the new Steiff Toy Factory (designed by Richard) to the United States of America.

At home Margarete and her family waited anxiously for news

of the bears' arrival. They had invested much time and money in the new bear. Would the Americans like it? After a few worrying weeks a telegram arrived from the USA.

'Teddy bears selling well in States,' it read. 'Will need more. Can you supply?'

Margarete was pleased but puzzled. 'Why does he call them *teddy* bears?' she said. 'They are Steiff bears.'

'It's something to do with their President,' said Fritz. 'Mr Teddy Roosevelt. I'm told he likes bears and so toy bears were given his name. Now, they are all called teddy bears.'

'I see,' said Margarete. 'But ours shall be different.' She was already working on another bear and inside the left ear she stitched a small button. 'See Fritz? Knopf im Ohr. That is how you will know a Steiff bear from any other. He will have a button hidden in his ear.'

'I'll do even better than that, my dear Gretel,' said Fritz. 'Do you remember how it all started? With your little pincushion? Well, I'll have a button made with an elephant on it, to remind us of your first stuffed toy, and his trunk will be 'S' shaped. 'S' for Steiff. What do you think of that?'

Margarete approved. 'Yes, I like that very much.'

As she trimmed the new bear, cuttings of golden mohair plush fell to the floor.

'Oh, look,' she said. 'Yet more scraps. Now, what are we to do with all these little pieces?'

Fritz put his arm around her shoulder.

'I should make some *little* teddys,' he said.

NOTE

After the initial order in 1903 of 3000 bears the Steiff factory produced a further 12,000 bears that year and, in 1908, exported more than a million.

The company was officially registered in Stuttgart in 1906 with Margarete and her three nephews as founders.

Margarete Steiff was born in 1847, died in 1909 and is buried in Geingen.

ACKNOWLEDGMENTS

'The Bear in the Window' by Anne Forsyth. Copyright © Anne Forsyth, 1993. Reproduced by permission of the author.

'Shooting Teddy Bears is no Picnic' by Abigail Harman. Copyright © Abigail Harman, 1993. Reproduced by permission of the author.

'Harold's Bear' by Pauline Macaulay. Copyright © Pauline Macaulay, 1993. Reproduced by permission of the author and Eric Glass Ltd.

'A Friend in Need' by Anne Goring. Copyright © Anne Goring, 1992. Reproduced by permission of the author and Dorian Literary Agency.

'Titanic Bear' by Pat Rush. Copyright © Pat Rush, 1993. Reproduced by permission of the author.

'The Battle of Jericho' by Peter Clover. Copyright © Peter Clover, 1993. Reproduced by permission of the author and Laurence Pollinger Limited.

'Confessions of a Bad Bear' by Allan Frewin Jones. Copyright © Allan Frewin Jones, 1993. Reproduced by permission of the author and Laurence Pollinger Limited.

'Look Me in the Eyes' by Jill Drower. Copyright © Jill Drower, 1993. Reproduced by permission of the author.

'Fit for a Princess' by Pat Rush. Copyright © Pat Rush, 1993. Reproduced by permission of the author.

'One Bear's War' by Elisabeth Beresford. Copyright © Elisabeth Beresford, 1993. Reproduced by permission of the author and Rosemary Bromley Literary Agency.

'Confessions of an Adult Bear Collector' by David Elias, 1993. Copyright © David Elias. Reproduced by permission of the author.

'The Teddy Bears' Picnic' by William Trevor. Copyright © William Trevor, 1980. Reproduced by permission of the Peters, Fraser and Dunlop Group Ltd.